Where the Heart Takes You

Where the Heart Takes You

Virginia Wise

ZEBRA BOOKS
KENSINGTON PUBLISHING CORP.
www.kensingtonbooks.com

ZEBRA BOOKS are published by

Kensington Publishing Corp.
119 West 40th Street
New York, NY 10018

All Kensington titles, imprints, and distributed lines are available at special quantity discounts for bulk purchases for sales promotion, premiums, fund-raising, educational, or institutional use.

Special book excerpts or customized printings can also be created to fit specific needs. For details, write or phone the office of the Kensington Sales Manager: Attn.: Sales Department. Kensington Publishing Corp., 119 West 40th Street, New York, NY 10018. Phone: 1-800-221-2647.

Zebra and the Z logo Reg. U.S. Pat. & TM Off.
BOUQUET Reg. U.S. Pat. & TM Off.

First Printing: January 2019
ISBN-13: 978-1-4201-4779-7
ISBN-10: 1-4201-4779-X

ISBN-13: 978-1-4201-4782-7 (eBook)
ISBN-10: 1-4201-4782-X (eBook)

10 9 8 7 6 5 4 3 2 1

Printed in the United States of America

To my husband because,
as with all great romances,
we were meant to be together from the beginning

Chapter One

Pennsylvania Backcountry, 1737

Greta Scholtz wandered past the stumps of freshly cut hemlocks. She raised the blade of her hand to her forehead and squinted into the sun. The old milk cow could be anywhere. Greta felt just as lost in the strange, new land. She frowned, hitched up her skirts, and slogged through the muddy clearing.

"Rose!" Greta cut her eyes toward the forest. "Rose, where are you!?" She hoped that the cow had not wandered beneath those dark, towering pines. Backcountry settlers fenced in their crops and let their livestock roam free to forage and fend for themselves. Cows and hogs grew fat and happy on the bounty of the forest—unless they met a hungry predator.

The otherworldly howls of a wolf pack had woken Greta during the night and she could not rest until she knew that Rose had escaped their hunger. The young woman scanned the shadowed underbrush that lay beyond the clearing and imagined the quiet, stealthy beasts that roamed the foothills of the Blue

Mountain. Here, at the far edge of the colonies, the New World teemed with bears, mountain lions, and bobcats.

A soft bell rang. Greta whipped her head toward the sound and grinned. "Rose!" She marched to the other side of the clearing, then hesitated before plunging into the old growth forest that separated her from the other settlers. *How can I overcome all of the dangers of the backcountry? If only Father were here.* But Father was not there. *And I will never see him again.* He risked everything to bring them to a land where they were free to worship as Amish, but he never laid eyes on the green hills of Pennsylvania.

Memories of the voyage pushed into Greta's mind. The small group of Anabaptists felt so full of hope when they boarded the *Charming Nancy.* After decades of persecution in Europe, Greta's people knew they would be safe in Pennsylvania. "William Penn made a place where everyone is free to worship as they see fit," Greta's father, Johannes, had explained. She remembered his smile as they plodded up the ship's gangplank with everything they owned stuffed into one small chest.

But Johannes Scholtz had not survived the voyage to see the Promised Land. He was not alone. One in nine passengers died on the voyage. Overcrowding, disease, and deprivation spelled disaster for the old and young. After they sailed, Greta heard rumors that profit-hungry trading companies preyed on German immigrants by crowding them into the hold like herrings. Others claimed that dishonest middlemen pocketed money meant to buy food for the voyage, condemning passengers to weeks of malnourishment.

Greta trudged toward the wayward cow. With her father gone, there was no man of the house to stand between her and backcountry predators. *I will learn to shoot a musket myself.* The other families in the tight-knit community would be happy to help her, but Greta wanted to show the settlement that she could handle the challenges of her new life.

And yet, here she was, chasing after Rose again. "I have to stop fearing the wolves." There was no one to hear her words but a deer that paused beneath a gnarled hemlock. The animal froze and stared at Greta with soft brown eyes. Greta cupped her hands around her mouth. "Rose! Come back!" The deer flinched, leapt across a rotten log, and disappeared into the forest.

No wonder the elders are pressuring me to marry. How can I possibly manage on my own? I do not want to be a burden on the community. But how can I settle for a loveless marriage with a stranger who takes me in out of charity? She sighed and pushed a stray lock of chestnut-colored hair under her prayer *kappe. And who do they expect me to marry, anyway? A widower twice my age? There are not many eligible bachelors out here, in the middle of nowhere.*

Greta emerged into a clearing and spotted her cow in the middle of the neighbor's kitchen garden, surrounded by crushed vegetables. A section of the fence that protected the crops lay broken on the ground. "Rose! No!" The cow raised her head, stepped forward, and flattened a head of cabbage with her hoof. Greta clenched her eyes shut and pressed a palm to her forehead. "Oh, Rose! What have you done this time?" She rushed through the front yard and grabbed the cowbell around Rose's neck. "Come on, Rose. Out of the garden! Please!" She glanced toward the cabin door. Greta had just arrived in the Anabaptist settlement, and this was not the way she wanted to make a first impression on her new neighbor. Rose chewed her cud and watched Greta with a dull expression. Greta pulled harder. The cow stood stock-still, then bellowed and took another step forward without warning. Greta lost her balance, fell backward, and landed hard in the mud. She groaned and wiped a splatter of dirty water off her face. *At least no one saw that!*

"I've seen pigs wallow in the mud before, but never a young lady." The deep, masculine voice startled Greta and she flung her head around.

A tall, broad-shouldered man stood over her. Dark eyes locked onto hers and Greta felt her stomach leap. She stumbled over her thoughts, unable to respond to his words. "Oh! I . . ." Her gaze moved from the man's eyes to his strong jaw, hardened features, and muscular build. Greta felt her face turn red and she looked down. "I . . . I . . . it is just that . . ." Greta shook her head and wiped her muddy hands on her white apron. The stranger leaned forward, close enough for Greta to catch the twinkle of amusement in his brown eyes. She cleared her throat. "Rose, she . . ." The man took Greta's hands and pulled her to her feet without any effort. His tall frame blocked the sun and she stood in his shadow, still unsure how to respond. She adjusted her prayer *kappe* and straightened her neck cloth, which modestly covered her shoulders and chest.

"Well?"

Greta frowned.

"Well?" the man repeated, and raised his eyebrows. Greta couldn't tell if the expression showed playfulness or irritation.

"My cow. She broke in."

"*Ja*, I can see that." The man offered a small half smile. "What do you plan to do about it?"

Greta hoped the smile was meant to make her feel more comfortable. *No, he must be making fun of me. I must look ridiculous with my muddy dress and trespassing cow!* "I . . . I will take care of all of this." Greta bit her lip. "I promise. I am sorry—"

The man nodded and glanced at the sky. "The day is almost over. And there will be no work tomorrow."

"I will come back after the Sabbath." Greta stared into the man's eyes, trying to decipher his emotions. "First thing."

"That will be much appreciated." The man tipped his hat and turned away.

Greta let out a breath of air as the tension in her shoulders relaxed. The man's gaze had felt so intense as he studied her. She wished she knew what he had been thinking. *Most likely, he is exasperated with Rose and me and is struggling to be polite. I must try harder to fit in here.*

Greta tugged on Rose's collar. "Let's go." The cow did not move. Instead the animal lowered her head and bit into a tarragon leaf. *Just when I thought I couldn't be any more embarrassed!* "Rose, come on!"

The man turned back around and raised an eyebrow. He strode over to Rose and grabbed her collar. The cow raised her head and stared at him. "Time to go, *ja?*" The animal lumbered forward. Greta's cheeks burned as she marched after Rose and the stranger.

"I don't understand . . . Rose usually—"

"*Ja,*" the man cut her off, and shrugged. "I will see you first thing day after tomorrow."

Jacob Miller frowned as he watched Greta Scholtz lead her cow into the forest. The memory of her steady gaze burned inside his mind. He had fallen into those lively green eyes and could not find his way out again. What was it about her that drew him in and would not let him go? *It must be the outrageous way that we met. She looked so ridiculous, sprawled on the ground with that adorable expression of shock on her face.* Jacob winced. He didn't want to find her—or any woman—adorable. His heart was still too raw. He shook his head and tried to force his attention back to his work. But his gaze lingered on the young woman as she strode across the clearing.

She must have felt humiliated, but she kept her head held high and promised to fix the problem instead of shying away. Though young and unprepared, she seemed eager to overcome the challenges of the backcountry. A familiar sense of loss flooded him. *I remember another woman like that.* He cut off the train of thought before the memories overtook him.

Remember, the Lord taketh away. . . .

Jacob knew that there was more to that verse. But after months of grief, he struggled to believe that the Lord giveth. Life in the backcountry felt like it was all take, and no give. Less than a year had passed since he had buried Marta with his own hands. He remembered shoveling cold earth over the grave and promising never to open his heart again. Jacob pushed aside the unwelcome warmth that Greta Scholtz forced upon him.

He needed to finish splitting a log before sundown. *What is the matter with you? Focus on your work.* But thoughts of Greta pushed into his mind as he struck his ax into the wood. He remembered the delightful sprinkle of freckles across her nose and cheeks. He remembered how she tried to look dignified as she lay sprawled in the mud. And he remembered the endearing quiver in her voice as she fought to overcome her embarrassment. Yes, that Greta Scholtz knew how to make quite an impression.

Jacob shook his head and let his smile drop back into a frown. He set down the ax and wedged a fat wooden peg into the crack he had hacked into the log. He wiped his hands on his knee breeches and picked up a massive wooden mallet. His face hardened as he raised the heavy mallet far above his head and swung it down against the peg. The force of the blow ricocheted into his shoulder and jaw. After enough blows the peg would force the wood apart. Then he would have to repeat the process again and again, down the entire length of the log.

Jacob sighed and swung the mallet down again. *Be practical. Prepare for winter. And, whatever happens, don't fool yourself into thinking that a captivating young lady can make things right again.*

Greta felt completely and utterly humiliated. The cowbell clanged as Rose followed behind her and the constant noise made her feel even more vulnerable and exposed. Even though she walked alone through the forest, Greta imagined everyone in the settlement hearing the bell, looking up, and laughing at her. She told herself that she was overreacting, but all she could think about was that man, standing over her with that hard, humorless expression.

Why did he stare at me like that? What was he thinking? She pressed her hands over her face and squeezed her eyes shut. *He was thinking about what a ridiculous woman I am! How could everything have gone so wrong so quickly!* Closing her eyes made everything worse because his image blazed inside her mind. His chiseled features . . . the way his hands closed around hers and lifted her without effort . . . his dark, mesmerizing eyes. Greta opened her eyes. The fact that she could not stop thinking about him made her as confused as his attitude did. *Whatever is wrong with me?* Greta felt her forehead. *Mayhap I am coming down with a fever. I must be delusional. Why else would that man make such an impression on me?*

She heard a shout and looked up. The six-year-old Fisher twins ran along the footpath that wound through the settlement. The woolen hosen on Peter's legs sagged, showing a sliver of bare calf beneath his knee breeches.

"Peter, pull up your hosen before you catch cold!"

Peter grinned and waved, then darted past without straightening his stockings. Greta shook her head, but smiled. Peter and Eliza's parents took sick and died on the *Charming Nancy* during the crossing. She remembered how she held the twins close and shared their grief as they endured endless days together in the dark hold of the ship. *If only I could take them in. They are alone in this harsh new world just like me.*

Greta sighed and gave Rose's rump a gentle slap. "Go on now. But watch out for the wolves, *ja?*" *If I had a husband, the elders would let us adopt Peter and Eliza.* She felt a stab of longing, then forced the emotion away. *I will not fall for the first man I meet in the New World. And I certainly will not fall for* that *man, no matter how much the elders think I need a husband. He could never be interested in me after today.*

The thought of that tall, broad-shouldered man with the amused half smile reignited Greta's embarrassment. She slunk across the clearing and flung open the door of a small log cabin. *I hope I never see him again. Except, that would mean never staring into those dark eyes again. . . .* Greta cut off the thought.

"My goodness, Greta." Ruth Yoder looked up from her mending with a startled expression. "Whatever has come over you?"

Greta sighed. "I'm sorry, Ruth. I've only been here a few days and I'm already disturbing your quiet evenings." Greta had felt like a disruption ever since she came to live in the small cabin. After the *Charming Nancy* arrived in Philadelphia, Greta and her fellow Amish made their way to the base of the Blue Mountain, at the very edge of the Pennsylvania frontier. The land had just opened for European settlement the year before and the new group joined a handful of Amish families who had already cleared land and put down roots in the wilderness.

The new settlers scrambled to house everyone and Greta felt fortunate that the group found her a cozy home with an elderly widow—although the elders made it clear that the arrangement was temporary. They insisted that the backcountry was no place for a single young woman and an old widow.

Ruth patted the bench beside her. "You are not disrupting, dear. I cannot tell you how lonely I've been since my husband died."

Greta sighed and slumped onto the rough, backless bench. No roads had been cut through the backcountry yet, so settlers had to leave their wagons—and furniture—behind. The benches, and almost everything else inside the cramped cabin, had been handmade from whatever materials could be found in the Pennsylvania wilderness.

Greta wiped her brow with the corner of her apron. "It is not an easy life here."

Ruth let out a long, deep breath. "No, it is not." She looked down. "I thought that, after so many years of hiding our faith, my husband and I would live out our old age in peace. But it was not *der Herr*'s will."

"And I thought my father would live out his years here too, free and happy."

A smile broke across Ruth's wrinkled face. "But I am grateful that you have come to me. It is wonderful that more Amish are finding their way to our little outpost."

"To think that this was all forest just a few months ago," Greta said.

"*Ja.* One year ago, when my husband and I arrived here, there was naught but trees and wolves."

"We will make a new life here. I know we will."

"*Ja.* You are so young, Greta. You have your whole life ahead of you. I can only imagine what *der Herr* has planned for you here, in the New World."

Greta looked away. *How can I manage without Father? I feel so alone in this strange, wild land.*

"What is troubling you, child?"

"I'm afraid that I have not gotten off to a very good start here."

"Oh?" Ruth raised an eyebrow. "What happened today? You certainly came into the house like a storm."

"I heard the wolves and went looking for Rose."

"Is she safe?"

"*Ja.*"

"No harm done, then."

"Well, not exactly." Greta sighed. "Rose got into the neighbor's kitchen garden."

"Oh dear. Which neighbor? Not Jacob Miller, I hope."

"If Jacob Miller lives beyond that stretch of forest." She motioned in the direction of his farm.

Ruth suppressed a smile. "He is a handful, that one."

"Well, that is one way to put it." Greta put her face in her hands. "I can never see him again. I just can't face him after . . ."

"After what? It can't be that bad . . . can it?"

"Oh, Ruth! I fell in the mud and there he was standing over me with this expression of . . . of . . . complete disapproval! It was the most embarrassing moment of my life!" Greta thought she caught a gleam in the old woman's eye.

"Most women would be eager to see such a handsome man again. Hmmm?"

Greta scowled. She hoped that Ruth did not think she felt an attraction to Jacob Miller. That would be preposterous after he caught her in such an embarrassing situation. Absolutely preposterous. Greta cleared her throat. "If he's handsome then I certainly did not notice."

"No?"

"No."

Ruth shrugged and turned her attention back to her mending. "Of course, dear."

Chapter Two

Greta and Ruth hurried to the Riehls' farm for the Sunday worship service. The countryside still swarmed with wildlife, but axes rang out every day as the settlers cleared the endless forest to make room for homes and crops. Greta's eyes lingered on the stumps that surrounded a stout log cabin. *Soon we will have a proper town, just like we had back home.* Her heart filled with pride at the progress made since she and the other *Charming Nancy* passengers arrived just a few days earlier.

Greta paused when they reached the crowd gathered in the next clearing. A handful of men in their best dress jackets and knee breeches chatted in the gentle autumn sun. Children laughed and chased one another. Homespun skirts swirled in a gray and white collage. Greta watched the simple, friendly scene and felt the warmth catch inside her chest. *This is why I came to America.*

A girl and a boy shouted and crashed into her with an enthusiastic hug.

"Greta!"

Peter tugged at Greta's skirts with sticky hands. "We've missed you!"

Greta wrapped her arms around him and squeezed. "And I have missed you!"

"You were always with us on the journey," Eliza added. "I wish it could be like that again."

Greta nodded her head. "*Ja.* But now you live in a cabin with a family. That is good too."

The twins shrugged. "*Ja.* But they cannot keep us forever. It is only temporary."

Greta's forehead creased. *Just like me. Without family, praying for a home of my own.* She forced a brave smile and tousled Peter's hair. "Don't worry. *Der Herr* has a plan for you." *And for me. I just don't know what it is yet.*

She took each child by the hand and they walked toward the gathering together.

"I don't think we could have crammed everyone into the Riehl cabin today," Ruth said as they strolled side by side. "It is fortunate that the weather is mild."

"*Ja.* Someday the menfolk will have to build us proper houses, large enough for services."

Ruth scanned a cluster of young couples. "And large enough for growing families."

Greta looked down. At twenty-four, she was on the verge of becoming an old maid. She had waited to marry so that she could work to help her father save enough money to come to the New World. Greta frowned as she remembered the years of sacrifice that ended in her father's death, rather than the fulfillment of his dreams. *Is there still a purpose for me here in Pennsylvania without Father?*

"Enough daydreaming," Ruth said. "Let's find a

seat." Ruth motioned toward the backless benches that the men unloaded from a cart, dragged into the front yard, and then arranged into two different sections, one for the men and one for the women. Greta noticed one of the men as he pushed the last bench into place. His back was turned, but she recognized something familiar about his broad shoulders and large, work-hardened hands. She frowned as the man turned around.

Jacob Miller's dark eyes met hers and he nodded without smiling. Greta gasped and shifted her gaze. *It looks like I was staring at him!* She felt her cheeks flush red as she stalked away. *Well, I was staring. But not for the reason that he thinks.* Greta clenched her jaw and settled onto a bench between Ruth and Eliza in the women's section. *As if I wasn't embarrassed enough already. I must put all thoughts of Jacob Miller out of my mind. This is most unbecoming!*

Greta refused to let her gaze wander to the men's side again. Instead, she opened the *Ausbund*, an old hymnal of Anabaptist German songs her people sang during every service. Greta's copy of the book had been passed down through the Scholtz family for years and the thin, brittle pages reminded her that she wasn't alone, even in the backcountry. She felt connected to her Anabaptist ancestors and to the families who worked beside her to carve out a living from the wilderness. She felt a familiar warmth as the congregation lifted their voices in song. The rich, a cappella melody drifted above the trees and into the crisp blue sky above.

Ruth looked at Greta and smiled. The old woman squeezed her hand and then closed her eyes. Greta knew that she was meant to be here, in a strange, new land. And yet, she still felt troubled deep inside. *I am so blessed to be here, alive and free. But I feel such a sense of loss without my father. And this land is so foreign and harsh. I miss the villages of southern Germany, the bustling, cobblestone streets, bakeries, and windmills. I feel so alone, starting over on my own. And even worse, I am a burden on the community. If only I could shoot my own game and plant my own fields!*

The three-hour service wound to a close after a sermon about the Israelites' journey through the wilderness and another a cappella song. The men rearranged the benches to create a makeshift table and the women heaped dishes onto the rough planks.

"I think I know what is in every pot on that table," Ruth whispered.

"Pumpkin mush and pumpkin broth. Same as we brought." Greta sighed. "I hear the men are going to build a bake-oven for the settlement this week. Soon we will have bread again. And maybe even cake, if we can get some cane sugar."

"Sugar." Ruth shook her head. "That would be a fine treat."

"Oh, look!" Greta pointed to a platter. "A turkey!"

"Ah, yes, I hear we can thank Jacob Miller for putting meat on the table today."

"I've never had a turkey before, Ruth! And it has been ages since I have had any meat." She breathed in the rich aroma of golden, greasy skin and felt her stomach rumble. *I should thank Jacob for the wonderful good meal.* But then she remembered the aloof look in his eyes as she lay stunned in the mud of his kitchen garden. *Better to avoid reliving that humiliation. I am probably the last person that he wants to speak to today.*

Greta inhaled the food as soon as she piled it on her wooden trencher. She only stopped chewing to smile politely at her neighbors and ask how they were managing. Most of them had journeyed together on the *Charming Nancy* and she felt a strong connection to the small group—and a fierce commitment to finish what they had started.

Ruth stepped aside to refill her plate and Abraham Riehl and Amos Knepp slid in to take her place beside Greta. Along with Jacob and Ruth, the two elderly men and their wives, Berta and Emma, had lived in the settlement the longest and had naturally fallen into a position of church leadership until the settlement could choose a bishop by lots.

"Greta. *Der Herr*'s blessings on this fine day."

"Indeed, Abraham. We *are* blessed today. It was a great joy to attend my first service in the New World."

The silver-haired man smiled. "It is a day that our ancestors could not have dreamed would ever come to pass."

Amos cleared his throat. "Greta, how are you faring?"

"I am fine. Ruth Yoder is very hospitable."

"*Ja*. It is not good for a woman to live alone."

"This is a challenging land," Greta agreed. "And Ruth must have been very lonely since her husband died."

The two men glanced at each other. "We are glad that you have found a nice home," Amos said. "But, how long can the arrangement last? Two women alone in the wilderness? There are so many things that you simply cannot do on your own."

"We will make sure that you have the help you need," Abraham said. "But—"

"Good. Ruth and I will manage quite well, then."

"*Ja.*" Abraham adjusted his wide-brimmed hat. "But, Greta, you cannot mean to stay on your own."

Greta looked down.

"You must be realistic. Besides, there are widowers in the community in need of a wife. You could find a good match that would benefit both parties."

Greta felt her stomach drop. Abraham made marriage sound like a business arrangement. She knew that many people married for practical reasons, but she did not want to be one of them. She longed for something more. "I had not considered getting married so soon."

"It is time to think about such things," Amos said. "Winter is coming and scratching a living out of the wilderness will only become more difficult."

I know that, as Amish, we must put others before ourselves; the good of the group before our own desires. But marriage . . . ?

"There are good men in need of a helpmeet," Abraham said.

Greta glanced around at the single men. She only saw a handful of elderly men and a few teenage boys. And Jacob Miller. She narrowed her eyes. "Who do you have in mind?"

Amos pulled at his beard. "Oh well. I am sure that I could not say." He raised an eyebrow and leaned in closer. "But Jacob is a fine man. Recently widowed. I imagine that you two could be good partners."

Greta balked. *They are trying to set me up with Jacob Miller? I am quite sure he is not interested in me.*

"Oh. No. I don't think . . . No. No, thank you." She

cut her eyes toward the handsome stranger. His tall frame and broad shoulders filled out his black waist-coat and dress jacket. The rim of his black beaver-felt hat sloped forward and hid his dark, brooding eyes.

"You must be practical, Greta," Abraham scolded. "We are not in Germany anymore. The backcountry is no place for a woman alone."

"I am not alone. I have Ruth Yoder."

"She cannot plant your crops or hunt game for you, Greta. You must think this through. You are an extra mouth for our community to feed. We only meant for you to live at the Widow Yoder's house temporarily."

"*Ja.* I understand." Greta averted her gaze, embar-rassed that she might be putting herself before the community. "I do not want to burden anyone."

"No." Abraham patted her shoulder with grand-fatherly reassurance. "Think about what we have said. Jacob is a good man."

Greta remembered the way Jacob had stared down at her with that unreadable expression after she fell into the mud. His eyes were so intense. . . . *Surely that look was one of disapproval.* Greta refused to begin her new life by throwing herself at a man who would surely reject her. She opened her mouth to comment and then closed it again. It was too much to explain. "*Ja.* I will think about what you have said."

"Good!" the men chimed in unison.

Greta kept her attention on Jacob Miller as the brethren sifted away from the Sunday gathering. *Is he in on this? Does he know that the church elders are trying to put us together?* Then a thought hit her like a slap. *Maybe he is not as disapproving as I assumed. Maybe he put them up to it.* Greta felt a strange flutter in her stomach at the thought. She could not understand what caused the sudden rush of emotion. *Indigestion,* she insisted to herself, and raised her chin. *It must be indigestion.*

But when Jacob strode away from the gathering without saying a word to her, Greta felt disappointed. *No,* she told herself. *This is not disappointment. This is frustration. I am just frustrated that I haven't made the impression I wanted.* Greta shook her head. *He is avoiding me—and no wonder. The last time he saw me I was sprawled in the mud like a hog. That is no way to make a good impression.*

Then again, why on earth would the church elders try to put us together if Jacob Miller did not approve . . . ?

Greta frowned as she watched Jacob saunter down the dirt path. She studied his casual gait and relaxed manner, the self-assured way he held his shoulders. *I wish I knew what that man was thinking.*

"Well, Greta. Do tell me what you are staring at." Ruth sidled up to her young friend with a devilish half smile on her lips. Greta jumped. "I . . . I . . . nothing. I am not staring at anything. I mean, not anything worth mentioning . . . I mean . . ."

Ruth chuckled. "We both know what you were staring at, dear. Or should I say *who* you were staring at."

"Oh. Oh no." Greta blushed and looked miserable. "How terribly forward of me. Please, tell me that no one else noticed. I didn't mean to stare . . . it is just that . . ." Greta adjusted her prayer *kappe.*

"Just what, dear?"

"It is just that Abraham and Amos think that I should marry Jacob Miller!"

Ruth shrugged. "It makes sense. You both need a spouse." She glanced at Greta with a sly, sidelong look. "And you obviously have feelings for him."

"Feelings!? Feelings?!"

"Yes, dear. Feelings."

Greta shook her head. "Feelings of embarrassment, you mean!"

Ruth raised an eyebrow. "Embarrassment? Not exactly."

Greta opened her mouth to protest and then shut it again. She closed her eyes and counted to ten. She took a deep breath. Ruth was still smiling when Greta opened her eyes. Greta counted to ten again. "I do not have any feelings beyond embarrassment when it comes to Jacob Miller!" She glared at his back until he disappeared around a bend at the end of the path. "We've only spoken once, and he stared at me as if he could not believe I could be so incompetent. I could never marry a man who thinks so little of me."

"Of course, dear. Whatever you say, dear."

Greta held her head high and stomped away.

Ruth caught up to her. "Do you know what my favorite Shakespeare line is, Greta?"

Greta gritted her teeth. "No. I can't imagine."

Ruth grinned. "*'The lady doth protest too much, methinks.'*"

Chapter Three

Abraham and Amos stood in Jacob's front yard when he arrived home from the service. Jacob shot the men a quizzical look.

"You got here mighty fast. You must have taken the shortcut through the Widow Yoder's farm."

The elderly men glanced at each other and shrugged. "*Ja*, well, we do have something to discuss with you, Jacob."

"But you left the service so quickly that we did not get a chance to speak to you after lunch."

"*Ja*. It was almost as if you were avoiding someone."

Jacob frowned. "Avoiding someone? Me? No. Just looking forward to a quiet afternoon of rest."

Abraham smiled. "Indeed."

"*Ja*," Amos added. "You work harder than any other man in the settlement. I am sure that Sundays are a welcome relief."

"*Ja*. They are most welcome." Jacob waited for the men to explain their hasty visit, but they only nodded and grinned. He sighed. "You mentioned that you wanted to discuss something with me?"

The elders glanced at each other. Neither seemed eager to be the first to speak.

"Well?" Jacob frowned.

"Well, Jacob, we know that these months have not been easy on you."

"*No*, they have not." Jacob's jaw tightened. The last thing he wanted was sympathy. "But I am not the only person who has lost loved ones this year. Or struggled to make a living in the backcountry."

Amos cleared his throat. "True. But you seem to struggle more than others to reconcile your fate with *der Herr*'s will."

Jacob clenched his jaw harder. His mouth tightened into a hard line. "I have not failed in my duties to the community. I have helped build and clear land. I will be ready to share from my crops this winter if any of our brothers or sisters runs short before spring."

"*Ja.*" Amos nodded. "We know that your work ethic is without fault. We know your commitment to our community."

Abraham put up a hand. "But it is not your work ethic that we are concerned about."

"It is your heart, Jacob." Amos tapped his own chest. "Your heart."

"Thank you for your concern," Jacob retorted. "But I am fine. My heart is fine."

"We find you much changed this past year," Abraham cut in.

"We know that you have always been serious-minded." Amos shifted his weight from one foot to the other. "But you do not fellowship with the brethren as you once did. You seem to struggle to trust again."

Abraham furrowed his brow and nodded. "Ever since Marta and the baby died—"

"I am fine." Jacob shook his head. "There is no need to talk of these things. I am not a burden to anyone. I have no conflict with anyone. This conversation is unnecessary."

Amos frowned and stroked his beard.

Abraham put up a finger. "Then let us add a pleasant topic to our conversation."

They are not going to drop it. But I don't need anyone's help. Jacob ignored the doubt he felt in the pit of his stomach. *I am doing fine on my own.*

"We have noticed a lovely young lady, newly arrived on the *Charming Nancy.*"

Jacob felt his chest tighten. He knew where this was going.

"There is no need to press the subject. As I have said, I am doing just fine on my own."

"I am sure you are, Jacob." Amos held up his hands, palms up. "But this young lady—I do not believe that you have met—she is certainly in need of a partner. What a blessing it would be for her to find a good man in this hostile country! She and the Widow Yoder will be alone all winter, and you must admit that is a most unsatisfactory arrangement."

Jacob sighed. "Let us be honest, brothers. You are trying to push a new bride on me because you think that I am bitter and lonely."

"We think this young lady needs a husband," Amos insisted. "Her father died on the crossing and she is without family."

Jacob raised his eyebrows.

"All right, all right," Abraham admitted. "'Tis true.

We worry about you, Jacob." The old man shook his head. "You are not the man you once were."

"Then the last thing I need to do is take a new bride."

The two elders paused as they searched for a retort. Jacob sighed. "Who is this potential bride, anyway?"

"Oh, she is living with the Widow Yoder. Greta is her name. A lovely girl."

"The Widow Yoder, you say?"

"*Ja.*"

"Just arrived?"

"*Ja.*"

"She didn't bring a cow with her when she joined the settlement, by any chance?"

"Oh, *ja*! We have heard that Rose has a habit of breaking through fences. Do mind your garden."

Of course. Jacob frowned. *Of all the women who could have wandered into my life, it had to be one that I cannot get out of my mind.* "I have had the, um, *pleasure* of making Greta's acquaintance."

"Then you know what a charming girl she is!"

"I am not sure 'charming' is the way I would describe our first encounter." And yet, *charming* was exactly the way she had seemed as those big green eyes stared up at him with that adorable look of dismay. Jacob pushed the thought away and reminded himself that her cow had destroyed hours and hours of his work.

Abraham waved his hand. "No matter. She is an ideal catch. Young and hardworking, with great strength of character."

Amos nodded. "You will find her charming in the days to come, I am sure."

"I do not have time to find any young ladies charming." Jacob swept his hand across his farm. I have to repair the roof tomorrow and begin harvesting. Old Bess has gone lame. And after nine months I have not had time to dig a well; I am still hauling water from the creek. Visiting young ladies is not on the agenda."

Amos shrugged. "You should add fence repairs to that list. Greta's cow has been in the Widow Yoder's garden, I hear. You cannot expect her to fix it on her own."

"She needs your help," Abraham said.

Jacob looked away. His eyes followed the path that cut through his clearing and into the forest. He remembered Marta's bare feet padding across the yard as the wind whipped her skirts. Jacob tried to recall the shape of her face, the soft expression she wore as she glanced back at him and smiled, but the details had faded. He felt a stab in his chest as he realized that his memories of her were weakening. *Forgive me, Marta. I will never forget you. Never. And I will never open my heart to another woman. I owe you that. No one will ever replace you and no one will ever take this pain away.*

He shook his head. "I will take care of the fence because it is my duty to assist a sister in need. But there will be no friendship, no relationship, and *certainly* no marriage."

"Hmmmm." Abraham ran his fingers through his beard. "It sounds as though she has made quite an impression on you, Jacob."

Jacob sighed, then chose his words carefully. "You could say that."

"One has to wonder why our suggestions have triggered such a strong reaction from you."

"I am not reacting strongly. All I want is to get this season's work finished and go about my business." *And to guard my heart.*

Amos smiled. "My mistake, then."

"I am sure that she has not made any impression, whatsoever," Abraham added.

"None at all," Jacob agreed, his face hard.

"Good."

"Good."

The men nodded and headed toward the path. Jacob stood on the front porch and frowned.

"Oh, by the way, Jacob." Amos turned around as he crossed the ruined kitchen garden. "I am surprised to see what a mess your garden has become. You always used to be so careful in your work."

Abraham frowned. "I hope that you are not struggling to keep up with your chores."

Amos nodded in agreement. "A good woman like Greta could certainly help with the workload. You cannot keep doing all of the chores that a wife should do. You will work yourself to death."

The men turned back around and shook their heads at the smashed vegetables.

Jacob watched them leave with his mouth agape. He could not find the words to defend himself against such ludicrous accusations.

Chapter Four

Greta woke up early and dressed quickly. She pulled a stay over the loose linen shift that she slept in. The stay wrapped around her upper body to provide support and enforce good posture. Greta frowned as she laced up the stiff, fitted cloth. *I want to hurry and get on my way. Putting on all of these layers takes too much time!* After the stay was in place, Greta shrugged into her bodice and tightened the laces down the front. Then she stepped into a petticoat and pleated overskirt and fastened them around her waist. The sun began to rise as she pinned an apron across the front of her garment and secured a neck cloth over her shoulders and across her chest.

Greta blew out the candle beside her pallet, walked to the hearth, and sat down on the three-legged stool to pull on her woolen hosen, tie them above her knee, and fasten her leather shoes. She splashed cold water from the wooden bucket onto her face, dumped the remainder of the water into the cauldron, and stoked the fire. The cauldron would hang above the flames all day so that there was always hot water on hand.

Greta noticed that sunlight had replaced the cabin's shadows. *It is getting late.* She pinned her long, thick hair into a bun and fastened a prayer *kappe* over the chestnut locks.

"Oh, my. You are already up and about and here I am, still abed." Ruth threw back the covers and rubbed her eyes.

Greta glanced toward the elderly woman's pallet. "I want to get an early start. Today is the day I have to face Jacob Miller. The earlier I begin, the earlier I finish."

Ruth laughed. "Fair enough."

Greta started for the door.

"Do not forget to wear your scoop! The sun will be bright today, I wager."

Greta nodded and reached for her wide-brimmed straw hat. Two ribbons hung from opposite sides of the brim and she tied them beneath her chin as she raced out the door. The ribbons pulled the brim downward to form a distinctive shape that gave the hat its name.

Greta arrived at Jacob's doorstep as the sun crested the tree line. She set her mouth in a tight line. *Let's get this over with.* The young woman swallowed, raised her chin, and knocked on the rough oak door.

No answer. Greta forced herself to breathe evenly and ignore the excitement she felt at the thought of seeing the aloof stranger.

She knocked again, louder this time.

"Hello? Jacob?"

Still no answer.

She hesitated and then knocked a third time.

"Enough racket, Greta. You don't have to keep pounding on the door."

The deep voice came from above.

"Oh!" The young woman's eyes shot upward. Jacob's face appeared over the eave of the roof. He held a wooden peg between his lips and a mallet in his right hand.

"It has been raining into the cabin." He motioned to a spot on the roof with his chin. "Just going to make a few repairs."

"What's that? I can't quite understand you."

Jacob pulled the peg from his mouth. He repeated himself with exaggerated enunciation.

"Oh. Yes. I see."

"Well, don't let me stop you, Greta. I'm sure you have plenty to do."

Greta thought she caught a twinkle in his dark eyes as he spoke. *Is he joking with me or is he making fun of me? Why can he not be more obvious with his intentions?* She hesitated.

Jacob frowned and set down the mallet. "Can I help you with something, Greta?"

Oh no, I've been staring again. She cleared her throat and forced a neutral expression on her face. "Yes. Yes you can."

He sighed. "Well? What can I help you with?"

"Oh. Right. Yes. I need help." *What is it about Jacob Miller that leaves me so flustered and tongue-tied?* She steadied her voice. "I have not brought any tools. I thought that I could use yours."

He waved toward the yard. "*Ja.* I left them by the

door." He turned to his work and then glanced back at Greta when she did not walk away. She put her hands on her hips and gazed back at him. "I wonder, Jacob, shouldn't you use nails to repair a roof? It must be quite time-consuming to whittle those little pegs. And I cannot imagine that the seal is nearly as tight."

Jacob raised an eyebrow. "And where would you suggest that I buy these nails, Greta? From the squirrels? Or the wolves, perhaps? There is nothing here but wilderness."

"Hmm. Right. Well, carry on."

Jacob looked down at the young woman with an astonished expression that morphed into a frown.

"After you finish with my tools, put them back where you found them."

"Naturally." Greta waited for Jacob to say more, but he turned his attention back to the peg in his hand. *Why can't he give me a few minutes of civil conversation? Am I really such a bother to him?* She turned away as she felt heat rising into her cheeks. *Of course I am—my Rose destroyed his garden. I've been nothing but a bother to him since the moment we met.*

Greta replayed their conversation over and over again as she replanted herbs. She told herself that it didn't matter what Jacob Miller thought of her. She told herself that she was completely unmoved by the chiseled features and the strong arms that pulled her to her feet without effort. The teasing half smile reappeared in her mind. The dark, unreadable eyes that stared into hers . . . *Regain your dignity, Greta! He barely takes the time to speak to you. And when he does speak to you, he maintains a careful distance. He clearly*

*thinks that you are a bothersome young woman, unfit for the
backcountry.* She speared the earth hard, then stopped,
put down the trowel, and smiled. *Well, if that is what
he thinks of me, I will just have to show him otherwise.*

Greta raised her chin with determination, picked
up the satchel beside her, and strode toward the
cabin. She rummaged through the packed food as
she walked. Until she felt an unexpected crunch beneath the heel of her shoe. Greta froze. Her eyes
moved from the satchel to the earth beneath her
foot. Another cabbage lay crushed on the ground.
She gasped and glanced up at the roof. Jacob was
not in sight. She exhaled a sigh of relief, wiped the
dirt and cabbage leaves off the bottom of her shoe,
and continued toward the roof.

"Jacob!"

No answer.

"Jacob!"

The mallet stopped its sharp rhythm.

"Jacob!"

"Are you injured, Greta?"

Greta frowned and stood on her tiptoes to get a
better view of the roof. "No."

"Is there a fox threatening the chickens?"

Greta cut her eyes to the hens. They pecked at the
dirt in tight, rapid movements. "No."

"A wildfire?"

"No."

"Then what can I help you with, Greta?"

Greta tried to read the tone of his voice. She
frowned and cleared her throat. *A nice home-cooked meal
will show him that I can manage just fine in the backcountry.*

"I have brought you refreshments, Jacob. We can share a late breakfast."

Greta thought she heard a sigh come from the rooftop.

"What is that, Jacob?"

"Do not weaken your resolve." He whispered the words to himself so that Greta couldn't hear. "Friendship is the first step toward something more. . . ."

"Jacob, are you talking to me? I cannot make out what you are saying."

"I am not hungry, Greta."

Greta stared at the roof. His gruff response cut into her. She forced a cheerful smile and rummaged through her satchel until her fingers closed around a greasy white cloth. "I am sure you will be hungry later. Here. Have some squash." She narrowed her eyes and flung the package into the air.

Greta waited to hear the thump against the handhewn wooden shingles. But the noise did not come. Instead, after a few beats, she heard a quiet splat on the far side of the house.

"You missed, Greta."

"Hmph." Greta put her hands on her hips and stalked around the cabin.

"If you are trying to impress the pigs, you have succeeded."

Greta heard a hint of amusement in Jacob's deep voice. She rounded the corner and saw the white cloth in the middle of a mud puddle where two fat hogs fought over bits of fried squash. Their glistening, upturned noses whuffled and snorted as they lunged for the food.

Greta turned on her heels and marched back to

the kitchen garden. *We will just pretend that never happened.* But she could feel Jacob Miller's eyes on her back the entire time.

The Fisher twins called on Greta the next evening. They announced that they had come to help with the evening chores, but Eliza knocked over the water bucket and Peter sloshed the corn cake batter into the fire. Greta just laughed. She didn't care that their efforts hindered more than helped. "I would rather enjoy an adventure with you than work alone without incident," she said as she tousled Peter's unkempt hair.

"Have you met your neighbor?" the boy asked as he set down a tin cup of milk. Greta wiped his mouth with her handkerchief. He wiggled to get away.

"Jacob Miller?" She nodded in the direction of his farm.

"*Ja.*"

"I have." Greta felt her cheeks flush at the memory. *Why does he fluster me so very much?*

Eliza smiled and reached for Peter's pewter cup of milk. "I like Jacob." She swallowed twice and set the cup down with a bang. "I bet you do too."

Greta wiped a drop of milk that had splattered on the table and changed the subject. "Who are you living with now?"

"With the Gruber family."

"Have the elders decided who you will stay with permanently?"

Peter sucked on one of his fingers and shook his head.

"The Gruber family is nice." Eliza shrugged and

set down the broom. "But they haven't enough room for us."

Greta counted off the number of Gruber children in her head. "No, I should think not. It must be quite a squeeze."

Peter nodded, his finger still in his mouth.

"We like Mrs. Gruber very much, but she really hasn't any time for us."

"No, I am sure that she has her hands full."

Greta wished that she could take them in. She frowned. *Children need a father.* . . . Jacob's face appeared in her mind. She frowned.

Greta shook the image from her mind and smiled at Peter and Eliza. "You need to get on your way or you will miss your supper." She pinched Peter's red, chubby cheeks and he giggled. Then his face dropped into seriousness. "But what if there is a fox on the path?"

"A fox? Why should that matter?"

"Because foxes might eat me."

"Peter is afraid of foxes." Eliza shook her head. "I keep telling him that he should be afraid of wolves instead, but he insists on being afraid of foxes."

"Oh well, perhaps it is best not to be afraid of either one."

Peter looked up at Greta with big eyes. "But foxes might eat me."

Greta smiled. "No, darling, foxes do not eat people. You are much too big for a fox to eat."

Peter popped his finger back in his mouth. "Mmm fhing fffxxss enn—"

"Take your finger out of your mouth, dear. I cannot understand you."

Eliza reached over and pulled his hand down. "I think foxes eat little boys," Peter repeated.

"Why would you think such a thing?"

"Because they have teeth."

"*Ja.* Hmmm. I suppose that is true. Animals with teeth *can* bite."

Peter nodded, his fears confirmed.

Greta shook her head. "No, no. That is not what I meant. I just meant that . . . Well, just think, even rabbits and chipmunks have teeth."

Peter's eyes widened. "Rabbits and chipmunks will bite me?"

"No. Of course not." Greta sighed. "Never mind. Foxes do not eat little boys. They do not eat people."

"Ever?"

"Ever."

Peter frowned, still unconvinced.

"Let's go before it gets dark, Peter." Eliza tugged on Peter's sleeve. "You always think that you see foxes in the dark."

Peter reached for Greta's hand. "Too late. Foxes are out now. Can you walk us to the Gruber farm?"

Greta could not resist Peter's sad brown eyes. "A walk would do me good. I have been in this cabin far too long."

Ruth raised an eyebrow. "You will spoil them." But then she smiled and shrugged. "Ach, what can it hurt? The poor dears."

Greta and the twins sang nursery rhymes as they walked under a cloudless sky, a thousand stars glittering down from a cold, dark dome. Greta stopped when they reached the Grubers' front gate. "Run along, now. It really is getting late and I must get back."

"You won't come in?"

"No, not tonight."

Greta watched Peter and Eliza skip to the front door. The oilcloth over the windows glowed a cozy yellow and Greta could sense the warmth inside. She imagined the roaring fire and the rich smell of roasted meat. The Gruber family would be sitting down to dinner with half a dozen children gathered around the table, the room full of chatter and laughter. Greta sighed and turned away. The cold cut more sharply than before and she raised the hood of her cloak. *Will I ever have a family of my own? A husband who will sit with me at our safe, warm hearth as the wind howls outside? Children who pull at my skirts, reaching up to be held?*

Greta tried to push the thoughts from her mind as she trudged back to the Yoder cabin. But she knew that she headed back to a house that was not her home. The thought dug into her heart. *I am grateful to have a roof over my head and a friend to share it with. But I cannot help but long for something more. . . .*

Greta watched her breath form tiny white clouds in the cold air and then disappear. She folded her arms beneath her cloak. A wolf howled in the distance and Greta shivered. She pulled her cloak closer and quickened her pace. The path loomed like a dark tunnel ahead. The oak branches quivered and reached like hands. She tried to walk faster, but her feet stumbled over roots and loose stones. *Here I am, wandering alone in the dark.* Fear and disappointment tugged at her throat and blurred her thoughts.

A scuffling sound pulled Greta's thoughts back to the path. She gasped and stared into the brush beside the dirt lane. Branches snapped. "Who is there?" No answer. She knew that bears and mountain lions roamed these wild hills. Another wolf howl rose toward the moon and melted into the dark sky. She hesitated and searched the shadows. Another branch snapped. Greta broke into a run. Her breath caught in her throat. Thoughts of teeth and claws and nameless night creatures flashed in her mind. She glanced back and strained to see a shape in the moonlight. Her feet kept running ahead, even though she could not see where she was headed.

Greta's body slammed into something. Something large and warm that grunted when she hit it. She shouted in surprise as a hand grabbed her arm and steadied her from the force of the impact.

"Easy now, I have you."

"Oh!"

"Calm down, now."

"Oh! It's *you*!"

"*Ja*. It's me." Jacob's tall frame blocked the path. He looked down at her with an amused expression.

"I was running."

"*Ja*. I noticed. You should look in the direction that you are running next time."

"*Ja*. But, there was . . . never mind." She shook her head. "Never mind."

"There was what?"

Greta raised her chin. "Nothing."

A branch snapped behind her and the bushes shook again. She jumped and grabbed Jacob's arm. "There! That's it. Something there, in the bushes!" She edged closer to him and lowered her voice. "A bear. I think it is a bear, *ja*?"

Jacob raised his eyebrows and pointed to the base

of the bush. A possum waddled onto the path, sized them up with beady eyes, then shuffled to the other side and disappeared into the woods. "There's your bear, Greta."

"Oh." Greta pulled away from him and straightened her prayer *kappe*. She cleared her throat. "Mmmm. Well. A possum. That was my next guess, of course."

"Of course." Jacob looked down at her with a wry half smile. "Are you all right? That was quite a thumping you took when you ran into me."

"Me? I am fine. Just fine." Greta brushed off her sleeves and smoothed her skirt. "You know, I would not have bumped into you if you had not been in the way. What are you doing out on the trail after dark, anyway?"

"I was after my supper."

Greta noticed the musket in his left hand. "Any luck?"

Jacob shrugged. "No. It got dark on me, so I guess I am in for another night of pumpkin stew."

"*Ja.* Well. Good night, then."

Jacob hesitated. He stared down at her. She could see the intensity of his gaze in the moonlight that reflected off his eyes.

Do not let yourself fall into those deep, mysterious eyes, Greta Scholtz! Maintain your dignity. You have embarrassed yourself quite enough already.

"I can walk you home."

Greta hesitated, surprised.

He gave his lazy half grin. "That is to say, you seem pretty spooked."

Greta flinched. *First he finds me in the mud, and now*

I cannot stroll down the path without fear! "Spooked? No. I am fine." She raised her chin and turned away.

"You did not seem fine a minute ago." His eyes twinkled. "When that bear—I mean that possum—showed up you seemed awful scared."

Greta whipped back around. "Jacob Miller, are you making fun of me?"

"Making fun? Why on earth would I want to make fun of you, Greta? You only ran away from an animal the size of my shoe. What's to make fun of in that?"

"That is quite enough from you. I will see myself home, thank you very much."

"Are you sure? What if you run into a squirrel? Or a chipmunk? How will you manage?"

"How will I manage?" Greta did not know if she should laugh. "Quite well, I imagine." Her tone had been too forceful. She felt hot and awkward. "Ach, you are joking. I didn't mean . . ."

"I never joke."

Greta stared at him for a few beats, then smiled. "You should not lie, Jacob Miller."

"I never lie, either."

"Oh."

Then he rewarded her with a nonchalant smile. Her smile widened into a shy grin. Jacob's expression dropped back to seriousness as he gazed at her awkwardly for a moment. He cleared his throat. "The night grows late. Let me walk you home, to ensure your safety."

Greta felt a catch in her chest. She looked down, then back up at his face. He stood so tall that she had to crane her head back to see into his eyes. A cloud passed over the moon and his face fell into shadow. Greta wondered what he was thinking. She realized that she wanted his company, if only for the short time it would take for them to reach the Yoder cabin. But she knew that small indulgence would only make his rejection more painful, if he did not feel the same way about her. *And how could he? Every time we meet I seem more trifling and incompetent.* "No, I cannot trouble you. I am sure that you must rise early on the morrow."

"*Ja.* That I do."

"Good night, then."

"It is no trouble to see you safely home, Greta." He placed a warm, steady hand on the small of her back. "In fact, I insist. After all, there are dangerous possums afoot tonight."

Greta laughed. She could smell the masculine scent of woodsmoke and pine on his coat as he steered her toward the Yoder cabin. She could not think of what to say and they walked in silence, the only sound the steady rhythm of Jacob's breath and the crackle of dried leaves underfoot. The silent, shadowed woodlands ran alongside the path, but Greta did not feel afraid. She sensed that Jacob would stand between her and any danger.

Jacob felt a twinge of disappointment when they reached the Yoder cabin. He realized that he didn't want to see Greta disappear through the threshold. There was so much that he wanted to say as they neared the door, but couldn't. *I should not have given us this time together. I will lead her to think that there could be a future for us.* Jacob nodded and turned away without saying good-bye. *And I know that there cannot be any future. Even though she warms my heart on a cold, moonlit night.*

Greta stared at him for a few beats, waiting for him to speak, then turned toward the cabin with downcast eyes. Jacob caught a glimpse of warmth and firelight as the door creaked open, then the world plunged back into darkness when it banged shut.

Jacob imagined Greta inside. He pictured her saying hello to Ruth as she hung her cloak on the peg and then warmed herself by the fire while she hummed a tune from the *Ausbund*. Jacob realized how much he wanted to be inside that cabin too. He could imagine himself pulling a chair beside her and the fire, relaxing in the heat from the flames as Greta laughed and he lost himself in her happy green eyes.

Jacob frowned and turned back onto the isolated path.

Chapter Five

That night, Jacob dreamed that a terrible storm caught him outdoors and he could not find his way home again. Water whirled and slashed through the air until it soaked his skin and he stood alone, shivering. He could feel his body shake from the cold damp. The soft *ping, ping, ping* of water hit his face in a steady beat until the sensation roused him from sleep.

Jacob's eyes flew open and he realized that it had rained into the cabin during the night. The roof had sprung another leak. A water droplet eased through an invisible crack above his bed and plummeted directly onto his forehead. Jacob sighed and wiped his face. Time to repair the shingles again.

From his vantage point on the roof, he could see across his and the Yoder fields, all the way down to the creek. Jacob heard a song carry on the wind and looked up from his mallet to see Greta strolling toward the muddy bank. She moved with a carefree joy that he could feel come alive in the rhythm of the song.

"Greta!" He cupped his hands around his mouth and shouted loudly enough for her to hear.

"*Ja?*"

"Do look out for flying squash on your way there. That seems to be a problem in these parts."

Greta jumped and the song cut off in the middle of a word. She spun around. "Oh! I did not know you were there!" She took a moment to gather herself. "Flying squash . . . ?" Then a memory flickered across her face. She frowned and turned back toward the creek. Jacob chuckled.

Greta stopped short when she reached the edge of the water. Jacob watched as she struck her forehead with the palm of her hand. *She just realized that she has forgotten the bucket.* Jacob watched her double back and smiled. He shook his head and raised the mallet as he wondered how such an absent-minded girl would ever make it in the backcountry. *She's got spirit. But that does not mean that she is cut out for this life. Marta had spirit too. But I brought her here and—*He cut off the thought. *The backcountry is no place for a woman like Greta Scholtz. This land is a place for loss and longing. Do not ever forget that.*

Jacob watched Greta disappear behind a stand of pines at the edge of the clearing. He looked down to hit a peg, then glanced back up and watched the young woman reappear at the edge of the creek. She tiptoed across the slick mud, to the edge of the cold, clear current. The sun sparkled off the rushing water and brightened her white apron.

Jacob paused, mesmerized by the way the light filtered through the trees to fall across her face. Dark, green pines loomed over her and swayed in the autumn breeze. Blue sky stretched above the scene, bright and crisp as the sea.

He frowned, picked up another peg, and forced himself to look away. He did not glance up again until he heard an angelic voice echo against the foothills. He recognized the old hymn that carried on the wind and felt something stir deep within his heart.

Greta's eyes flicked up and she caught him watching her. She grinned. Jacob swallowed. *Now she'll think I'm interested. And I am definitely not interested. I cannot be interested!* He felt a tickle of doubt in his gut. *I was not staring because I am interested. I was staring simply because she is a making such a racket. You cannot help but notice her.*

Greta continued to stare up at him and grin. He frowned at her. She ignored his reaction and marched forward with her head held high. Ja. *She definitely thinks that I am interested now.*

Greta's attention stayed on Jacob instead of on the path. Her foot caught on a root and she tumbled forward, hit the ground, and sprawled across the grass like a slain goose. Jacob waited for Greta to pick herself up, brush off, and carry on. He sighed. *Oh, Greta. Why did you ever come to the backcountry? Can you not see that you are woefully unprepared?* His stomach tightened at the thought of Greta, alone against the wilderness. He shoved the thought from his mind. *She cannot be my responsibility. I already failed a woman once. And I will not fail another.*

Greta pushed herself out of the dirt. She wiped her mouth with her forearm and struggled into a kneeling position. Her body jerked and she collapsed to the ground again. One hand shot to her ankle.

Jacob threw down the mallet. *I think she is hurt.* He flew down the ladder and rushed to her crumpled body. She looked so small and fragile against the green weeds and overturned water bucket. Jacob wanted to smooth back a loose strand of her hair and whisper to her that everything would be all right. He stopped himself from dropping to the ground beside her and taking her in his arms. He shoved his feelings away.

"We really must stop meeting like this, Greta. I am beginning to think that you prefer wallowing in the mud to my company."

"Perhaps I do, Jacob." She turned her face upward and the paleness of her skin startled him. He noticed her clenched teeth and tight lips.

Jacob took off his beaver-felt hat, ran his fingers through his hair, and set the hat back on his head. "Are you hurt? Do you need my assistance?"

"No. I am fine. I do not need help." She pressed her hands against the earth, struggled to rise, then gasped and collapsed back onto her knees. Jacob tried to take her hand.

"No, Jacob. I can manage on my own." She waved him away and tried to push herself up again. Jacob lowered himself to the ground and put a hand on her shoulder. He pressed down gently but firmly.

"That is enough, Greta. You have proven your point. But I cannot let you walk on your own."

"I said I am fine." Tears formed at the corner of her eyes. She swallowed hard and forced them back.

"Greta, I insist."

She drew in a shaky breath. "Very well, then. Only because you insist."

Jacob leaned closer. "What hurts?"

"My right ankle."

He cleared his throat and rubbed the back of his neck. "I will need to assess the injury."

"That would be most improper."

"We are on our own, Greta. There is not a doctor for hundreds of miles. Someone has to make sure that it is not broken."

Greta grimaced and shook her head. "Isn't there someone else?"

Jacob swept his hand to the left and right. "Do you see anyone else? We are surrounded by wilderness."

Greta looked up and saw only the soaring forest and endless sky.

"But . . ."

Jacob shrugged. "I could leave you here in the mud and walk for help. My horse went lame this week, so I cannot ride. It would take a long time. I would rather set the bone now, before the swelling makes it too difficult."

"Set it? You would set my bones, here in the middle of a field?"

Jacob shrugged. "*Ja.*"

Greta looked unconvinced.

"The truth is, I am the closest thing there is to a doctor around here. I am the only person I know of who has set broken bones before."

"You?"

"Yes, me."

"Whose bones?"

"Well, I had an old hunting dog. Best dog you ever saw. She got caught in—"

Greta put up her hand. "Jacob. Are you telling me

that your experience comes from setting the broken leg of a dog?"

"*Ja.*"

Greta exhaled. She shook her head. She exhaled again.

"Very well, Jacob, proceed."

Jacob cleared his throat. "You'll need to remove your hose."

"Remove my hose!"

Jacob shuffled his feet and looked away. "I can hardly check the injury when it is covered by a thick layer of cloth."

"But . . ."

Jacob shrugged his shoulders. "It is up to you, Greta. We can leave it as it is, but that is a risk. If you walk on a broken bone . . ." He sighed. "You could end up with a permanent limp."

Greta pursed her lips and raised her chin. "Very well. Turn your back."

"*Ja.*"

Jacob turned around and kept his eyes on the ridgeline beyond the clearing. Greta pushed aside her pleated overskirt and petticoat and untied the ribbon that held the woolen hose above her right knee. She rolled the black fabric down her calf and exposed her ankle, then readjusted her skirts so that only a tiny sliver of skin showed between her shoe and the hem of her dress.

"All right. You may turn around now."

Jacob kneeled beside her foot and studied the bruised, puffy flesh. He let out a low whistle. "This is much worse than I thought. The swelling . . ." He cut his eyes to her face, then back down to her wounded ankle. *She is a lot tougher than I thought. Most men would be bawling like babies right now. And to think, she tried to get up on her own, without my help.*

"I apologize, Greta, but I must feel the bone."

Greta nodded her permission and clenched her jaws against the pain.

Jacob laid his fingers against her ankle and blushed at the impropriety of the situation. Greta flinched, but his large, rough hands felt surprisingly comforting.

"Try and move it for me."

Greta grimaced and moved the foot up and down.

"Good. Now left and right."

She tightened her lips and moved the foot from side to side. His warm, reassuring hand stayed on the bruised flesh. He nodded. "It is not broken."

Greta managed a quick smile of relief. "You are sure?"

"*Ja.* Pretty sure." He set her foot down, returned her smile, then stood up and turned his back. Greta pulled her hose above her knee again and tied it in place. She took a moment to rearrange her skirts and straighten her prayer *kappe.*

"Okay."

Jacob turned back around and crouched beside her. "We've got to get you home."

Greta shook her head. "I cannot walk."

"No. A sprain can hurt worse than a break. You are in for a difficult few days."

Greta sighed. "Then how will I get home? You said that your horse went lame."

Jacob did not answer. Instead he slid his arms

around her waist and lifted her into the air. She gasped.

"I didn't expect . . . you . . ."

"Shhh. It is fine." He pressed her against his chest and held her as easily as a child. "You weigh less than a feather." Something felt so right about drawing her close, warm and safe in his arms. He looked down at her wide green eyes.

"Am I hurting you?"

"No." Her voice came out in a whisper. "Not at all."

Greta laid her cheek against his shoulder and breathed in the scent of pine and earth. She could feel his muscles flex beneath the homespun shirt. The warmth of his flesh burned against her face and arms through the linsey-woolsey cloth. His heart beat against her ribs. She closed her eyes and relished the feeling of safety that flowed over her.

Jacob cut the distance quickly and when she opened her eyes again they were already at the cabin. Ruth Yoder stared in surprise as they strode through the door. Jacob brushed past her and headed for the nearest bench. He set Greta down, then slid a second bench toward her.

"Here. Keep it elevated." He helped her lift her foot onto the seat while Ruth hovered beside them. "What happened?"

"I fell." Greta shrugged. "Clumsy as always."

"It is not broken."

"That is a relief." Ruth pressed a hand to her heart. "A broken bone out here in the backcountry . . ." She shook her head and did not finish the sentence.

"Give her a few days. She will recover on her own."

Ruth nodded and hurried to the corner of the cabin where she stored herbs and foodstuffs. "I have vinegar to bring down the swelling."

Jacob nodded, his expression hard and unreadable.

"And I will brew her some tea." Ruth smiled. "It is not real tea, of course, only redroot."

"A cup of redroot will do her good, I am sure."

"*Ja.* I have grown fond of it." Ruth laughed. "Of course I have almost forgotten the taste of real tea."

"As have I. But redroot will serve her better. It can bring down swelling, I have heard."

"I have heard that as well. There is a wealth of medicines hidden in these woods, if you know where to look."

Jacob gazed down at Greta, as if he would say something, then nodded and turned away, a serious expression on his tanned face. He strode out the door and pulled it shut behind him. Greta stared at the closed door. She could still feel the gentle strength of his embrace, the warmth of his chest through his homespun shirt as he carried her home. She could still feel the comfort of his low, soothing voice.

Ruth studied her with a raised eyebrow. "Well, Greta, what do you think of Jacob Miller now?"

"Oh, I . . . I don't . . ." She bit her lip and shook her head.

"You don't what, Greta?"

Greta broke into a grin. "I don't know what to think."

"Oh, I think you do."

Greta blushed and looked down, but her heart was still smiling.

They heard a knock at the door a few minutes later. Ruth opened it to find Jacob's large frame blocking the doorway. He wore a wooden shoulder yoke with two buckets of water suspended from it. "This should last until tomorrow." Jacob crossed the small cabin and set the buckets down beside the fireplace, careful not to let the liquid slosh over the sides. "And the cow is in the barn, safe and sound for the night."

"Thank you, Jacob, for taking care of everything."

"*Ja.* We are Amish. What else would I do?"

"*Ja.* Amish. Of course." Greta looked at her lap, flustered. *He seemed so attentive, so caring. I thought maybe . . .* She pushed the thought from her mind, embarrassed. *No, you are being presumptuous. He is just doing his duty. Why else would he attend to a girl who seems so outrageously incompetent?*

When Greta looked up again, Jacob was already gone.

Jacob could not stop glancing back at the cabin. The settlers used oilcloth instead of glass, so he could only make out a haze of light and shadow where Greta sat. A soft voice drifted through the oilcloth and he imagined the laughing eyes and lively spirit that went with it. He frowned and forced himself to look away.

That night, as he stoked the fire and gazed into

the glowing coals, Jacob wondered why Greta had stumbled into his path. He shook his head and pushed away the obvious answer. *No. Absolutely not. Oh* ja, *she can be captivating—but that is completely irrelevant.*

Jacob sighed, unfastened his leather shoes, and pulled off his woolen hosen. Walking through muddy fields kept his feet and calves uncomfortably damp, so he laid the woolen hosen across the hearth to dry.

Jacob sighed again and picked up his Bible. He flipped through the worn pages as he searched for confirmation about his attitude toward Greta. *I know what happens when you fall for a sweet young woman and dare to dream of a happy future.* He turned to the list of births, marriages, and deaths recorded on the first page of the book. His finger ran over the hand-written words as he whispered the name of his wife and son. Jacob Jr. had lived just a few hours after Marta's death. *There would have been a midwife to call if we had still been in Germany. They might have lived. But instead we were here, alone in a strange, hostile land.*

He closed his eyes and tried to push away the surge of guilt that threatened to overcome him. *I chose to bring my family here. I chose to expose them to the perils of the backcountry.* He swallowed hard. *I chose to come here for a higher purpose. How could it have ended like this?*

Jacob remembered the bold excitement he had felt to be one of the first Amish families to set down roots in the New World. He and Marta journeyed from Germany's Rhine Valley a year before the *Charming Nancy* set sail. He thought that his family would pave the way. Instead . . .

Jacob closed the Bible and stared into the dying fire. The flickering light danced against the cabin's rough log walls and cast moving shadows across his face. He felt alone in the wilderness, even though his neighbors' cabins peppered the forest with warm, inviting hearths and familiar faces.

Chapter Six

Greta did her best to hobble around the house and complete her chores. But each step sent a stab of pain through her ankle. She frowned when Ruth shuffled into the house with her back bent under a load of firewood.

"Ruth, you should not do that. It is too much for you." Greta wondered how the elderly woman had managed on her own since her husband died.

Ruth shook her head. "Greta, you worry about me too much. I am fine. Just rest and take care of the spinning. You can do that sitting down."

Greta collapsed onto a bench and picked up the handheld drop spindle from the mending basket. She fed a portion of wool around the shaft, then dropped and rotated the spindle. Gravity and the spinning motion worked together to transform the piece of wool into yarn. Greta glanced up from her work to check the water bucket by the hearth. Almost empty. She hated to think how Ruth would struggle to haul water back from the creek.

A loud knock interrupted Greta's thoughts. Ruth

opened the rough oak door and grinned. "Jacob! What a pleasant surprise."

Jacob nodded, but did not smile.

"Hello, Jacob." Greta felt her cheeks redden as he swept his eyes past her. She looked down and felt her heart beat faster. *Has Jacob come to call on me? The way he carried me home yesterday . . . That twinkle in his eye when he looks at me . . . Maybe . . .* She glanced back up but his attention was on the bucket by the hearth. She studied his tall frame and serious expression. She remembered the way it had felt when he swept her into his strong arms and carried her all the way home. She blushed harder and focused on turning the drop spindle.

Jacob rolled up the loose sleeves of his long linen shirt and picked up the bucket without looking her way. "Just stopped by to take care of a few chores." He noticed the pile of sticks stacked beside the bucket and frowned. "Ruth, you should have waited for me."

She shrugged. "I hate to be a burden."

"You are no burden, Ruth. You have earned your rest."

Ruth chuckled. "You and I have lived in the back-country longer than most. We know how to work."

"*Ja.* That we do. And you have put in enough work for a lifetime. Time to let others help you for a change." Jacob hurried out the door before Ruth could respond.

Jacob sighed as soon as he left the cabin. He had done his best to avoid Greta, but ignoring the young woman did not cleanse her from his thoughts. Whenever he gazed at her pretty, blushing face, he felt drawn to her, despite his firm resolve. Her sparkling green eyes danced across his mind. She had looked so pleased to see him, so hopeful and expectant . . . Jacob shook his head. *I should not encourage her. The elders have already made their thoughts on the matter clear—they want me to take her for a wife. But they do not understand. I am responsible for Marta's death. And I won't be responsible for any harm coming to another naïve young woman. I am not the man that she needs. No matter how enchanting she seems . . .*

Jacob drew a bucket of cold, clear water from the creek and trudged back to the cabin. Next, he split logs and hauled in a good store of firewood. "This should last a while," he announced as he stacked the last cord by the hearth. Greta watched him under lowered lashes and waited for him to return her stare. He didn't.

"Thank you, Jacob." Ruth stirred the big black cauldron that hung over the fire by a chain. "Stay for dinner." The rich, earthy smell of pumpkin wafted through the tiny cabin. "It is not much, but we would like to share."

Jacob shook his head. "I best be getting back to tend to my own chores."

Ruth nodded. "Thank you again."

"No need to thank me, Ruth. It is our way to help one another." Jacob turned on his heels and strode through the threshold. Greta watched him until the door shut with a bang. She was still blushing, but this time her cheeks were red from embarrassment instead of sheepish hope.

"Oh, Ruth! He never once spoke to me. Not one time!"

"Hush, Greta. Oilcloth is not soundproof, you know. The shutters are open."

Greta lowered her voice to a whisper. "You would think I had the plague!" She turned the drop spindle so forcefully that it nearly flew from her hand. "I just do not understand! After the way he took care of—"

A half smile appeared on Ruth's lips. "After the way he took care of whom?"

Greta didn't answer.

"Funny you should care so much, dear. I thought that you were not the least bit interested in the man. Is it not a relief that he has ignored you?"

Greta's eyes flashed. She slammed the drop spindle into the mending basket. "I never said . . . that is not . . . !"

Ruth did not answer. She just stirred the cauldron and grinned.

The Fisher twins knocked on the door early the next morning. They ran to Greta's side as soon as Ruth let them in. "We heard you got hurt, Greta!" Peter shoved a bouquet of wildflowers in her face. Greta sneezed and grinned. "Oh, thank you!"

"Let me put that in water for you." Greta gasped at the sound of Jacob's deep, comforting voice.

"Jacob!"

His large frame hovered in the doorway and blocked the long rays of the morning sun.

"Do come in!"

Jacob nodded. The smell of woodsmoke and spices welcomed him as he entered the small cabin. He smiled at Peter. "That was a nice thing to do, young man."

"It was my sister's idea."

"Very thoughtful of you, Eliza. Lovely flowers from a lovely little girl."

Eliza beamed and reached for his hand.

Greta smiled at the warm scene. *What a wonderful father he would make! He is so gentle and kind with the children.* Jacob looked up and caught her watching him. He cleared his throat and looked away. Greta frowned. *Stop dreaming impossible dreams. Remember neither one of you is interested in the other.*

"We have to go get our chores done before breakfast," Eliza announced, and bounded away.

"Good-bye!" Peter flashed a grin and followed his sister.

The twins' absence left the cabin unnaturally quiet. Jacob cleared his throat and walked to the fire.

"The weather is turning." He rubbed his palms together. "There is a chill in the air. The first snow will fly within a fortnight, I think." Jacob made sure that his eyes did not stray from the fireplace. But he could still feel Greta's presence across the room. He picked up the bucket and hurried away from the captivating young lady.

"Stay for breakfast." Ruth motioned him back toward the hearth. "Pumpkin stew again."

Greta wrinkled her nose. "I hope I never see another pumpkin again as long as I live!"

"We are fortunate to have anything in our pot." Ruth glanced at Greta with a kind but chastising look. "Do not forget how blessed we are to have full bellies. My husband and I came here a year ago with naught but a bag of corn, a bag of nails, an ax, and an iron spider for cooking atop a campfire. We started with almost nothing. And look how much *der Herr* has blessed us." She waved her hand through the air. "It is all a Plain woman needs."

To the outside observer the tiny cabin looked humble: a hard-packed dirt floor, rough log walls, a few herbs hanging from the rafters, a handmade table with two benches, and a shelf beside the hearth that held two wooden trenchers and one pewter cup. There were no beds, only pallets on the floor that the women rolled up during the day to create more space in the cramped room.

"*Ja.*" Jacob nodded. "Those were difficult days. We are blessed to have enough food." He felt a stab of remorse as he realized how rarely he had thanked the Lord since Marta's death.

Greta shrugged. "Well, we were certainly blessed with plenty of pumpkins."

Jacob could not help but chuckle. "*Ja.* It is good that there has been enough for all the newcomers."

"More than enough." Greta let her gaze linger on Jacob as she spoke. He laughed again at her dry humor and their eyes locked. Jacob felt himself fall into her warm green eyes and pulled his attention away. He grabbed the bucket and made a beeline for the front door as Ruth watched with a knowing expression.

When Jacob returned with the water, Ruth ladled a serving of pumpkin stew onto a wooden trencher. She lifted the trencher and held it under his nose.

"You must eat a good breakfast for your efforts." Jacob glanced at Greta. Sweet-smelling steam curled up from the stew and warmed his face. He hesitated and tried to pass the trencher back to Ruth. She kept her hands on her hips and shook her head. "No. You will eat with us."

"There is no fighting you, Ruth."

She heaped another portion of stew onto the second wooden trencher and then nodded for him to take both trenchers to the table.

He set the second trencher in front of Greta and settled onto the bench across from her. There were just two short benches in the cabin, so Ruth remained on the three-legged stool and tended the fire. She only owned two trenchers, so she would have to wait until the others finished before she could eat.

"Ruth, come eat first," Greta insisted. "I will wait."

Ruth shook her head. "No, I am comfortable here by the fire. It is too cold at the table. You go on and eat." Greta raised an eyebrow. She knew what Ruth was doing. *First the elders try to set me up with Jacob, and now Ruth is too!? I can make it just fine on my own, thank you very much.* And yet, she found herself glancing up at the handsome widower sitting across from her. His presence felt strangely comforting. He was a man of few words, but his thoughtful actions and rich brown eyes spoke volumes.

Greta tried to pull herself back from her emotions. *Do not be silly, Greta. Jacob is only doing his duty to his neighbor. He would help anyone in the settlement. His kindness is not personal.* But she dared to hope as she peered up at him and felt her heart quicken.

Jacob shoveled the stew into his mouth without stopping to look up. Greta searched for something to say as she scraped her spoon against the trencher. *He refuses to look at me.* The only noise came from the crackling of the fire and the sound of metal thumping against wood. *Think of something clever to say! Think, think, think!*

Jacob set his spoon down with a satisfied sigh.

"Thank you, Ruth. You have always been a good cook."

Ruth made a dismissive gesture. As an Amish woman, she was careful to avoid pride and immediately deflected the compliment. "I am just using the abilities that *der Herr* has given me."

Jacob nodded. "Indeed."

"Anyway, after my Hans died, it is a pleasure to cook for more than one."

An expression of regret passed over Jacob's face. "Hans was a good man."

Ruth sighed and stirred the cauldron. "*Ja.* Hans was a good man."

"And he lived to see a new life in a new land for our people."

Ruth nodded. She smiled a faraway but happy smile. "We had wonderful good years together."

Jacob nodded. "When the fever came he died peacefully, knowing that you had a good roof over your head and a good crop in the field."

"*Ja.* I lived a full life with my Hans. I am content now." She moved her eyes to Jacob. "But you, Jacob, you are still a young man."

"Thirty-five is not too young."

"You will think otherwise when you are my age." Ruth grinned before letting her face drop back to a serious expression. "You are too young to live as if your life is over."

Jacob's eyes hardened. He shook his head. "I work. I have joined my neighbors to create a new settlement for our people. I do not live as though my life is over."

Ruth sighed. Her eyes moved from Jacob to Greta, then back to Jacob. "Oh yes. You go through the motions. But life is not about actions only." She tapped her heart. "It is about something deeper."

Greta stared at Jacob and wondered what pain hid beneath his aloof demeanor.

"We all miss Marta." Ruth spread her hands. "But life must go on."

Jacob pushed his bench back with too much force and stood up from the table. "I am doing all that a good Amish man should do. What more do you want from me?" He shook his head and started for the door.

"I want you to find peace again. And consider the possibilities for your life. You are still very much alive, Jacob, even though Marta is not. You still have a life to live."

Jacob paused and stared at Ruth. He opened his mouth, then closed it again. Greta watched his jawline sharpen as he clenched his teeth. He stood in silence for a long moment, then turned and walked away.

"Jacob!" Greta longed to run after him.

"Let him go, child." Ruth turned back to the fire. "Let him go." She sighed and shook her head.

"I wish there were something that I could do."

"Do not worry. I feel sure that you will help him."

"I will?" Greta narrowed her eyes. "I actually threw fried squash at his head a few days ago, you know."

Ruth's eyes softened. "You, my dear, are an answer to my prayers for that man. You might be able to reach him."

"Why, Ruth? What happened?"

Ruth stood up from the three-legged stool and picked up the broom. "His wife, Marta, died in child-birth. And the baby died a few hours later. He blames himself. He thinks that she would have lived if they had stayed in Germany, where he could have fetched a midwife for her."

Greta thought about Jacob's guarded eyes. "I think that I understand him better now." *He must feel even more lost and alone than I do.* She frowned. "He has been distant, but I thought . . ." She looked down. "I thought it was me."

Ruth shook her head. "No."

"He hides feelings well. He works hard and asks nothing from anyone."

"Oh yes, he does work hard. But I think that he uses work as an escape. If he keeps busy he does not have to think or feel." She shrugged. "He is running from the past. But the only way to heal is to face the loss, then move forward into the future." Ruth looked at Greta with a knowing expression, but said no more.

Chapter Seven

Jacob breezed into the Yoder cabin and saw an empty bench where Greta usually sat with her drop spindle.

"Where is she?"

"I could not keep her inside any longer." Ruth shrugged and stoked the fire. "I guess she is well enough. But it would be better if she rested that ankle for another day or two."

Jacob grunted in agreement. "She's gone to the creek?"

"*Ja.*"

"I will help her haul the buckets back."

Fall leaves crunched under Jacob's boots as he strode across the clearing. He saw Greta emerge from the forest with her back bent under the weight of the yoke.

A rabbit scampered over a log, shot past Greta, and fled into the forest that lined the clearing. Jacob smiled.

"Do be careful, Greta. That rabbit looked dangerous."

Greta jumped. "Oh! I didn't know you were there."

Water sloshed against her apron as she readjusted the heavy wooden yoke. The rabbit startled at the commotion and zigzagged away in a different direction. "Dangerous?"

"Almost as dangerous as that possum that stalked you in the dark the night you almost knocked me over." He shot her a wry look. "I feel certain that you remember."

She looked away and shifted the weight of the yoke.

Jacob shook his head. "Hand over the buckets, Greta."

"I can manage." She wanted to show Jacob that she was able to handle life in the backcountry—even if she did run in terror from a possum.

"Are you sure? Because a mouse might run across your path. And then what would you do?"

Greta laughed.

He lifted the yoke from her shoulders. "I am glad to see that you are getting better."

"*Ja.* As am I." She smiled. "Now I can chase Rose when she wanders into your yard again." Jacob stared at her for a moment and Greta felt her stomach tighten. *There I go, saying the wrong thing again.* But Jacob's serious expression gave way to a smile. She giggled and their eyes met. Greta felt a connection as their eyes lingered on each other for a moment. Then Jacob's face fell back into seriousness. He cleared his throat and pulled his gaze away.

Greta sensed that his grip on her arm loosened. *He is fighting the connection that we both felt.* She frowned. *How do I reach this man? Ruth must be right— he is so busy running from his feelings that he cannot let anyone in.* She tried to think of what to say as they trudged across the field side by side. The fact that he kept his hand on her arm made her feel awkward and content at the same time.

They reached the cabin before Greta could come up with the right words. *Next time I will think of something to say that will help him.* She bit her lip and wished that she had a quicker tongue.

The handsome widower pushed open the door and helped Greta to her bench. *"Danke."* She stared up at him with a hopeful expression. He set down the water bucket and turned away.

"Greta is back on her feet so I think we can manage on our own now, Jacob." Ruth picked up the bucket and poured the water into the cauldron that hung over the fire. "But I do hope you will come again soon. Just for a visit."

Jacob smiled. "I will be back on the morrow."

Greta felt her stomach jump. She dared to grin at him again.

"I need to mend your fence. The elders tell me that Rose breaks into your kitchen garden as well as mine. I cannot allow you two to go hungry, can I?"

Greta thought she caught that familiar gleam in his eye. The look made her feel warm and fuzzy inside. *But what if I am misreading him again? What if he is just doing his duty? Perhaps he is only helping us because the elders suggested it.* Greta felt her face flush and she looked down.

Greta did not look up again until she heard the door close. "I wish I knew what that man was thinking! Every time I think he might be interested I am filled with doubt." She looked down. "And no wonder.

I find myself falling short every day. Perhaps I should never have come."

"Nonsense. You are doing just fine. It takes time, is all. You will find your way."

Greta nodded and picked up her drop spindle.

"But, speaking of Jacob—"

"Oh, Ruth. I think that is enough about him."

Ruth put up her hand, undeterred. "He needs to realize that life is for living. And that *der Herr* still has a plan for him."

"*Ja*. 'Tis true."

"Good. So it is settled."

"Settled? What is settled?"

"You will take lunch to him tomorrow while he repairs the fence. That will give you the opportunity to sit with him and talk. Get to know each other. I believe he will soon admit that he harbors an affection for you."

"Oh, Ruth, I do not know. I must not appear too bold for his attentions."

"Nonsense. Offering him a hot meal after he labors on our fence is perfectly reasonable."

Greta hesitated. She opened her mouth, then closed it and shook her head. "Very well."

Ruth beamed and nodded. "Good."

Greta did not respond. She wondered if he would greet her with his charming smile or with that aloof gaze that pushed everyone away.

Gold and red leaves shimmered along the tree line and whispered in the wind. Greta smiled and breathed in the cool, crisp autumn air while she strolled toward the split rail fence. She swung her basket of food and sang a tune from the *Ausbund* as she navigated the mud and wild grasses.

Her song faltered and her stomach tightened when she caught sight of Jacob. *The day is too beautiful to feel discouraged. There has been a spark growing between us, hasn't there? Surely I am not the only one to feel it.* True, she felt a small, nagging apprehension in the pit of her stomach, but that was easily pushed aside.

Greta smiled and waved when Jacob noticed her. He nodded and turned his attention back to the fence. *No matter. He is just busy.* Greta raised her chin and forged across the clearing.

She smoothed her skirts and straightened her neck cloth as she drew near.

"Jacob!"

Jacob nodded again but kept his eyes on the wooden post in front of him.

"I have brought lunch." She thrust the basket into his face.

"You are enthusiastic today, Greta." He gave a small half smile and pushed the basket away from his nose.

She stared back at him and waited. Jacob slid a split rail into place. He pushed it into position and brushed his hands. "Would you like to dine with me, Greta?" He kept his eyes on the fence line as she gazed up at him.

"*Ja.* Of course." She blushed at her forwardness. "I mean, Ruth made two servings, one for each of us." She swallowed. "I have been cooped up for so long. I thought it would do me good to be outside again. A little sunshine and fresh air . . ."

"Hmmm." Jacob picked up another split rail and hoisted it into position. He jostled the beam until it felt secure, then wiped his forehead with his handkerchief and surveyed the morning's work. The repairs on the fence looked nearly finished. He nodded. "Wonderful good."

"*Ja!* Wonderful good. I knew you would agree. I brought . . ." Greta stopped. She clamped her mouth shut. *Wait, was he saying that the fence looks wonderful good? I thought he meant dining with me would be wonderful good. Oh no.* Greta cleared her throat. She could feel her cheeks burning. "*Ja.* That looks like a good day's work on the fence." Her voice cracked. "Thank you for repairing it."

Jacob looked down at her with an expression she could not decipher. *Is it confusion or amusement? Why do I care so much anyway?*

"What have we got there?" Jacob nodded toward the basket.

She whipped a blanket off the top of the basket and shook it out. The wind caught the cloth and it flapped against the air. Greta struggled to smooth the blanket down, but the cloth fought her like a mischievous child.

"Here, let me help you." Jacob grabbed a corner and pulled the blanket taut between them. Greta smiled and lowered her corner toward the ground. But they both let go too soon and the blanket flew from their fingers, caught by the autumn wind like a kite.

"Oh!" Greta dashed after the wayward cloth, but every time she drew near the wind whisked it away again, as if they were playing a game. "This is harder than chasing down a piglet!"

Jacob followed behind and Greta cringed to think how ridiculous she looked as her prayer *kappe* flapped loose and her skirt whipped in the wind. But, when she glanced back, he was laughing. Laughing! She allowed herself to laugh too. She felt a wild revelry, like a schoolgirl just released from a long day hunched over a desk. They ran side by side, lunged for the blanket, and grinned. The wind died down for an instant and they both caught the cloth at the same time. Jacob's warm fingers fumbled against hers. Greta felt a strange excitement at the touch and pulled her hand away. The moment of carefree joy gave way to awkward tension.

Greta looked down and gathered the blanket. They walked back to the basket in silence as the fall leaves crunched beneath Jacob's leather boots. Greta's hand still burned from the touch of his warm fingers.

Greta unpacked the picnic as Jacob spread out the blanket and weighed it down with his mallet and a split rail. Neither spoke. *I did not expect to see him laugh. He can be so merry if he lets himself.* She served Jacob a corn cake and tried hard to maintain a neutral expression. Greta could feel him watching her as she handed him the trencher. She wondered what he was thinking. *His stare is so powerful. So full of hidden thoughts.*

"Tell me, Greta, how are you adjusting to the backcountry?"

"Oh, just fine, I suppose. Ruth has been very kind."

She shrugged. "As have you. We could not have managed without your help."

"Your ankle no longer pains you?"

"No. Thank you for asking." She kept her eyes on her trencher. *Is he just being polite, or does he really care? Truly, he has shown signs of affection. . . .* Jacob looked out over the clearing as they chewed in silence.

"What are you thinking about?"

He frowned. "Nothing."

"You look as if you are pondering something."

Jacob's frown deepened. "I was thinking that I am enjoying our picnic."

"Oh." Greta felt her heart beat faster. She swallowed and tried to breathe evenly. "I . . . I was not sure. You do not look as though you are enjoying it."

"No?" He gave a small smile. "I suppose I have forgotten how."

Greta liked the warmth that came into his eyes when he smiled. She looked down and tried to calm her drumming heart. "*Ja.* I have heard that you have had a difficult trial this past year."

He shrugged and kept his eyes on the tree line. Greta sensed the shift in his mood and set down her trencher.

"I am sorry, Jacob."

Jacob sighed. The hardness returned to his face. "As am I."

"The church elders say that you are much changed this year."

Jacob continued to stare into the distance. A tendon in the side of his neck twitched. He took a long time to gather his thoughts before he responded. "Why did you call on me today, Greta?"

Greta wondered what happened to the man with the twinkle in his eye who had winked at her the day before. His expression had turned to stone.

Her stomach tightened as she felt the conversation slip out of her control. "I just . . . I wanted to . . . Are you all right, Jacob? Truly?"

"I am fine, Greta."

"You do not seem fine, Jacob."

He sighed. "Why do you say this? Why are you here, Greta?"

Greta stared at Jacob's eyes. They still gazed into the distance, as if she weren't there. She wanted to reach out and run the back of her hand across his face and tell him everything would be all right. Her breath caught in her throat as she realized that her feelings for him had developed into something that she couldn't push away.

"Because . . . because I care about you!" Greta blurted the words out before she could stop herself. Her pale cheeks turned a bright crimson. Jacob did not respond, but she thought she saw him flinch. She bit her lip and tried to think of a way to take back the words. "I mean, I care about you as I would any brother or sister. We must look out for one another in this strange land." She knew that he did not believe the excuse. If nothing else, the deep blush on her cheeks and the sharp rise and fall of her chest gave her true feelings away.

Jacob turned to look at her. His face looked as distant as a stranger's. He hesitated, as if trying to find the words. "Greta. I am sorry that I have given you the wrong impression. That is my fault."

Greta sucked in her breath. She felt her stomach

drop out from under her. The world felt as if it were moving in slow motion. *This cannot be happening.* "No. I never thought . . . I mean . . . I do not . . ." Greta wanted to run away and hide. *I should never have let myself believe that he had feelings for me.*

Jacob took a breath and let it out slowly. "Good. I am glad we understand each other."

"*Ja.* Of course." But the expression on her face contradicted her words.

Jacob swallowed and looked away again. "Greta." His voice sounded soft and distant. "I have no intention to court you. I hold no affection for you."

Greta gasped. "Oh!" She jumped up and smoothed her skirts. *How could I have misread him so?* "Very well, Jacob Miller." Jacob did not acknowledge her words. He sighed and looked down.

Greta threw the trenchers into the basket as tears pricked at her eyes. Jacob stood up so that she could gather the blanket. His face looked unreadable. *But I know what he's thinking. He told me plainly!*

Greta replayed the conversation in her head as she ran back to the cabin. The memory of his words cut into her chest like a callous blade. *How could I have misread him these past few days? How could I have been so foolish?*

She raised her head. *Fine, Jacob Miller. You will get your wish. I will have no affection for you, either. None whatsoever.* "And it will be your loss, Jacob Miller! Your loss!" Greta felt so consumed with hurt and humiliation that she shouted the declaration across the clearing. In the distance, Rose raised her head and stared with large black eyes.

Greta stormed into the Yoder cabin and shook her

head. Ruth sighed and set the straw broom aside. "I see that your conversation did not go well." Greta did not answer. Instead she burst into tears.

"There, there now. Let it out."

"I had it wrong! Terribly wrong!" Greta pulled her apron to her face to cover her soggy eyes. "Oh, Ruth, I am so embarrassed!" She cried harder.

"Now, now. Go ahead and tell me what happened."

"He is cold and aloof and . . . un-Amish!"

Ruth stifled a smile. "'Un-Amish' is not a word, dear."

"Oh, Ruth! Have a little sympathy!" The words came out muffled from behind the apron.

"Hmmm. Well, the truth is, I am afraid that he is not the only one engaged in un-Amish behavior."

"You just said that 'un-Amish' is not a word!"

"That is right, dear. Anyway, calling a brother un-Amish is not exactly Amish behavior either."

"Ruth! You are only making it worse!"

Ruth smiled. "I do not think that Jacob Miller meant what he said today."

Greta hiccupped. She pulled the apron from her face. "You don't?"

"No. I have seen the way he looks at you."

Greta shook her head. "But he was completely clear today. He said that he holds no affection for me!"

"He said those words?"

"*Ja!*"

Ruth frowned. "Give him time."

"That will be easy. I do not intend on seeing him again. Ever!"

* * *

Jacob's heart felt like a rock within his chest. He replayed his conversation with Greta again and again. His cold, hard words echoed inside his mind. *"I hold no affection for you."* He felt ashamed of the statement. And he knew that it was a lie. *But it is for the best.* He pushed aside the feeling of warmth that Greta brought when she gazed up at him with her sparkling green eyes. The way her grin made him feel alive again. *No. You know better. Nothing good can come of your feelings for Greta Scholtz.* He wished that he could have been kinder, gentler. But he had done what he had to do. *I cannot let her believe that there could ever be a future for us. It is for her own good. I will not fail another woman like I failed Marta.* He nodded and set his face into a hard mask. *I have done the right thing. I just wish that it did not hurt so much.*

A hard knot twisted inside Jacob's stomach as he did his chores. Greta's expression of shock and dismay pressed into his mind. *She looked so innocent and hopeful as we dined, before her face fell as I said those cold, hard words.* Jacob was so distracted that he knocked over the water bucket while he stacked the firewood by the hearth. He frowned as the water transformed the hard-packed dirt into mud. Then, when he hauled a bag of corn into the loft for winter storage, he cracked his head on the rafter. Jacob sat down hard and rubbed his scalp until he stopped seeing stars. He shook his head. *Why is it so hard to push Greta Scholtz away?*

Jacob sighed and went to check on the pumpkin stew that bubbled in the cauldron. He stepped in the mud in front of the hearth and his frown deepened. *I should have let her down more gently.* He stirred the stew and contemplated his next move. *I should apologize. No, that would only encourage her. And the worst thing that I can do is to encourage her. Leave her be, for her sake.* He scooped out a spoonful of stew, slurped the hot broth, and wrinkled his nose. *Needs some sugar. And nutmeg.* But those luxuries were long gone. Just like his hopes for a better future.

Chapter Eight

Greta slid the wooden paddle into the newly built community bake-oven. She pulled out a warm loaf of bread, breathed in its rich, nutty aroma, and smiled. Barbara Gruber passed by and stopped to peer over Greta's shoulder.

"I think that should bake a little bit longer, don't you?"

Greta's smile evaporated. "It looked done to me."

"Give it a bit longer." Barbara nodded and continued on her way. *I know she is trying to help, but her advice only highlights how incompetent I am!* Greta slid the loaf of bread back inside the oven and pushed a log into the flames. She wiped her hands on her apron and picked up her drop spindle, determined to be industrious as she waited.

"Ah, Greta, how do you do?" Abraham stopped at the bake-oven and tipped his hat.

Greta looked up from her spinning and smiled. "Very well, thank you. It will be a great joy to taste bread again."

"*Ja.* That it will. I am very pleased that the bake-oven

is completed. It seems that every day we build something new!"

Greta nodded. "We are on our way to becoming a proper village! Why, I can only imagine how much we will have accomplished by this time next year!"

"Indeed." Abraham paused. "But, these advances cannot be made without effort."

"No. Clearly not."

Abraham nodded and stroked his beard. "And we all must do our part, mustn't we? We must partner together in order to grow our settlement and support one another."

"*Ja.* We must all do our part."

Abraham grinned. He nodded. "So you have agreed to—"

"Greta! What a pleasure." Amos trotted toward them, his hand on his black beaver-felt hat to keep it in place as he hurried down the dirt lane.

"Hello, Amos." Greta spoke politely, but she did not smile. She knew a setup when she saw one. "What a surprise to see you here."

"*Ja! Ja!* What a surprise. All of us here, together." Amos grinned and nodded.

Abraham cleared his throat. "*Ja.* Well, Greta and I were just enjoying a little chat about our settlement." He glanced at Greta. "And she was just telling me that she has agreed to marry."

Amos clapped his hands together. "*Wunderbar!*"

Greta felt the heat rise in her cheeks. "Oh no! I did not mean . . . that is not what I said, exactly . . ." She shook her head. "There simply is no one suitable. Simply no one at all!"

"There is Jacob Miller, Greta!" Amos threw up his hands. "He has been visiting you daily!"

Greta looked mortified. "I did not realize that Jacob's comings and goings were under such close scrutiny."

"Oh, Greta, do not take offense," Abraham cut in. "As you said yourself, this is a small settlement. How can we not take notice of what is happening?"

"Indeed." Greta swallowed as she fought to keep her composure. "And what, if I may ask, is happening?" Jacob's words from the day before rang in her head. *He holds no affection for me!*

Amos threw up his hands. "Why, Jacob Miller is courting you, of course!"

Greta pinched the bridge of her nose and counted to ten.

"Greta? Do you have a headache? My wife has just mixed an herbal concoction that you should try."

"No." She shook her head. "No, thank you, Amos. My head is quite well."

"Good. Now, about Jacob Miller. Are you betrothed yet?"

"Oh, Amos, he is not even courting me!"

Amos looked surprised. "No? Are you sure?"

"I am sure that I would know if I were being courted."

The two elders stroked their beards.

"Perhaps. Perhaps not. It seems a very good match."

"*Ja.* A very good match," Amos echoed.

"I am sorry to disappoint you, but Jacob simply is not interested in me."

Amos waved his hand. "Not interested? Preposterous."

"Preposterous," Abraham repeated. The two men shook their heads and frowned. "The truth is, Greta, you have responsibilities that go beyond yourself. We cannot expect for our humble settlement to survive if we do not join forces for the greater good."

"Jacob needs a wife and you need a husband."

Abraham nodded in agreement. "It is a good match. And, since he is courting you—"

"But I already told you that he is not courting me!"

Abraham blinked. "But, Greta . . ."

"I am sorry, Abraham, but we are simply not a match. There is no way around it. He and I are not suited to be in the same room together, let alone share a life together!"

The elders' frowns deepened. Abraham raised an eyebrow. Amos shook his head and extended his hands palms up, in a pleading gesture. "Well, if that is the way you feel, I suppose we could consider a match between you and Mr. Hertzberger. He's recently widowed, you know. . . ."

Greta grimaced. "I prefer a husband who is young enough to still have a few teeth left."

Amos shrugged. "He is getting up in years, that is true, but he is a good man. A good match."

"Not as good a match as Jacob Miller, mind you," Abraham cut in. "But Mr. Hertzberger is a good man."

Greta let out a long, slow breath of air. "*Ja*. I am sure that he is delightful." She counted to ten as she struggled to maintain a polite expression.

"Well, you must marry someone." Amos shook his head. "There is just no way around it."

A group of children shouted and ran past the bake-oven. Greta glanced past Abraham, to the grinning, carefree faces. Suddenly, she had an unexpected idea. A brilliant, perfect idea.

"I believe I have a solution."

"So you will marry?" Amos leaned closer. "You must admit there really is not another option."

"No."

"But, Greta, you cannot allow yourself to be a burden. Who will provide for you during the long, lean winter months?"

"As I said, I have a solution. Who is teaching the children to read?"

The two men glanced at each other and shrugged. "They have their parents."

"But their parents are busy, are they not? The daily tasks are endless. I cannot believe that there are enough hours in the day for them to provide an adequate education." The elders listened without commenting. Greta took a deep breath and pressed on. "And I am sure that you will agree that we all must learn to read in order to know *der Herr*'s Word. Not to mention the *Ausbund* and the *Martyrs Mirror*. Those are works that have been foundational to our faith, *ja*?"

The men nodded.

Greta grinned. "Well. I will do it. I will teach them."

Abraham rubbed his chin. Amos tapped a finger against his lips.

Greta's heart pounded as she prayed for their approval. *This could be the answer to my dilemma!* "I believe I could be quite useful, even though I am on my own." She glanced from one man's face to the other. "I could earn my keep, anyway."

"Excuse me." Maria Stoltzfus approached the trio with a basketful of dough. Three young children clung to her skirts. "I need to get to the bake-oven."

Greta took the young mother's sudden appearance

as a sign. "Maria, what would you think if I offered to teach your children to read?" An expression of surprise passed over the disheveled woman's face. "I would welcome it, I suppose." She laughed. "I haven't the time. That is for certain." She bent to wipe a child's nose and pull another child's thumb from his mouth. She straightened back up and nodded. "*Ja.* I would welcome it."

"Splendid!" Greta turned back to Amos and Abraham with a hopeful expression.

The two elders hesitated and then nodded their agreement.

"I had hoped for a more suitable arrangement," Amos admitted. "A good marriage would have been ideal, but . . ."

"Then it is settled!"

The men glanced at each other and nodded again. "*Ja.* I supposed it is settled."

"On a trial basis," Abraham added.

"*Ja.* On a trial basis," Amos agreed.

"*Wunderbar*! I will not disappoint you." Greta watched Maria's children as they huddled around the mouth of the oven. "I will do my very best!" She felt a surge of excitement as she imagined helping those young, innocent minds learn and expand.

Maria turned around. "Greta?"

"*Ja?*"

"You have bread baking?"

"*Ja.*" She grinned and nodded.

"Then why is there still wood burning inside the oven?"

Greta's face fell. "I don't understand."

"To get the right temperature for bread you have to pull the burning logs out before you put in the dough. Otherwise . . ." Maria slid the wooden paddle under Greta's loaf and pulled it out. "It is a bit over-done, dear."

Greta's smile fell. Her first loaf of bread in the New World was burnt to a crisp.

Greta searched the settlement for the Fisher twins. She could not wait to share the news with them. Greta found them trudging down the main path, each of them balancing a yoke with water buckets over their shoulders. She hitched up her skirts and hurried toward them with a wide grin.

"Peter! Eliza! How would you like to come to my cabin every day? I am going to have a school!"

They rushed into her arms. "Where have you been? We haven't seen you in ages."

"I am sorry! There has been so much work to do since I twisted my ankle."

"*Ja*. We have been minding the fires to burn the brush so that the men can build more cabins and plant more crops."

"*Wunderbar*. You are very good workers."

Peter raised his chin. "We have cleared out the forest all the way to the creek."

Greta beamed. "One day we will have real streets again, paved with cobblestone. And houses with more than one room!"

"For now, I will just be happy to have a school." Eliza gazed up at Greta and slipped a small hand around her arm.

"Me too, Eliza." Greta smiled, straightened the girl's prayer *kappe*, and laid her palm over the child's hand. "Come over tomorrow afternoon, after your work is over." The children nodded, picked their buckets back up, and headed on their way.

Greta felt a growing sense of excitement as she went from cabin to cabin and recruited more families to join her makeshift school.

"Where will you meet?" Jonah Gruber asked after she knocked on his door and explained her plans. The Grubers' six-year-old son, Christian, looked up at Greta with big brown eyes.

"I thought we could meet at the Widow Yoder's cabin."

Jonah nodded. "But we cannot do without him for very long. He is needed."

"I suppose it could work if he gathers the kindling and hauls an extra bucket of water before he leaves," Barbara Gruber said as she wiped her hands on her apron and crowded into the doorway.

"*Ja.* And, we will have less need of him during the winter months. I doubt we can spare him at all come spring."

"Our lessons will be short. I will not keep him from his chores too long."

"And"—Barbara Gruber leaned forward—"I understand that you will likely be occupied with more important things by spring."

"More important things?"

"Why, marriage, obviously!"

"*Ja.*" Jonah nodded. "We are all pleased to hear of Jacob's affections for you. It is a blessing to see *der Herr* lay down a new path for his life."

"Oh." Greta cringed inside. *Not this again.* "Jacob is a good man, I am sure."

"*Ja*, a good man," the couple repeated in unison.

"But we are not planning to marry."

Barbara looked confused. "But, dear, he visited you every day for two weeks." She glanced at her husband. "Not that anyone was paying attention." Barbara cleared her throat. "It is just that, well, we are all eager to see Jacob move on with his life and he seems, we heard . . ."

Greta shook her head. "I am sorry to disappoint you, but his visits were purely out of concern for my welfare, mine and the Widow Yoder. He simply came to take care of the chores until my sprained ankle mended. Now that I am back on my feet he keeps to his own farm."

Jonah shrugged. "Ah, well. As we said, Jacob is a good man."

Barbara nodded. "A hardworking man."

"It is just like him to see that his neighbors are well cared for."

"*Ja.*" Barbara shrugged. "We will see what *der Herr*'s will is in the matter."

Greta frowned but did not argue. *Why does everyone think that Jacob and I are the perfect match?! Is it just because he and I are both available? Does no one realize that he wants nothing to do with me? When will this humiliation end?*

"I suppose that you need to know him well to form a true opinion of him," Barbara admitted. "His spirit is not as warm as it once was."

"*Ja.*" Jonah sighed. "But he is still the same good man. Even if he tries to pretend otherwise."

"Pretend?" Greta tilted her head and drew her eyebrows together.

"He has a loving heart beneath that tough exterior."

"That thought has occurred to me."

"Because it is true." Jonah nodded.

"He just needs a good woman to remind him that there is still a plan for his life," Barbara added.

"*Ja.*" Jonah nodded. "I am sure that he is interested. He just has not told you yet."

"*Ja,*" Barbara echoed. "He is interested."

"I appreciate your advice, but Jacob simply is not interested in me." Greta looked down. "He has made that clear."

The Grubers glanced at each other but did not reply. Their expressions made it plain enough that they did not believe her. There was an awkward silence until Greta took a deep breath and forced a smile. "Now, about teaching Christian to read. Could you send him to the Widow Yoder's cabin once his chores are completed each day? I will send him home in time for his evening meal. I will only keep him for an hour or two. Can you spare him that long?"

"Just an hour or two?" Jonah tugged at his beard.

"*Ja.*" Greta glanced from him to Barbara.

"All right," Jonah consented. "But just for a season, mind you. Come spring he will be in the fields with me from sunrise to sunset."

"*Ja.*" Greta broke into a relieved grin. "I understand."

Greta stood a little bit taller as she walked away from the Grubers and headed toward the next farm. It felt good to be of value to the community. "Who needs marriage? I can earn my own keep and make my own way. And what a difference I can make!"

A small, nagging feeling threatened to break her resolve. *Maybe there is something to everyone's insistence that Jacob and I are meant to be. Maybe teaching the children is just* one *part of what* der Herr *has planned for me. . . .* She shook her head and pushed the question away. *Today is a day to be happy and encouraged. Not to obsess over a man who told me that he wants nothing to do with me.* Greta took a deep breath, raised her chin, and put all of her focus on recruiting another young mind to her little backcountry school.

Chapter Nine

Barbara turned toward her husband and nudged him as they watched Greta walk away. "Perhaps it is time that you returned that hammer to Jacob."

Jonah ran his fingers through his beard. "I do believe that you are right." He winked at his wife and headed over to his friend's farm with the borrowed hammer in hand. He found Jacob behind the cabin, splitting firewood.

"Hello there, Jacob." He held up the hammer. "I am returning this to you."

Jacob shrugged. "I ran out of nails weeks ago. I am only using a mallet and pegs now."

Jonah shrugged. "Well, here it is, regardless. Thank you for lending it."

Jacob nodded. "Happy to do it."

Jacob waited for Jonah to leave, but his friend hovered behind him. Jacob set a thick piece of wood atop a tree stump and raised his ax. He swung the blade down and heaved the wood in two. Jonah still did not leave. Jacob sighed and tossed the two halves onto the woodpile. "It is nearly time for dinner. Care to join me?"

"I would be delighted."

Why do I get the feeling that Jonah is here with an ulterior motive?

"There is not much. Just cold corn cakes."

"Cold corn cakes sound perfect."

The two men relaxed in the warmth of the fire as they chatted about the weather and the likelihood of a good crop of winter wheat.

"We need to put more flax in the ground, in addition to the wheat," Jacob added, and lifted his arm. "My sleeve is worn through."

Jonah studied the fabric and nodded. "*Ja.* 'Tis the same in our household. We all need more flax to spin into linen."

Jacob picked up his corn cake. "Food before clothing, I suppose. There is so much to be done. It is a mammoth task to start from scratch."

"*Ja.* But what a blessing the New World is!" Jonah swept his hand in a wide arc. "Our forefathers could not have imagined such bounty."

Jacob nodded and wished that he felt the same enthusiasm. He looked into the distance and waited for his friend to leave.

Jonah cleared his throat and set down his pewter plate.

"Greta Scholtz came by our farm today."

Jacob felt the corn cake stick to his throat. He swallowed hard and forced it down.

Jonah shook his head and smiled. "She has spirit, I tell you."

"Does she?" Jacob pushed a crumb across his plate. "I really had not noticed."

Jonah looked at Jacob with a skeptical expression that Jacob ignored. "She is starting a school."

"A school?"

"*Ja*. She seems to think that she will never marry." He shrugged. "She wants to support herself and be an asset to the community."

Jacob looked away.

"Seems strange, a good woman like her convinced that she will not marry."

Jacob shrugged. "Not everyone finds the right person."

"Sometimes finding the right person is not the problem."

Jacob sighed. "What are you getting at, Jonah?"

"Well, since you mention it, I cannot help but notice how suitable you and Greta are for each other. But, the poor girl is convinced that you are not the least bit interested." Jonah laughed. "How ridiculous is that?" He shook his head and looked Jacob in the eye. "You must come clean with her, Jacob. It is not fair to let her think that you have no feelings for her."

Jacob let out a long, slow breath of air. *Do not falter now. No good can come from a relationship with Greta Scholtz. No matter how enchanting she is.* "But I have no feelings for her, Jonah."

Jonah flinched with surprise. "I find that hard to believe."

"Believe it."

"How can you be so sure?"

Jacob shook his head. "Trust me, Jonah. I hold no affection for her." He pushed his plate away.

"I heard that you were courting her."

Jacob laughed and shook his head again. "It seems

that people are hearing a lot of things about me since Greta Scholtz arrived."

Jonah frowned. "You never courted her?"

"Never." Jacob gave Jonah a hard stare. "And I do not intend to."

Jonah rubbed his chin. "You are sure?"

Jacob threw up his hands. "I think I would know if I were courting a woman."

Jonah grunted and shrugged. "Fair enough."

Jacob frowned. "I know that people have been . . ." He paused, searching for the right word. "*Encouraging* us to court. But I have never courted Greta Scholtz and I never intend to. As I said, I hold no affection for her."

"None at all?"

"None." Jacob paused. He knew that it was wrong to lie. But he told himself that a lie was the only way to protect Greta. And himself. *I cannot bear to fall for another woman and lose her again. And she is better off without a man like me, who leads his wife to disaster.*

Jonah sighed. "Well, you are a grown man, Jacob. I suppose that you know what you want."

"*Ja.* I suppose I do."

Jonah picked up his beaver-felt hat and left in a somber mood. Jacob latched the door behind his friend, settled back in front of the fire, and stared into the dying embers. The room felt thick with memories of his wife and tiny son. He stoked the fire and watched the sparks flash against the dark air.

Jacob sighed and ran his fingers through his hair. *How much longer can I run from how I feel?* He stared into the fire until the light faded from the ashes. *I loved Marta—I will always love Marta.* Guilt flooded into Jacob. He closed his eyes. *I cannot bear to let Marta go. And yet, how long can I hold on to someone who is gone?*

Jacob frowned and hurried to his feet, almost knocking over the three-legged stool. He shrugged into his coat and picked up the ax by the door. Jacob knew how to avoid facing the issue. *Splitting a few logs should do it.* An icy wind whipped across his face as soon as he opened the door. He braced himself and headed into the cold, dark night.

Greta stood at the table in the dim, early morning light to skim and strain the milk she had taken from Rose before dawn. She remembered her father as she set aside the wooden bucket and unpinned a soiled apron from her bodice. Before he died he told her to take the money sewn into the lining of his coat and buy a cow when she reached America. She poured a cup of fresh, frothy milk into a cup and recalled the warmth of his work-worn hand as she held it on the *Charming Nancy. Father's last thoughts were for my future. I will find a way to succeed here, for him. Even if I have to do it on my own.* She had almost given up and left Rose on the trail as the group of settlers hacked their way through the forest. Greta had to push and coax the animal across creeks, through thick brush, and down steep ravines. But finally, the party reached their destination with a disgruntled milk cow in tow. *I did not give up then and I will not give up now.*

A child's eager shout drifted in through the oil-cloth that covered the window. Greta set the tin cup down and tried to make out movement through the hazy cloth. "Whatever could be causing such excitement?"

"Go see and let me know," Ruth said as she splashed a bucket of water into the cauldron that hung inside the large fireplace.

Greta heard another high-pitched shout and hurried outside. The Fisher twins galloped through the clearing that encircled the cabin and motioned for her to follow.

"A new family has arrived!"

Greta clapped her hands and grinned. "*Wunderbar!*"

Peter's wool hose sagged below his knee as he pumped his chubby legs to keep up with his sister. Eliza held her hand over her *kappe* to keep the starched fabric in place as she dodged a fallen tree, then glanced back at Greta with an excited smile. "Hurry up!"

Greta could not maintain the twins' pace, but she followed their shouts and laughter down the footpath that wound through the settlement. The morning spread bright and brisk around her as she felt an eager anticipation at the promise of new neighbors who would help their Amish village survive.

By the time she reached the center of the settlement, the twins had already greeted the newcomers and rushed back to their morning chores. Greta spotted a solitary cart across the clearing from the smokehouse. A young woman stood in a graceful pose with her hands clasped at her chest as she surveyed her surroundings. Greta caught a flicker of concern on the woman's face, but her remarkable beauty outshone the negative expression.

Greta held up her hand and called out a greeting.

The woman turned and smiled. Her striking blue eyes shone in contrast to her coal black hair and fair skin. *"Wunderbar.* I was beginning to wonder if we had found the right place. My grandmother and grandfather have gone in search of the bishop, but the only people I have seen are two small children, running about like wild animals."

Greta laughed. "The Fisher twins. And I am Greta Scholtz."

The woman smiled a polite, yet careful smile.

"We haven't a bishop yet," Greta continued. "But I am sure that we will draw lots for one soon. Our settlement is growing quickly. And now, we have another family!"

"I am Catrina Witmer. From Philadelphia." She looked past Greta and searched the clearing with her eyes. "Is there any place to rest and refresh? It has been a terribly long journey. And I have seen nothing but trees, dirt, and squirrels the entire way."

"We are so very glad that you have made it to us!"

"Ja." The woman's face looked strained beneath her perfect features. She leaned against the cart and smoothed her neck cloth. "I thought we would never arrive."

"You came alone? Just you and your grandparents?"

"We had a guide, but he has already pocketed his wages and gone. Gone where, I cannot imagine." She waved a hand toward the forest that towered around them. "Where is there to go here?"

Greta laughed. "You will get used to the wilderness. It is not the empty place that I once thought. The forest holds wild foods to forage, and game for our table, and ancient hemlocks taller than you could imagine anything could grow. Everything we need is here." Her eyes swept across the tree line. Greta had not realized that the backcountry had truly become home until that moment. "You will grow to love the wilderness, the stark beauty and even the quiet isolation."

Greta noticed that something other than the ancient forest had caught Catrina's attention. Greta followed Catrina's gaze and frowned. The newcomer was watching Jacob stride out of the woods as he headed toward the smokehouse.

"Well, it seems that you are right." Catrina smiled and straightened her posture as she watched the tall, masculine figure in the distance. "Perhaps we are not so isolated after all."

"Oh. *Ja.* Well, that is not exactly what I meant."

"No?"

Greta cleared her throat. "Your parents did not join you?"

"What?" Catrina pulled her attention from Jacob. "Oh. *Ja.* They stayed in Philadelphia. They own a shop and, well . . ." She shrugged. "They are not Amish."

"Oh." Greta's brows knitted together. "They are not, that is to say, I do not mean to pry but, they are not . . . ?" She did not want to say the words.

Catrina laughed. The sound was soft and feminine like tiny bells. "No. They are not shunned. They were never Amish. My grandparents converted late in life, after my mother had married and moved out of the house."

"But you have been baptized in the faith?"

Catrina shook her head. "Not yet." Her gaze returned to the other side of the clearing. She watched Jacob disappear inside the smokehouse. "Is he spoken for?" Her eyes stayed on the empty doorway, even though she addressed Greta.

"Jacob Miller? Oh. I don't . . . I could not say. . . . He is not courting anyone, but he is recently widowed and is not interested in—"

Catrina smiled a soft, knowing smile. "Not interested? We will see about that, Greta dear."

"Oh. I don't . . . I mean, I suppose . . ." Greta didn't know what to say. Her stomach dropped at the thought of the beautiful stranger setting her sights on Jacob. *Her* Jacob. *No, not my Jacob.* Greta frowned and twisted the ties of her *kappe* in her fingers.

A hesitant expression marred Catrina's face. "Forgive me, Greta. I have been too bold. Has he showed you any promise of affection? Perhaps you have been hopeful that he will court you? I am sure that there are few eligible men here."

"Promise of affection?" Greta's frown deepened. "No. He is not . . . Jacob Miller is . . ." She searched for the right words. "He has shown no interest in courting since his wife—"

"Then you have no expectations?"

"Of courtship?"

"*Ja.*"

Greta cleared her throat. She hesitated. "No."

Catrina smiled. "I have decided that we will be great friends, Greta. Surely there are not many other women our age here?"

"No. Only us."

Catrina's smile broadened.

Greta looked away. She felt the heat rising in her cheeks.

"I do believe that it is time for me to meet Jacob Miller." She giggled. "I could use help unloading my belongings. And he is the ideal candidate for the job."

"Oh." Greta swallowed. "Oh, I see."

Catrina set a soft, delicate hand on Greta's arm, but her gaze stayed on the smokehouse door. "Thank you, dear. Lovely to meet you." Her eyes lit up as Jacob strode out of the smokehouse and into the sunlit field. Catrina flashed a dazzling smile and lifted her free hand in a graceful wave. Jacob tipped his beaver-felt hat and nodded. Greta wished that she could read his expression from across the clearing, but his chiseled face remained guarded. Greta stared at Jacob for a few beats, then murmured a quick good-bye to Catrina and slipped away into the forest.

Her heart beat far too fast for a woman who claimed to have no desire for a man's affection.

Chapter Ten

Greta woke up early the next morning filled with happy excitement. *Today is the first day of my new school!* Then her mood dropped like a stone when the fog of sleep cleared and she remembered the way Catrina Witmer had watched Jacob the day before. *Mayhap I should have admitted my feelings to her. I could have discouraged her.*

Greta sighed and slid her woolen hose up her legs, then tied them above her knees. She did not want to touch the cold, rough earth beside her pallet with bare feet. She shook her head and rose from the warmth of the quilt. The chilled morning air struck her through her thin shift and she shivered. *It matters not. I should accept that Jacob has no affection for me. But the thought of him with another woman feels like a heavy stone in my chest.* She frowned as she remembered the newcomer's remarkable beauty. *I should not begrudge her a good match. It is not her fault that Jacob has rejected me. I should not have allowed myself to develop feelings for him. I must set Jacob Miller aside and move on.*

"You seem troubled this morning." Ruth looked

up as she stirred a bowl of cornmeal and water for the morning's corn cakes. Greta had told Ruth about Catrina's arrival the day before, but she had not disclosed her obvious interest in Jacob. Greta forced a smile. "All is well."

"I am surprised that you are not more excited at the arrival of another young woman your age."

Greta looked away. "The children will be here this afternoon. There is much to do beforehand. I must hurry."

Ruth studied Greta's frown and started to speak, but closed her mouth instead and continued to stir the corn cake batter. She shrugged. "We will speak more of Catrina later, mayhap."

Greta's frown deepened. "Mayhap. But I would rather think of my plans for today." The cold air made her fingers fumble as she laced the ties of her bodice.

"It seems odd to bring all the children here and run a school. It is not our way."

Greta looked up, concerned that Ruth did not approve. But the elderly woman smiled. "Oh well. A new world calls for new ways, I suppose."

Greta grinned as she secured her long, shining hair and fastened her white *kappe*. "That does not sound like you, Ruth. What is next? Will you suggest that we give up our Plain ways to wear lace and buttons, or for our men to grow their mustaches like soldiers?"

Ruth laughed. "Oh, Greta!" She shook her head. "But, all joking aside, it is a good thing to see you help the children."

"And being useful."

"*Ja.* It is not easy to be a woman on her own."

Greta sighed. "It seems so easy to be a man. Take Jacob." She waved in the direction of his farm. "He is on his own, just like me, but he can live alone and support himself. He is strong enough to plow his fields and he can shoot his own supper."

"True." Ruth stoked the fire. "But he is still expected to marry. For the good of the community. We all must think of the community, not just ourselves."

Greta sighed and walked to the window. She stared through the oilcloth and tried to make out the shape of the trees that stood between her and Jacob's cabin. "I want more from a marriage than that." Greta wanted to explain but didn't know how. She remembered the way her heart beat like a drum in her throat when Jacob gazed down at her with a twinkle in his dark eyes, or the way her stomach leapt when he flashed his sly half smile.

Ruth chuckled.

Greta turned abruptly from the window to Ruth. "Is that funny to you?"

"Just imagine Jacob Miller trying to spin his own flax, or make lye soap out of ashes, or mix an herbal remedy for the croup."

"Oh. *Ja.* I suppose he needs help too." Greta looked down. "But he does not want that help to come from me." She took a deep breath and let it out. "I was never interested in him, anyway." Greta felt a pang of guilt at the lie.

Ruth raised an eyebrow. "You are sure about that?"

"I know when somebody is disinterested."

"And aloof," Ruth added.

"And aloof," Greta said.

"And guarded."

"And guarded." Greta nodded.

"And handsome."

"And handsome." Greta laughed as soon as the words escaped her lips. "You tricked me! I did not mean . . ."

"Of course not, dear." Ruth pulled the iron spider off the coals and checked the corn cakes. "Of course not."

Greta frowned and set the table. She let the trenchers bang against the wood and Ruth clucked her tongue in gentle reprimand. The young woman sighed and threw up her hands.

"All right. Let's just say that I have feelings for him. Just for the sake of argument."

"*Ja.* Just for the sake of argument."

"Let's just say that I am interested in Jacob. *Mildly* interested, mind you. *Barely* interested."

"But interested."

"Theoretically."

"All right. Theoretically."

"So." Greta cleared her throat. "Let's just say that I am interested. What good would it do? He has made his feelings clear." Greta felt an unexpected flood of emotion. She clenched her jaw and tried to force it back down. "Do you not remember, Ruth? Last we spoke he said that he had no affection for me."

Ruth frowned. She poured the corn cake batter into the iron spider that sat atop the burning coals in the hearth. The surface sizzled and earthy steam billowed upward as the batter spread across the hot metal. "Sometimes people say things that they do not mean. Especially if they are afraid to admit how they really feel."

"Maybe." She put her hands on her hips and leaned forward. "Or maybe he feels nothing for me."

Ruth sighed and shook her head, but did not argue the stark declaration.

Jacob looked up from his field of winter wheat when he heard the shout. The stalks of grain rippled in the wind like the waves of an earth-colored sea. He cupped a hand over his brow to shield his eyes from the low afternoon sun. A group of children ran along the footpath that wound past his farm and into the old growth forest. He smiled when he realized where the children were headed. *Greta's little school is underway.* Jacob wiped the sweat from his brow as he watched the carefree scholars laugh and play on their way to their studies.

He remembered his last conversation with Greta and cringed. *I said things that I should not have said.* He felt that familiar rush of pain that appeared anytime he was tempted to draw closer to Greta Scholtz. He watched the children disappear into the forest and sighed. *My grief and anger over Marta has become a prison.* He swallowed hard. *And yet, I still do not think I am ready to let go.* He could feel his heart harden as he remembered his wife and son. He closed his eyes. *Help me, Lord. I am so afraid that you will allow everything to be taken from me again. How do I trust you as I once did?*

Jacob turned back to his work as he wrestled with memories of Marta, his floundering relationship with *der Herr,* and his feelings for a spirited schoolteacher that could no longer be pushed away.

* * *

The children arrived at the Widow Yoder's cabin full of smiles and chatter. They offered a polite hello, sat down in a semicircle around the hearth, and gazed up at their new teacher. Ruth sat in the corner of the cabin, out of the way, mending a torn bodice. Greta cleared her throat. *Where to begin?*

"Welcome, children. I am so glad that we are blessed with this opportunity." Seven pairs of eyes stared up at her, waiting. Greta felt her face flush. She forced a smile.

"First, we need to assess your reading and writing skills." Greta drilled each child and sorted them into groups by skill level. She tested their knowledge of the ABCs with her copy of the Bible and the *Ausbund*, since these were the only books that any of them owned. The dirt floor served as a tablet, a twig for a pen.

By the end of the lesson, Greta's nervousness transformed into confidence and her heart warmed with a newfound sense of purpose. When dusk fell on the cabin she could not believe how fast the minutes had flown past. "It is time for me to send you home, children." She collected the books and helped the younger children fasten their cloaks.

"I look forward to seeing you all tomorrow."

Christian handed Greta a butternut squash as she waved them out the door. "Here, Greta. This is for you."

"Thank you, Christian. This will make a lovely dinner."

"Mother says that we must feed you for teaching

us. At least until you get married." His brow creased in concentration. "You are the lady who is going to marry Jacob Miller, aren't you?"

Greta's mouth fell open. Christian peered up at her with big brown eyes. She stared back at him for a few beats, unable to voice a response. All of the children stopped wiggling and stared back at her. The room fell into complete and painful silence.

Gretel Gruber reached up and tugged on her teacher's skirt. "*Ja*, Greta, aren't you supposed to marry Jacob?"

The smallest girl, Anna Stoltzfus, jumped up and down and clapped. "Oh! I love weddings! There are cakes and pies and roast beef at weddings!" She grabbed Greta's hand and squeezed. "Do marry soon, Greta. I have not had cake in forever!"

"There will not be any cake," Christian admonished. "There cannot be cake without sugar. And there is no sugar."

The little girl's face scrunched up and she began to cry.

"Oh, dear." Greta rubbed the child's back. "Oh, no. No crying, Anna."

"But I want cake. And now there will be no cake."

"There can still be roast beef," Christian said.

Anna snuffled and wiped her eyes. "Roast beef?" She smiled and wiped her eyes again. "I do like roast beef."

Greta put out her hand. "Oh, no. I am sorry, dear. But there will not be any roast beef. Or cake. Or pie."

The little girl began to wail again. "Not even a dried apple pie?"

"No, dear. Not even a dried apple pie." Greta

pinched the bridge of her nose. "There will not be pie or cake or roast beef because there will be no wedding."

Anna stopped crying and looked up. "But, everyone says that there will be a wedding." The children nodded in unison.

Greta put her face in her hands and groaned.

Ruth stood up from a bench in the corner and made a shooing motion with her hands. "All right, children, that is enough for today. Out with you all, before you miss your supper." The children filed outside and skipped down the path until their shouts disappeared into the cold evening air. Greta shut the door and collapsed onto a bench. She shook her head. "Well, I never." She shook her head again.

"Do not pay it any mind, dear," Ruth said as she looked up from her mending. "Children say the funniest things."

"So it is not true, then. Everyone in the settlement is *not* saying that Jacob and I will be married?"

"Oh no, dear. Of course they are all saying that."

Greta put her face in her hands. Soon the entire settlement would learn that Jacob had rejected her.

Chapter Eleven

Greta tried to push aside all thoughts of Jacob Miller the next day. She decided to distract herself by doing the laundry and spent the morning hunched over a cauldron of boiling water in the crisp autumn air. Lye soap burned her nostrils as she stirred shifts, stays, woolen hosen, and neck cloths with a big wooden paddle.

"The children will be here soon," Ruth reminded her when the sun began its downward arc. Greta frowned and pushed back a lock of hair that had fallen across her face.

"What a mess!" Greta shook her head as she surveyed her stained apron and muddied skirt. "Sometimes I think that doing the laundry just creates more laundry!" She sighed and shook her head again. Ruth smiled, patted her shoulder, and headed to the kitchen garden.

Greta leaned over the side of the cauldron to hoist out the wet laundry. Her fingers found a grip on the bed linens in the dull, murky water. She pulled, but the waterlogged fabric caught beneath other garments and wouldn't budge. She clenched her fingers tighter and used her body weight to pull backward. Greta strained until the linens shot upward. The momentum threw her backward—and into strong, familiar arms.

"We really must stop meeting like this," Jacob said as he steadied her, then stepped back.

"Oh!" Greta's hands flew to her face and she stuffed loose strands of hair back under her prayer *kappe*. "I did not . . . I did not expect you." She wiped the sweat off her forehead and smoothed the front of her bodice. "Where did you come from?" *Why does he always appear when I am at my worst?*

"We are neighbors, if you had not noticed. 'Tis a short walk from my place to yours."

"But how long have you been standing there?"

"Long enough to wonder if you were trying to knock me down intentionally."

Greta blushed. "Oh." She cleared her throat. "No. Of course not. Thank you for catching me."

"I would not blame you if you did try to knock me down, you know."

"Oh." She looked up at him with a startled expression.

Jacob stared at her and she felt herself melt into the dark pools of his eyes. "After what I said to you."

Greta studied his face, unsure of what he meant or how to respond. Her heart fluttered against her rib cage like a sparrow's wings. *Is he trying to take back what he said to me? Is he trying to tell me that he does hold some affection for me?* The air between them felt tight with anticipation. "What do you mean, Jacob?"

Jacob opened his mouth to say more, then closed it again. A sad expression passed over his face. Greta thought he seemed lost and alone, even though he stood so tall and strong and looked so capable. *How can a man who has trekked across the wilderness and built a cabin with his own work-hardened hands look so vulnerable?* Greta wanted to reach out, take his broad, strong hands, and tell him that all would be well. Instead, she gazed into his guarded eyes and waited. He stared back. Greta's heartbeat pulsed in her ears. She sensed a deep longing beneath his hardened features.

Jacob's expression changed and he shifted his feet. The moment was gone.

"You have a spot there." Jacob pointed to her cheek. She frowned and rubbed at her face while she tried to maintain a dignified expression.

Jacob gave a slight smile. "Still there."

She kept rubbing.

"*Ja*, now you are just spreading the dirt around." Jacob pulled a handkerchief out of his pocket and wiped her face. "There we go."

Greta looked back down at the cauldron. She felt embarrassed and uncertain. *Did I imagine the connection I felt when he looked at me? Why did he push the moment away? Why is he here?*

Greta looked up and met his gaze again. She felt a magnetic pull as their eyes connected. Time stood still. The noise of the birds and movement of the wind through the trees dropped away. There was only the intensity of Jacob's dark, mysterious eyes.

A swirl of skirts and an enthusiastic hello interrupted them. "Oh Greta, darling!" Catrina ran toward them and clapped her hands together. "You must introduce me!"

Greta sucked in her breath, startled. She cleared

her throat and forced a polite smile as the world snapped back into place. She was suddenly aware of her bedraggled appearance next to Catrina's clean white apron and perfectly smoothed hair. "I didn't expect to see you here, today."

Catrina laughed. "I came to call on you. We are going to be great friends, remember." She switched her attention to Jacob. "Now, you were about to introduce us."

"Oh. *Ja.* Of course. This is Jacob Miller." Her gaze lingered on his chiseled, unreadable features before she turned back to Catrina. "And this is Catrina Witmer, newly arrived from Philadelphia with her grandparents. And new to our faith as well."

"Hello, Mr. Miller." She gazed up at him through thick black lashes. "How delightful to meet you."

"Call me Jacob. Plain folk don't put much stock in titles and such."

Catrina nodded and continued to gaze up at him with a flawless smile.

Jacob did not return the smile. "I trust you had a safe journey?"

"It was terrible! Just terrible!" She placed a delicate hand on Jacob's arm. "I have never felt so alone. How wonderful it is to be amongst people again."

Greta studied Jacob's expression as Catrina chattered like a bright, happy bird. Greta tried to decipher what Jacob thought of the newcomer. His face remained distant and he did not laugh when Catrina threw back her head and giggled.

Greta watched the interaction carefully. *Maybe he is not swayed by her beauty. He called on me for a reason today.*

"I must get back to my work," Jacob interjected

when he found a break in Catrina's enthusiastic monologue.

"Oh, must you?"

He sighed. "*Ja*. I only came round to deliver Greta's milk cow. She has been sampling my kitchen garden again."

"Oh. Rose." Greta cringed. *Of course. He called because he had to return my cow. I should not have assumed that there was more to his visit. He made his feelings clear last we spoke.*

"I brought her back here to release her so she doesn't go straight back to my cabbages." He flashed an impish grin. "Maybe she will sample your cabbages instead."

Greta managed a weak smile. "Thank you."

Jacob hesitated and Greta thought he might say something. But instead he tipped his black beaver-felt hat and strode away. She watched the tall, solitary figure cut across the clearing and disappear into the shadows of the hemlocks. She leaned against the smooth metal cauldron and stared at the empty tree line. Catrina chatted about something in a merry voice, but Greta did not notice. She felt cold and empty inside.

Greta's mind felt heavy with thoughts of Jacob as she tried to teach the children that afternoon. She kept asking herself over and over again why he held no affection for her. *What is wrong with me? Am I that unlovable?* She ran through her interactions with the aloof widower and felt her stomach sink with each memory. *What could I possibly offer him? I cannot keep my cow out of his garden, I am afraid of possums, and every time he sees me I fall into his arms—quite literally! He must think that I can barely function. He comes to my rescue nearly every day, it seems.*

Greta frowned and turned the page of the *Ausbund*. The thin, yellowed page whispered beneath her finger. She tried to focus, but an image of Catrina Witmer came to her. Greta remembered the woman's flawless skin, raven black hair, and piercing blue eyes. *Surely it is only a matter of time before Jacob finds affection for her and her beauty. If only I had something to offer. Some way to show him that I can do something right. Maybe then he would develop affection for me.*

Greta sat up straighter. She had an idea. Her mind raced as she considered if she could pull it off. A small smile appeared on her lips. She would manage it. She had to. *And Jacob Miller will have to take notice of me!*

"What are you thinking about?" Anna tugged on Greta's skirt. "You were daydreaming, weren't you?" The little girl pointed to the dirt floor. "I spelled out 'bat' and I got the 'bee' right, but you did not notice."

"Oh, Anna! That looks wonderful! Very nice." Greta smiled. "I am sorry that I was not paying attention. My mind was elsewhere."

"Where was it?"

Greta laughed and tapped little Anna on the tip of the nose. "Funny you should ask, darling. I was thinking of sugar. And you know what we make with sugar, don't you?"

"Cake!"

"*Ja!*"

"Are you going to make a cake?" Anna jumped up and down. "You are getting married after all, aren't you! I knew it! Cake! Cake for everyone!" The children jumped up and down and shouted.

"Oh, no!" Greta shook her head. "I am not getting married." She held up her hand to ward off the shouts of disappointment. "But I am planning to bake a cake."

"Cake!" The children shouted in unison and jumped up and down again.

"Greta, you should not get their hopes up." Ruth shot her a warning look from the corner of the cabin. "You know that there is no sugar to be had."

Greta nodded. "*Ja. Ja*, I know. But I have an idea." She bit her lip and thought for a moment. "Wouldn't it be perfect to bring a cake to the next worship service to welcome the Witmer family?" *And impress Jacob.*

The children squealed in delight.

"Now. All of you run along. We will end class a little bit early today so that I can get started." She helped the children into their wraps and sent them on their way with a grin.

Ruth shook her head as soon as the door shut. "Greta, what are you up to?"

"I have a plan." Greta grabbed her cloak from the peg and fastened it around her shoulders, then picked up one of the wooden water buckets.

"And? What is this plan of yours?" The elderly woman looked skeptical.

"Just wait. You will know as soon as I get back."

Greta raced across the clearing, toward the edge of the forest. "If I can just remember where it is . . ." She slowed when she reached the tree line and studied the branches. "Hmmm. I knew that I saw it here somewhere." She passed Rose and patted her on the shoulder. "Do you remember where it is, girl?" The cow raised her head and stared with disinterested eyes as she chewed her cud.

Greta walked until she reached the edge of the Yoder farm. "That's funny. I did not remember it being quite so deep in the woods." She frowned and squinted at the tree branches.

"Oh look, Rose, there it is!" Greta broke into a wide grin as she rushed to a large bush. "There is a beehive in there, Rose! And do you know what bees make? Honey!"

Just think how happy I will make everyone when I bring a cake to the service tomorrow. Jacob will have to admit that he is impressed. She heard a small, nagging voice remind her of a foundational Amish belief: *Pride cometh before a fall.* She ignored the thought. *Just imagine the look on his face when I serve him cake! He will have to admit that I am worth his affection.* She raised her chin and felt a thrill of victory.

Greta eased up to the hive. "Okay, Rose. What now?" Greta did not hear the cowbell and glanced back over her shoulder. Rose had disappeared. "Hmm, well, I am sure that I can figure this out on my own." She picked up a stick and studied the hive. *I will just give it a little poke and see what happens.* She shuffled forward. *I am sure that it will be fine. The bees are probably hibernating . . . right?*

Greta gave the hive a good jab with the stick. Nothing happened. "*Ja.* Hibernating." As soon as she said the words an insect zipped out of the hive, straight for her. Another followed. Then another and another. Greta leapt back. She felt a sharp pinch on her arm. "Ouch!" A second insect dive-bombed her face.

"Wait! That's not a bee!" A cloud of wasps poured out of the hive, full of wrath and ready for vengeance. Greta screamed, hitched up her skirts, and ran.

Jacob heard a sharp cry pierce the autumn air and took off running. He knew that voice. His heart pounded against his chest as he raced across the wheat field and jumped the split rail fence. "Greta! Greta!" She stumbled out of the woods and into his clearing in a wild, zigzagging motion. Her shrieks echoed off the Blue Mountain as she slapped at her face and hair. "Greta, are you all right?"

"Run, Jacob! Run!" She veered away from him and waved her arms. "Save yourself!" Jacob did not listen to the crazed young woman. Instead, he ran toward her even faster, until he drew close enough to see the mob of wasps that swarmed around her. "Do not come any closer! They will get you, too!"

Jacob lunged for her and grabbed her hand. "No! This way! If you go back into the woods they will not stop until you are dead!" He pulled her toward his farm and tried to dodge the painful stings. They clambered over a split rail fence, hit the ground running, and flew across the field.

"In here!" He pulled her into the pigsty.

"But the pigs! The mud!"

"*Ja!* The mud!" He picked Greta up and tossed her into the watering trough. "You will thank me for this. I promise." She landed with a splash and gasped as slop sprayed into her face. "Put your head down!" Greta held her nose, squeezed her eyes shut, and pushed her face to the bottom of the trough. Jacob grabbed handfuls of mud and smeared it across her back and neck.

As soon as he had completely covered Greta's

body in mud, Jacob dropped to the ground and rolled in a puddle. The wasps circled for another minute, then pulled back and buzzed away.

Greta lay stunned in the trough. Her prayer *kappe* drooped off her head and her chestnut-colored curls unfurled about her face in a wet, muddy mess. She wiped the slime and water off her mouth and spit. She spit again. She pushed herself into a sitting position. Dirty water streamed off her bodice and ran into her lap as she reached for her *kappe.*

Jacob lay sprawled on the ground beside her, covered in mud. A fat sow wandered over, grunted, and sniffed at his face. Greta stared at Jacob and the pig as she fumbled with the prayer *kappe.* She pushed it over her hair, but dirty water poured out of the fabric and streamed down her face. She groaned, snatched it off her head, and wrung it out. Greta stuck it back on her head and locked eyes with Jacob. He pushed the pig aside, sat up, and rubbed mud off his face.

"Well, Jacob Miller, I believe the first time we met you said something about my 'wallowing in the mud.'" She flashed a smile. "Looks like I am not the only one." And then she began to laugh.

Jacob looked surprised for an instant. Then he broke into laughter too. They laughed and laughed until the tears streamed from their eyes and their bellies ached.

Jacob waited until the laugher faded before he stood up and offered her a hand. "I am sorry that I had to throw you in the trough. I had no choice, really."

She took his muddy hands in hers. "Surely we could have run into the cabin."

He shook his head as he lifted her out of the trough. "Not airtight enough."

Greta shrugged and adjusted the soggy prayer *kappe*. "Well, we are both alive. I guess that is all that matters." She smiled. "I never thought that I would say this, but thank you for throwing me in the pigpen, Jacob."

Ruth gasped when Greta strode into the cabin. "My goodness, child! Whatever happened?" The old woman jumped up and the ball of homespun yarn in her lap rolled onto the dirt floor. "You look like a monster!"

Greta just smiled.

"Greta, what on earth happened?"

"Something wonderful." She danced across the floor.

"What?"

"Jacob Miller threw me into the pigpen."

"What?"

"Jacob Miller threw me into the pigpen." Greta pulled off the wet prayer *kappe* and tossed it on the hearth to dry. "Well, first there were wasps. Hundreds of wasps. And then, all of a sudden, Jacob was there. And then we were in the pigpen together and we were laughing and . . ." Greta broke into a grin. "Don't you see, Ruth? He rescued me! He braved a swarm of wasps to pull me to safety." She hummed to herself as she picked up the bucket of water. "You should have seen us laughing afterward. He was rolling in the mud like a pig, I was hanging out of the trough, dripping wet, and we just . . . well, I guess you had to be there."

"Clearly." Ruth clucked her tongue. "I thank the Lord that Jacob brought his hog in from the woods for the slaughter."

"Indeed. If his hog were still free to forage there would have been no place to hide."

Ruth shook her head. "What were you doing going around a wasp's nest, anyway?"

"Well, I . . ." Greta looked sheepish.

"You weren't looking for honey, were you?"

"*Ja*. I thought they were bees."

Ruth slapped herself on the forehead. "Oh, Greta!"

Greta shrugged. "So there will not be any cake, obviously. But I just might have discovered something better than honey."

"What?"

"That Jacob Miller holds affection for me after all."

"Well, well. What a surprise." Ruth smiled and picked up her mending basket. She did not look surprised in the least.

Chapter Twelve

Greta felt a surge of excitement as soon as she woke up the next morning. *Everything has changed. Ja, he claimed to have no affection for me, but there was a spark between Jacob and me yesterday. Definitely a spark. That was not just a rescue—it was something more. Something wonderful!*

"Greta, just where do you think you are going?" Ruth stood over Greta's pallet with her hands on her hips and shook her head.

"To my chores. Where else?"

"Oh, no you're not."

Greta frowned. "The vinegar we put on the stings drew out the poison. I really do feel all right."

"Hmmph. Do not be ridiculous. Bed rest for you. At least until that swelling goes down."

"Swelling? How bad is it?" She patted her face with her fingertips. The flesh felt hard. "Now that you mention it, it does hurt a little bit." She tried to smile, but her cheeks were too rigid to form a grin. "Ouch."

"*Ja.* Ouch is right. Now get back under the quilt and rest."

"But—"

"No buts about it."

"But—"

Ruth held up her hand. "I know that you are eager to see Jacob again, but you need to rest."

"Eager to see Jacob?"

Ruth shook her head. "Please stop the charade, dear. He has made a most dashing impression."

"It was quite a rescue."

"Hmmm. Well, today you are so swollen that you look rather like a piglet—all shiny pink skin and beady eyes."

Greta pressed her fingers beneath her eyes. The skin felt hard and puffy. "Oh! I cannot possibly see him like this! I really do look like a piglet, don't I?"

"A very sweet piglet."

"But a piglet nonetheless."

"Stay home and rest. I thank *der Herr* that you did not have an adverse reaction to the wasps' poison. Some people do, you know. It can be fatal for them."

"So this is not an adverse reaction?"

"No. Just some swelling and redness. It will go down soon. Rest today and you will soon mend. I know you are looking forward to seeing Jacob again after your . . ." Ruth paused as she searched for the right word. "Successful interaction yesterday. But you must look after your health."

Greta let out a contented sigh. "This 'successful interaction,' as you call it, is a good sign, don't you think?"

"Actions do speak louder than words."

Greta considered the situation and her grin fell back into a frown. "Except that Jacob is a chivalrous man. He would never leave a woman to fight off a swarm of wasps alone, no matter who she is." She went over the event in her mind. "He would have rescued anyone in my situation."

"True. But it seems that this was more than just a rescue, judging by the shine in your eyes."

Greta beamed. "I have never laughed so hard. And over such a foolish thing . . ."

"*Ja.* Laughing over being thrown in a pigsty and chased by wasps. I would say there is something between you two."

Greta looked sheepish. "There is something between us, Ruth. There just has to be! The way I feel when he is near . . . I do not know how to describe it." Greta bit her lip. "He brings out such emotion in me. And even when I think that he holds no affection for me I cannot wait to see him again!" She smiled at the memory of the two of them floundering in the mud like hogs. "And when he drops that guarded manner of his, well . . ." She shook her head, still smiling. "We sure do make each other laugh."

Ruth smiled. "I am so happy that Jacob is coming around. Although it should not have taken being chased by a swarm of wasps!"

Greta's face dropped back into a serious expression. "Well, we still do not know that he is interested in me. Remember, he has said the opposite. It might have just been a fleeting moment of passion due to the excitement and shared danger. People react to danger in strange ways, you know."

"Enough. I am leaving before you talk yourself in circles."

Greta pulled the covers up to her chin and snuggled down into the warmth. She sighed, closed her eyes, and drifted into a satisfied slumber, convinced that things were finally headed in the right direction.

Greta woke when she heard the cabin door open and close. She climbed out of a dream, yawned, and watched Ruth hang her cloak on the peg and set a basket onto the dirt floor. The old woman shuffled to the hearth and stoked the fire.

"I will brew us some redroot tea."

"That sounds lovely." Greta listened to the familiar clink of metal against metal and the slosh of water poured into a cup. The small cabin filled with the humid scent of dried leaves and damp earth. Greta studied the blobs of light and shadow that filtered through the oilcloth window as she waited for the tea to steep. Her thoughts hovered on yesterday's rescue and the feel of Jacob's strong hands as he tossed her to safety.

A knock on the door brought her back to reality.

"Oh! I look a fright." Greta struggled to get up from her pallet on the floor, horrified at being caught in her shift in the middle of the day.

Ruth put up a hand. "Do not fret, child. I do not intend to let anybody in." She opened the door a crack. A draft of cold air and a sliver of sunshine fell across the dirt floor.

"Well, what a pleasant surprise."

Greta studied the back of Ruth's head, but she could not see who was there. She strained to hear the conversation, but could only make out Ruth's side of it.

"No. I have put her to bed."

A low murmur from the other side of the door.

"*Ja, ja*. She is fine. Nothing some vinegar and bed rest cannot cure."

More murmuring.

"Ah! *Danke*! What a fine supper we will have now."

Another murmur.

"No. Do not worry. And thank you again." Ruth shut the door, turned around, and held up a fat rabbit for Greta to admire.

"Jacob brought us supper."

Greta's heart thumped against her chest. She wished that she had seen her handsome rescuer herself.

"How does he look? Is he okay?"

"*Ja, ja*. He is fine. He only got a few stings."

"So he is not a fat piglet, like me?"

Ruth chuckled. "He seems fine. A few stings here and there, but no worse for the wear."

"Thank the Lord."

"*Ja. Der Herr* has been good to you both. It could have gone very badly for you two."

"*Ja*."

Ruth set the rabbit down by the hearth and checked the sack of root vegetables. "I think we have enough carrots to make a nice rabbit stew."

"Perfect." Greta sighed. "I wish that he could have come in for a visit."

Ruth shook her head as she counted out a few carrots. "He could not stay, even if you had been properly dressed. He is on his way to the new Witmer farm. Or what will be the Witmer farm. There is much work to be done to clear the land and build the cabin. And, in the meantime, Jacob is taking them some of his wheat stores."

"He is a thoughtful man."

"It is our way to help one another."

"*Ja.* He is a good Amish man."

"*Ja.*"

"I cannot help but wonder what will happen now." Greta glanced at Ruth with bright eyes. "Yesterday morning I was convinced that there was no future for Jacob and me. But now . . ." She smiled. "Well, things seem different now, *ja?*"

Greta did not teach school the next day. "You do not want to scare the children, dear," the elderly woman explained. Greta touched her swollen face and sighed. "I feel much better."

"Glad to hear it."

"I think that I will be ready to see Jacob soon."

Ruth raised her eyebrows. "You may want to wait another day or two."

"That bad still?"

Ruth shrugged. "I would say that you might not make your best impression." They both laughed.

"I am feeling well enough to get back to work though." She grabbed the bucket and headed for the creek. The rich scent of woodsmoke drifted through the forest and met her at the edge of the clearing. Greta heard the sharp thud of axes and smiled. She knew that the men were bringing down the dark woods that separated her from Jacob. She hummed a happy tune as she picked her way between the hemlocks. A deeper voice joined hers when she neared the water. Greta paused, cocked her head, and then spun around. "Jacob Miller!"

"Hello there."

"You are clearing the land between our farms?"

"*Ja.* Soon there will be no place left for the wolves and bears to hide."

"I look forward to fetching water without fear of wild animals!" Greta grinned, then remembered her distorted features as their eyes met. "Oh, wait. Oh no!" She tried to pull her cloak over her face. "Jacob, I look a fright. Really, you mustn't . . ."

Jacob smiled. "Do not be silly, Greta. I've come to give you a hand."

"But I will scare you away if you see me. I look like a piglet."

"Greta." He shook his head. "Don't. I am not concerned with how you look."

"You're not?" She lowered the cloak. "Even though I look like this?"

Jacob shrugged. "I prefer witty banter to a pretty face."

Greta blushed and looked down.

"And besides, that swelling will go down soon enough. And then you will have both beauty and wit." Greta blushed even more. She raised her eyes and Jacob met her gaze with a grin. "But for now, you *are* rather frightening."

"Jacob Miller!" She punched his arm and he pretended that it hurt. But the grin did not leave his face.

"If you stop attacking me I will draw the water for you."

Greta smiled. "Very well." She held out the bucket. But when he reached for it, she spun around and dashed away.

"Hmmm. Nice try." Jacob took off after her, dodging stones and tall grass as he cut the distance between them. Just as he reached her, Greta collapsed to the ground in a heap.

"Greta! Have you twisted your ankle again?" Greta waited a few beats, then jumped up, laughed, and raced away. "Very tricky!" Jacob leapt after her. He overtook her quickly and lunged for the bucket. She was laughing too hard to keep her grip and, as their eyes met, he pried the bucket from her fingers. An unexpected seriousness fell over them as they each gazed deep into the other's eyes. Jacob cleared his throat and looked away. Greta smoothed her prayer *kappe*.

"I will just, uh, give you a hand here." His voice sounded awkward and unsure.

"*Ja.* Thank you." They walked side by side toward the edge of the creek. "You have a way of appearing at the right time, you know."

Jacob shrugged. "I stopped by the cabin to check on you, and the Widow Yoder told me you had already left to collect the water."

"I . . . I wanted to tell you . . ." Greta swallowed, unsure of what to say. "I wanted to tell you that I am glad that you were there yesterday. Thank you for saving me from the wasps."

Jacob smiled. He felt his heart grow warm. *I would never let any harm come to you.* "It was nothing."

"And thank you for the rabbit. Will you stay for some stew? It is the least that I can do. . . ."

Jacob stared into Greta's hopeful eyes. He felt himself make a decision. *I want to be near this woman every day. I want to be happy again. I want to trust der Herr with my future again.* He nodded and knew that he was committing to much more than a meal. "I would like that."

Greta flashed an excited smile.

"But we have to finish taking down the stand of trees beside my field. And then I must help the Witmers. They have a great deal to do before the snow flies." A flock of birds exploded into the air as a loud crash echoed through the forest. Jacob glanced back toward his farm. "There goes another tree. I cannot leave the others to do the work. I have to go." *But I will be back soon, Greta Scholtz. And I will sit you down over a nice dinner and tell you how I really feel. I have waited this long. Waiting another day or two will not hurt.*

Chapter Thirteen

Greta's stomach fluttered with anticipation Sunday morning. She took longer than usual to adjust her prayer *kappe* and straighten her neck cloth. She checked her apron for stains and shook the fabric to loosen the wrinkles. The white cloth snapped in her hands like a sail.

"Ready?" Ruth asked as she rose from the three-legged stool as Greta pinned the apron to her bodice. "Taking your time this morning, I see."

Greta ignored the comment and rushed outside. Ruth followed a moment later with a basket in her hand. "You forgot the bread to serve after the service."

Greta shook her head. "I do not know what is wrong with me today."

"I think that I might have an idea."

They walked in silence as the frozen grass crunched beneath their feet. The sunrise cast golden streaks of light across the frosty clearing and made the ice crystals sparkle. But Greta did not notice the beauty of the morning. She was too busy going over her last interactions with Jacob Miller. *His manner toward me has definitely changed. Now I am certain that he did not mean it when he said that he held no affection for me.*

It was too cold to sit outside, so the settlement crammed into Jacob's one-room cabin for the service. The fire crackled as they lifted their voices in song. Greta felt cozy in the warm cabin as she drifted away with the rhythmic melody. She cut her eyes to the side without turning her head and stole a secret glance at Jacob. A gentle smile formed on her lips as she dared to hope that he was on the cusp of declaring his true feelings for her.

Greta tried to listen to the service, but her mind drifted. Every thought strayed back to the handsome widower no matter how much effort she made to pay attention. Her eyes cut to Jacob again and again, then flicked back to the front of the room before anyone noticed.

Jacob felt distracted throughout the service. His attention—and his gaze—wandered to Greta. He tightened his jaw and pulled his eyes away. Again.

His thoughts drifted back through their time together. He chuckled inside when he remembered the first time he had ever seen her. She looked so ridiculous sprawled in the mud. And then there was the time she threw a squash at him. *I might have deserved that one.* Or the way they both ended up covered in pig slop and mud to escape the wasps.

Jacob sighed and glanced over at Greta again. She sat still as a statue as she focused on the sermon, a gentle expression on her soft, kindhearted face. *I have fought and fought this. And I am so relieved not to fight it anymore.* He closed his eyes. *It feels so good to finally give in and trust you again, Lord.*

Catrina's gaze flicked over to Jacob. She caught him staring in her general direction and moved her eyes back to the front of the room, a soft, sultry smile on her full red lips. Jacob frowned. *Catrina thinks that I was looking at her.* He did not allow his eyes to wander to the women's side of the room again for the rest of the service.

After the three-hour service wound to a close, the men pushed the backless benches into the center of the cabin and the women piled them high with meat, bread, and vegetables. The space around the table filled with elbows and loud voices as the small congregation tried to move around the tiny cabin, wooden trenchers in hand.

Greta scooped up a spoonful of roasted carrots. "I am glad that we have managed to grow more than pumpkins."

Ruth picked up a slice of squash and grinned. "I agree." She reached for a slab of venison. "Our settlement has come a long way since you arrived."

"And even further since you did!"

"*Ja.* Those were long, lean months." Ruth nodded at her trencher. "But look how *der Herr* blesses those who persevere."

"Amen."

The women made their way to the edge of the room as they searched for enough elbowroom to eat comfortably. Greta's eyes skimmed the gathering, looking for Jacob. She saw him at the back of the line, letting the others go ahead of him. *Just like Jacob.*

Greta nibbled on a carrot but barely noticed the sweet, earthy flavor. Her attention stayed on the tall, chivalrous man on the other side of the crowd. *Will he bring his plate over here once he gets his food? He does want to eat with me, doesn't he?*

Jacob waited with his pewter plate in hand as he listened to the happy murmurs of his neighbors. He felt the deep loneliness that he had carried for so long dissolve amidst the soft laughter and warm familiarity. So many people had reached out to him over these long, difficult months. But one person had made the difference. He looked up and searched for Greta's green eyes and freckled nose.

I cannot wait another minute to tell her how I feel. I had planned to wait until the right moment. But I will not put it off any longer. He worked his way across the room. But so many families stopped to say hello that it was slowgoing. He nodded at Barbara Gruber and Maria Stoltzfus as they discussed cures for a winter cough. He tipped his hat at Abraham and Amos as they chewed on fat chunks of venison. Peter Fisher ran through the crowd and bumped into Jacob's knee. The little boy looked up with big round eyes and Jacob patted him on the head and sent him on his way.

Greta kept track of Jacob's slow progression across the room. He looked tall and self-assured in his dark dress jacket and waistcoat. *He keeps heading this way . . . is he coming to eat with me?* She picked at a slice of venison as she studied his movements. Jacob took another few steps her way. *Ja, he is coming over here. He is coming to eat with me!* She looked down at her trencher and tried to concentrate on her food. *Do not let him see you watching him! You must act surprised and nonchalant when he gets here!* She smoothed her neck cloth and took a deep breath. *Calm. Maintain calm.* But her heart beat so fast that it felt as if it would fly from her chest.

Jacob made his way across the rest of the room, until he was almost to Greta's side. She beamed and opened her mouth to say hello—but Catrina slid between them before Greta could form the words. She had not noticed that the beautiful newcomer was hovering behind her and the appearance caught her by surprise. Catrina flashed a sweet smile and Greta felt her heart drop into her stomach. *Wait. Was Jacob on his way to see Catrina instead of me?* Greta's appetite disappeared and she lowered her trencher. She swallowed and looked up at Jacob, uncertain.

He opened his mouth to speak, but Barbara Gruber slipped in between them. "Greta, dear. Just who we have been looking for. Come here for a moment. We really must talk." Barbara took Greta's elbow and steered her away from Jacob and Catrina. Jonah Gruber followed close behind his wife. He looked uncomfortable. Greta glanced back at Jacob as Barbara led her away. Jacob's and Greta's eyes connected and she realized that he was watching her. She felt a renewed surge of hope. *He isn't paying attention to Catrina.*

"Greta, are you all right?" Barbara frowned and stared at Greta's face. "I heard about your incident with the wasps, but my goodness, you really do look a fright! I did not expect quite so much—"

"Is this what you wanted to talk to me about?" Greta interrupted, her eyes still on Jacob. She did not want to be reminded that Catrina looked even more beautiful than her than usual.

"No." Barbara cleared her throat. Her fingers fidgeted with her *kappe* with nervous energy. "Jonah and I have been discussing something."

"What?" Greta ripped her attention from Jacob and turned her head to Barbara.

"I should say that Jonah has been talking to Jacob, actually, and . . ." Barbara's voice trailed away. She looked at Jonah and poked him in the ribs with her elbow. He cleared his throat and rubbed the back of his neck. Barbara prodded him with her elbow again. "You should be the one to tell her, Jonah. You heard it firsthand."

"*Ja.* You are right. I heard it firsthand." He shuffled his feet and rubbed the back of his neck again. Greta's gaze moved past Jonah's shoulder and followed Jacob as he left Catrina's side. *Catrina did not hold his attention very long.* Jacob's eyes met Greta's again and she smiled.

"The thing is . . ."

"Greta?" Barbara leaned in closer. "Are you listening?"

Greta pulled her eyes away from Jacob's. "*Ja.* Of course."

"Greta, I have to apologize," Jonah said in a low voice. He wore a miserable expression on his face.

"Apologize? Whatever for?"

"I am afraid that Barbara and I have misled you. We were misled ourselves, you see. And we thought that we were doing the right thing, but we were wrong. And now we are afraid that we have given you false hope and made a mess of things."

"What? I am sorry, but I simply do not understand what you are talking about." Greta's eyes flicked across the room again as she searched for Jacob.

"Greta. Remember the conversation we had last week when you told us about your school?" Barbara placed her hand on Greta's elbow. "We thought that Jacob planned to marry you."

Greta felt her stomach drop. "*Ja.*"

"We misled you. I am so sorry."

"What do you mean?"

Jonah cleared his throat. "I spoke to Jacob about that."

"He had to return a hammer," Barbara cut in. "It isn't as if he went just to"—she waved her hand—"to speak about your personal affairs."

Jonah frowned. "Right. As I was saying, Jacob made it clear that Barbara and I—well, the whole settlement, I suppose—have it wrong. He is not . . ." Jonah swallowed hard and glanced at his wife. She nodded, her face somber. "He has no interest in courting you."

"Oh." Greta blinked. She cleared her throat. Her stomach twisted as she processed Jonah's words. *But, I was so sure. . . .* Her eyes shot across the room again, searching frantically for Jacob. She saw him leaning against the wall of his cabin, his face turned down, a shadow over his dark eyes. He looked alone and unreachable. Greta turned back to Jonah. "Are you certain that he still feels this way? Over the past few days we . . ." Greta struggled to find the right words. ". . . We drew closer."

"Ach. Greta. I am sorry. But I am certain his feelings

would not change day to day. He is not fickle. When he sets his mind on something it is done. And he was very clear that he holds no affection for you." Jonah's face looked pained. "None whatsoever." He shifted his weight from one foot to the other and looked away.

"Oh. Oh, I see." Greta's mind sifted through the events of the past few days. She had been so sure that they had made a connection. "But he seemed to connect with me in such a way that . . ." Greta shook her head. She would not humiliate herself by insisting that the connection had been there for him too.

Jonah shifted his feet again. "*Ja.* Jacob is a good man. He is a good friend. I understand how you could have felt that it was more, but . . . it is only friendship. I am sorry." Jonah looked at his wife. "I did not want to break her heart."

Greta felt the room crash down around her. *It does not matter what you felt, or thought he felt. Here is the truth of it, plain and simple. You must listen to the truth, not entertain false hope for a man who clearly wants to be left alone. You are a friend to him. Nothing more. The only connection he feels is platonic.* Greta cleared her throat again. She wished that she could be anywhere but in that room, hearing the laughter and chatter of the close-knit families around her.

Greta forced a smile. She even managed a small, shaky laugh. "Break my heart? Goodness no." She would not let anyone see how much the truth hurt. She could not save her heart, but she could save her dignity. "I feel the same way that he does, so that works out just fine." She told herself that even if the words did not feel true now, she would make them true. She would push all affection for Jacob Miller from her heart. Forever. It was the only way. It was what he wanted.

Jonah's eyes snapped to Greta. "Oh? I thought . . ."

"Greta, are you quite sure?" Barbara stared at Greta thoughtfully.

"Yes. Quite sure."

Barbara exhaled. "I am so glad to hear you say that, Greta. I feared that we had given you false expectations. We thought that you had fallen for him."

Greta shook her head. "No. Of course not. I just thought . . . well, there for a few days I thought that he had fallen for me."

Jonah grinned and shrugged. "Ah, well. I am glad we did not let this misunderstanding go too far. The situation could have become quite complicated."

Barbara laughed. "Could you imagine if you had both gone on thinking that the other one was interested when neither one of you is? What a mess we might have made!"

"*Ja.* What a mess." Greta's voice sounded flat. She heard herself mumble an excuse and hurry for the cabin door. She needed to get away from the stuffy room and the laughing couples that surrounded her. Her long, heavy skirts swished against her calves as she wove through the crowded room.

Greta glanced behind her as she yanked the door open. Cold, crisp air whisked past her as though it had been waiting for a chance to invade the warm, cozy cabin. Jacob caught her gaze from across the room and moved toward her. Greta could not hold back her emotions any longer and the tears welled in her eyes. She rushed through the door before the handsome widower could reach her. *I will not let him see me cry. I will never let him know how I really feel.* Hot tears blurred Greta's vision as she hurried across the muddy yard and vanished into the dark, towering forest.

Catrina waited until the door shut behind Greta, then slipped in to take her place beside Barbara and Jonah.

"How are you settling in?" Barbara asked. "You have met Greta?" She glanced across the room, but Greta was already gone. "You must be about the same age."

"*Ja.* She has been very welcoming. I am sure we will be friends." A look of concentration marred Catrina's perfect features. "I thought that Jacob Miller might have spoken for her. After all there are so few eligible men." She cleared her throat. "What I mean to say is . . ." She gave a sheepish grin and hid her face in her hands. "Oh! I do hope that I do not sound too bold. I just could not help overhearing your conversation. Is it true that Jacob has no intention of courting her? And that she holds no affection for him?"

"*Ja.*" Jonah nodded. "'Tis true."

"I understand your boldness, dear." Barbara smiled knowingly. "A woman must know if a man is eligible. And I can assure you that he is. What's more, he is in need of a good woman!"

"Oh. Oh my." Catrina flushed. "Is that so?" An expectant smile spread across her rose-colored lips.

Jacob frowned when he saw Greta rush to the door. The expression on her face troubled him. He wove through the crowd and hurried after her. His feelings for her flooded him and he knew that he could not push them down any longer. *She feels the same way about me that I do about her. I can see it in the way she looks at me. Her eyes are full of expectation and innocence. She looks ready for life to begin, and I can see in her face that she wants me to be a part of that life.* He remembered how, during their picnic, the words spilled from her mouth before she could stop them. "*I care about you,*" she had said. *And I care about you, Greta Scholtz. This is the right moment to tell her how I truly feel. I only wish that it had not taken me so long to let her into my heart.* He let the door bang shut behind him, pushed his beaver-felt hat onto his head, and set his face like a flint. *I am going after her right now. I cannot wait another moment.*

A friendly shout stopped him.

"Jacob!" The door whined open on its leather hinges. There you are." Jonah balanced a wooden trencher full of corn cakes and squash on his palm. He slapped his friend on the back with his free hand. "Going somewhere?" Jonah bit into a soft, greasy corn cake and chewed.

"*Ja*, I cannot stay. I have to speak with Greta." He started toward the woods that separated his property from the Yoder farm.

Jonah put a hand on his shoulder. "Wait." His mouth was full of corn cake and the word sounded thick and muffled. He held up a finger, chewed another few times, then swallowed. "I have to tell you something about her."

"Oh?" Jacob raised his eyebrows. He felt a surge of expectation.

"*Ja*, I just spoke with her." Jonah wiped his mouth. "Such a silly misunderstanding."

Jacob's feeling of expectation shifted to concern. "What misunderstanding?"

"You and Greta. I felt so bad about leading her on. Barbara and I figured we ought to set the record straight." Jonah took another bite of his corn cake. Jacob frowned.

"Set the record straight?"

Jonah motioned vaguely, then swallowed. "The fact that you are not interested in her. I—well, everyone, to be honest—have been telling her otherwise. It seemed cruel not to clear the record."

Jacob's chest tightened. "And how did Greta react?"

"Oh, that's the good part. She was not upset at all. Relieved is more like it. She even smiled. Barbara was ready to console her, but there was no need. She is not interested either."

"Not at all?"

Jonah shook his head. "Not at all. Quite a relief, I know. Now you can both move on without any misunderstandings."

"Oh. I see." Jacob felt as though the ground had dropped out from under him. He forced a guarded expression onto his face and hardened his eyes.

"I knew you would be glad to hear."

"*Ja*. What a relief." The words came out in a distant monotone, but Jonah did not notice. He slapped Jacob's back again. "See you around, Jacob."

Jacob managed to maintain his neutral expression as he watched Jonah slip into the crowd of smiling brethren. Jacob shivered. He had not noticed the cold before. A heavy, familiar emptiness settled into his chest. *All of this time, she was never interested?* His jaw tightened. *And why should she be? How could a woman like Greta Scholtz want anything to do with me? She is so trusting, so innocent.* His molars ground together as he stared at the empty path that Greta had taken into the woods. *I could never be what she needs. Not after I already failed one woman. And she knows that. I must let her go.*

Chapter Fourteen

Greta felt restless and alone. Her mind drifted to Jacob no matter how hard she tried to focus on her chores.

"You are much too distracted, Greta," Ruth said as she turned her drop spindle. "How many times have you had to rip out your stitches this morning?"

Greta frowned as she bent over her sewing. Her neck ached and her eyes blurred. "Too many times. I cannot seem to stitch a straight line."

Ruth smiled. "Put it away, then. Go fetch us some redroot. We need to collect a basketful before the snow flies."

Greta tossed the quilt square aside and stretched her back. "A wonderful good idea."

"Check the edge of the path down by the oak grove, before you reach the Gruber cabin. I wager you will find some there."

Greta grabbed a basket, pulled on her cloak, and dashed outside before Ruth could finish her sentence. She breathed in a deep breath of cool, clear air. The seasons hung between fall and winter as the settlement waited for snow to cover the brilliant orange and gold leaves with a dispassionate white blanket. Greta felt her life suspended between seasons as well, as the cold, hard truth about Jacob smothered the brightness and expectations she once had.

Greta found the redroot growing between the oak grove and the roadside, where the conditions were ideal for the shrub. The cold bit at her cheeks as she gathered her skirts and stooped to pick the small leaves. The *thwack* of an ax and the low shouts of men interrupted her. She smelled the acrid, woodsy scent of smoke and realized that the men were clearing land and burning the brush.

She imagined the humble settlement growing and growing until they had cobblestone streets and real houses—with two stories and glass windows—just like her home in Germany. And sugar! She grinned at the thought and hurried to check on the progress.

Beyond the next hill she found a clearing full of flashing axes, bonfires, and stacked logs. Greta hurried to the bustling work area, but her excitement evaporated when she rounded a crackling bonfire and saw beyond the hazy billow of smoke. Catrina stood close beside Jacob. A sliver of shining locks peered out from the edges of her prayer *kappe,* hinting at the dazzling mane beneath. She wore the same style of somber bodice and long, unadorned skirt that the rest of the women wore, but her beautiful features stood out despite her Plain attire.

Catrina held a bucket of water in her hands as she stared up at Jacob with her striking blue eyes. He sipped from a ladle and gazed down at her with an amused expression on his chiseled face.

It is nothing. She is going around and giving all of the men a drink of water. There is nothing between them. But Catrina didn't leave after Jacob finished his drink. The empty ladle hung from his hand, and yet she still lingered. She batted her thick black lashes and giggled. He returned her smile. Greta studied the casual slouch of his body as he leaned against the tree. She noticed the way he grinned at the woman; the expression seemed so natural, so relaxed. *He has never been so at ease around me.*

A hot, flustered feeling crept up Greta's body. Her mouth went dry. She swallowed hard. *Is this what happened to the affection that I thought we shared? He has given it over to Catrina?* Greta wanted to run all the way back to the Yoder cabin. But she stood riveted in place, her eyes glued to the smiling couple. The raven-haired woman giggled again. Then she reached for the ladle and her fingers brushed against Jacob's as she took it from him. She let her fingertips linger against his for a long moment before she dropped her hand.

Well, I never.

Greta had had enough. She spun around to leave when she heard Catrina shout her name. She froze, then slowly turned back around. There was no hiding now.

"Greta, dear! Why, it is almost as though you were trying to slink away. Do come say hello."

Greta squared her shoulders and forced a polite smile as she marched across the clearing. *Remember, Catrina does not know that you had hopes for a match with Jacob. You told her yourself that you held no affection for him. She means well, even if her kindness feels like salt on the wound. Just maintain your dignity and never let her know the truth.*

Catrina's features melted into an exaggerated look of sympathy as Greta drew near. "Oh." She set down the bucket and ladle, reached for Greta's hands, and held them in her own. "My goodness. Are you all right? I did not get a chance to speak to you at the worship service yesterday. But we have all been so very concerned." Catrina looked to Jacob. "She looks . . . terribly unwell."

Greta frowned and pulled her hands back from Catrina's. The woman looked confused, as if she didn't understand why Greta seemed irritated.

"I am perfectly well, thank you." She lifted her chin a fraction. "Thankfully, Jacob was there when the wasps attacked. He came to the rescue." Greta narrowed her eyes and studied Catrina's reaction. "Did you know that he risked his life to save me?"

Catrina smiled and gazed up at Jacob. "I am not surprised. He looks like a hero, does he not?"

Jacob shifted his weight from one foot to the other and looked uncomfortable.

"*Ja.* We ended up in the pigsty together. It was quite an adventure."

"Oh, my. How very . . ." Catrina maintained her smile as she searched for the right word. "How very *provincial.*"

There was an awkward pause as Greta stood trapped between Catrina's sugary-sweet smile and Jacob's discomfort. She felt completely inadequate beside the woman's flawless skin, shimmering blue eyes, and delicate hands. Everything Catrina did seemed graceful and deliberate. *She is the absolute opposite of me.* A hot, burning shame reddened Greta's cheeks. *Who did I think I was? I cannot compete with this woman. Especially when I look like a beady-eyed, swollen-faced pig!*

Jacob frowned and rubbed the back of his neck. "Greta, I have been concerned for your health as well. How are you faring?"

Greta wanted to appear self-confident and independent. "Very well, thank you. Healthy as a hog, really." Greta cringed inside. *Healthy as a hog? Why on earth did I say that? Especially when I look like one!*

Catrina gave an amused look. "You really should see to those stings. Have you tried vinegar?"

"Vinegar? *Ja.* Certainly. Lots of vinegar."

"*Ja.* I can tell. Vinegar does have a powerful scent!" She glanced at Jacob and then looked back to Greta. "Do look after yourself. Perhaps you should be lying down. . . ."

Greta wanted to sink into the ground. She had never felt so unattractive or self-conscious. Jacob frowned again. "I think that you are making a splendid recovery. Tough as nails, if you ask me."

Greta mumbled a quick good-bye and hurried away. She heard Jacob call out to her as she fled. His voice sounded kind and soft and she almost turned back around. But she forced herself to keep her eyes straight ahead and her head held high.

Greta's skirts whipped against her ankles in a tight rhythm as she stalked home. The humiliation and disappointment wrapped around her tighter and heavier than her cloak. *Foolish. Foolish. Foolish.* She shook her head. *How could I have ever thought that he would choose me over the perfect Catrina Witmer?*

Greta took a deep breath and let it out slowly. "I really thought that Jacob and I had something, Lord. And now . . ." Greta spread out her hands. "It hurts, Lord. It really hurts to think that he likes that woman more than me." Greta closed her eyes. "I know I should not speak badly of others. Especially to you." She sighed. "But it is so hard not to feel jealous. She clearly has stolen any affection that Jacob might have ever had for me."

Greta shook her head and walked a few yards in silence. She shook her head again. "It is hopeless, Lord. How can I ever compete with Catrina Witmer? She is perfect in every way! Not a hair out of place, her skirt and bodice did not have a single wrinkle or stain. And her face! She is gorgeous. Absolutely gorgeous." Greta narrowed her eyes. "I bet she is a great cook, too. I bet she never burns the bread." Greta kicked a loose stone into the woods and stomped the rest of the way home. She stormed into the cabin and slammed the door. Ruth looked up from the stocking she was mending. "Let me guess. You ran into Jacob and Catrina."

"How did you know?"

Ruth raised an eyebrow. "I have seen the way she looks at him."

"*Ja.*" Greta yanked off her cloak and threw it on the peg. "You should have seen her! If she has her way, they will be married within a fortnight!"

"*Ja.* I have seen her. And I agree." Ruth rubbed her chin. "The question is, what are you going to do about it?"

"Hmmph. I am not going to fight over him like a dog looking for scraps! That is for sure! If he wants her than he can have her." Greta stalked across the room and collapsed onto a bench. She put her face in her hands. "It is just so deeply unfair. Jacob and I had finally gotten through to each other and she comes and steals him away!"

"What makes you so sure that she has stolen him?"

"Pffft. Did you see her? She is perfect. Perfect in every way." Greta motioned at herself. "And I am . . . well, I am . . . ME!" She threw up her hands. "I rest my case. It is hopeless."

"You know that there are more important traits than a beautiful face and alluring eyes." Ruth raised her eyebrow. "As a Plain woman you should know that."

Greta scowled. "There is nothing about me that will outshine Catrina."

"How about your strength and perseverance? Your devotion to a Plain lifestyle? Your kind heart and giving nature?" Ruth held up her hand. "I really should not say any more. I do not want to tempt you to pride."

Greta laughed. "You do not have to worry about that! My self-esteem could not get any lower right now."

Ruth patted Greta on the knee. "Just try to remember what character traits are Plain and pleasing. Cultivate those and do not worry about anyone else. If Jacob chooses a pretty face and flirtatious manner over strength of character, then he clearly is not worth catching."

"Truer words have never been spoken!"

"Good. 'Tis confirmed. Just be yourself and do not worry what Jacob Miller or Catrina Witmer think of you."

Greta awoke early the next morning, ready for baking day. She mixed and kneaded, let the dough rise on the hearth, then punched it down and kneaded it again. "It is a blessing to have enough wheat." She blew a strand of loose hair from her eyes and kept her hands elbow deep in dough.

"*Ja.* You are lucky that you came when you did. My husband and I went months without wheat, waiting for that first crop to be harvested."

Greta wiped her hands on her apron. "I best hurry if I want to get my turn at the bake-oven. Barbara Gruber will have it stuffed full before I get there if I am not careful."

"With all of those mouths to feed she must have quite a few loaves to bake."

"Indeed."

"And she is feeding the Fisher twins, too, is she not?"

"*Ja.* The poor dears. They still have not found a permanent home. The Gruber family has been good to them, but they cannot keep them forever, not when they already have six children of their own."

"No. But I am sure *der Herr* has a home for them. We just do not know where it is yet."

"*Ja.* He certainly does." Greta felt a tug on her heart. "I wish . . ."

"You wish what?"

"I wish that we could take them in."

Ruth set down her mending and nodded.

"*Ja.* I have thought of it."

"You have?"

"Often." Ruth put out her hands, palms up. "But how would we support them? The odds and ends that you earn from teaching are just enough to keep the two of us fed." The old woman shook her head. "No. We would become an even greater burden on the community. Those children need to find a home with a mother and father who can give them more than we can."

"*Ja.* I have thought about it too. And have come to the same conclusion."

"Well, do not fret. The good Lord will have his will in the matter." Ruth picked her mending back up and nodded toward the door. "Now, you better run along before Barbara takes over the entire bake-oven."

The dough-filled basket pulled at Greta's arm as she trudged toward the center of the settlement. She stopped and set the load down for a moment to stretch her back. *It is going to be a long walk.*

"Good morning, Greta."

Greta recognized Jacob's deep, comforting voice behind her. Her heart fluttered and she tried to push the feeling away. She turned and offered a distant smile. "Good morning, Jacob. I trust you are well."

"Very well, thank you. But it is for your health that I am concerned."

"I am well enough, thank you."

"Recovered from the wasps, then?"

"*Ja,* I would say so." She stared up at his dark,

guarded eyes and felt a strange sense of loss. *Our conversation sounds so formal and uncertain, as if we were strangers. What happened to the happy banter we once had?* They stared at each other through a long, tense pause. Greta readjusted her grip on the basket. Her stomach felt like a hard knot.

"I am headed in the same direction," Jacob finally said.

"And how do you know where I am headed?"

He pointed to the dough in the basket and raised his eyebrows.

"Right. Of course." Greta laughed, then forced her face back into a neutral expression. "And what takes you in my direction today?"

"I have to seal the walls of the smokehouse before the slaughter."

"So we shall have ham this winter?" Greta smiled at the thought, then caught herself. "Not that I expect you to share. I just meant . . ." She looked away.

"I will save you the best cut."

"You will?" Her face lit up.

"I have plenty to share. Many households will welcome a break from wild game during the coming months."

"*Ja.*" She frowned. *He is giving ham to everyone. His offer means nothing.*

Jacob motioned to Greta's basket. "Let me carry that for you."

"That is kind of you to offer, but I can manage just fine, thank you." Greta didn't want to show any weakness. Not when Catrina seemed so capable and perfect. *I will show him that she is not the only one who can manage!*

"Can you? Because it looks like you can barely hold it up."

"What?" She raised the basket higher and tried to hide the tremble in her triceps. "You see, I am more than able."

"There is no need to put on a show, Greta. Just let me carry the basket."

"No, thank you, Jacob. As I have said, I can manage perfectly well on my own."

Jacob exhaled. "Very well, Greta." He motioned up the path. "Lead on."

Jacob watched Greta struggle with the weight of the basket and shook his head. *How did we end up like this? I was so sure that she held as much affection for me as I do for her. How did she slip away from me to become so distant? One moment I was ready to declare my intent to court her and the next moment I learn that she never wanted my affection. How could I have been so wrong?*

His studied Greta's graceful stride as she walked to the bake-house. She kept her chin held high, despite her obvious struggle with the overloaded basket. Jacob shook his head. *I cannot help myself. There is something about Greta Scholtz that pulls me in. She has a spark that cannot be extinguished. Maybe it is her independent streak, her strength of character. Maybe it is that she makes me laugh. And there is her caring nature, obviously. I have heard how patient and loving she is with the settlement's children.*

He heard himself laugh. *She cares for the settlement's children, widows, and orphans—just not for me.*

"Are you laughing, Jacob?"

Jacob frowned. He had not meant to laugh out loud.

"Do I amuse you, Jacob? Is there a joke at my expense?"

Yes, Greta, you amuse me very much. He clenched his jaw. "I was just thinking . . ."

"*Ja?* About what?"

Jacob shook his head. His face tightened into a mask. "Nothing. It was nothing." They walked the rest of the way in silence.

Jacob stopped when he reached the smokehouse. Greta nodded a polite good-bye and walked across the clearing to the bake-oven. She snuck a glance at Jacob as she started a fire on the oven floor. She watched him roll up his loose linen sleeves and pick up a shovel. Greta turned back to her work before he noticed her staring. She added larger pieces of kindling to the growing flames and then slid a log into the fire. She stoked the rising flames, sighed, and snuck another glance in Jacob's direction. He looked up and his eyes locked on hers. She gasped, turned her attention back to the oven, and made a show of stoking the fire.

Jacob cringed when Greta caught him watching her. *Do not give her the wrong idea.* He scowled and speared the ground with his shovel. *Why can't I keep my eyes off that girl?* He pushed the blade deeper into the damp earth and brought up a shovelful of red clay. He cut his eyes to the bake-oven, grimaced, and forced his attention back to his work. Jacob kept his gaze on the red clay, but he could not keep his mind from wandering. *She has made it clear that she holds no affection for me. I should leave her alone and let her be.* He sighed. *If anyone understands the need to be left alone, it is I.* He grunted and speared the earth again and again with all of his strength. The aggressive action did not alleviate his emotions; it only made him feel tired and hot. He stopped and wiped his brow with his sleeve.

"It does not matter how I feel. She is not interested, so that is that." *I never should have let it get this far. I knew better.* Marta's face flashed in his mind. He remembered the pain of that loss—and the promise he had made never to let anyone in again.

He felt a gentle tug at his heart, a familiar warmth that he had not allowed in for months. He sighed and closed his eyes. "Lord, I tried to reopen my heart." He hesitated and then shook his head. "But it looks as though I was wrong to try." He speared the ground again. *Maybe Greta's rejection is for the best. As long as I am alone I cannot lose anyone again.*

Greta returned to the bake-oven after the sun had trekked a quarter of the way across the sky and the fire had time to burn down to ashes. She made a tremendous effort not to look toward the smokehouse. Her resolve lasted all of three minutes. She glanced over her shoulder and saw Jacob pressing red clay between the logs that formed the walls of the narrow building. She frowned and brought her attention back to the oven before he could catch her staring. Greta slid the wooden door aside and thrust her arm inside to judge the temperature. She counted to seven before the heat forced her arm back outside. *Longer than five counts, but fewer than fifteen. The temperature should be right.* She picked up the iron peel, which was shaped like a flat shovel, and scraped the ashes out of the oven. Next, she grabbed the hearth broom, dipped it in a bucket of water so that the bristles would not catch fire, and swept the remaining ashes from the oven floor. *Finally, the oven is ready for baking.* Greta slid the dough onto the oven floor with a wooden peel, shut the little wooden door, and wiped her hands. *Perfect! Just wait, Jacob Miller. I can manage just fine on my own!* She snuck another glance at the smokehouse. Slick red mud covered Jacob's muscular forearms as he continued to seal the walls. Greta smiled with anticipation as she walked away and hummed under her breath. *I will give him a loaf of bread just so that he knows what he is missing!*

When Greta returned later in the afternoon, the warm, nutty aroma of baking bread welcomed her. *See, Jacob? I do not need your help. I managed to make three fine loaves of bread all on my own, thank you very much.*

She thrust the wooden peel inside the oven, anxious to draw out a fresh, perfectly baked loaf. Greta heard footsteps coming her way and straightened her posture. She cleared her throat and smoothed her skirts. She slid the peel under the warm brown bread and pulled it out. Her faced beamed with pride at her domestic success. "Ah! Just right!" Jacob strode by as she raised the loaf of bread and she looked up. *Perfect timing!*

"Well, Greta, it looks like you could have used some help, after all."

Greta's mouth fell open in surprise.

Jacob nodded toward the bread. "Take a look at the other side." She flipped the loaf around and saw that it was burnt black as an iron skillet. She pursed her lips, tossed the bread into her basket, and spun around on her heels. "Good day, Jacob." Jacob tipped his beaver-felt hat and watched her storm off down the path.

Greta shook her head and laughed as soon as Jacob was out of sight. *Pride cometh before a fall. And as a Plain woman, I should certainly know better than to gloat!* She shrugged. *I guess that is what I get for trying to impress Jacob Miller!*

The children returned to school the next day and they brought more food than usual. "Our mothers said that you had an accident and that we should give you extra." Christian crept forward. "Are you all right?"

Anna leaned closer to Greta and stared at her teacher's face. She squinted with concentration. "Will you always be this ugly?"

"Oh. Anna. That is not a very nice thing to say."

"I am sorry. But you look so . . . funny."

Greta laughed. "You should have seen me a few days ago. I was as pink and swollen as a fattened pig."

The children giggled and eased closer, hungry for hugs. "We missed you!" Eliza and Peter both shouted. Greta pulled her students close and wrapped them in her arms. "I am so glad to see you all again!"

Anna snuggled close. "And I am glad that you will not always be this ugly."

Greta laughed. "Me too." After a moment she sat back and looked her students in the eyes. "But you must understand that outward beauty is not important. It is a beautiful spirit that is pleasing to *der Herr.*"

Peter looked up at Greta with a serious expression. "Miss Witmer is very beautiful on the outside."

"Hmm. Well, yes. I suppose so."

"*Ja*, she is very beautiful." Eliza nodded solemnly. "Have you seen her? She has black hair and blue eyes. Mama says that is a very unusual combination."

"That is true. I guess."

"So, does that mean that she is beautiful on the inside, too?" Peter asked. "Because that makes sense. The inside should look like the outside."

"Hmmm. Well. I could not say as far as Miss Witmer is concerned. I mean, I am sure that she is a . . . um . . . a lovely person but, as a general rule, we should not judge the inside by the outside. A beautiful outside does not mean that a person has a beautiful spirit."

"Huh." Peter frowned. "That does not make much sense."

"Maybe not, but it is true. And as Amish, we take inner beauty very seriously. That is why we dress simply and live simply."

Peter smiled. "I think that you are very beautiful on the inside, Greta. Even though you are not as beautiful as Miss Witmer on the outside."

"Oh. Thank you, Peter." Greta looked down and adjusted her neck cloth. She forced a smile. "That is very kind." Greta changed the subject, but as she recited the ABCs aloud she could not help but wish that she were as beautiful on the outside as the stunning Catrina Witmer.

Chapter Fifteen

Greta felt a quiet dread the entire way to the worship service. She kept hearing Catrina's laughter as she and Ruth walked along the narrow path that cut through the woods to the Gruber cabin. The last, stubborn leaves clung to oak branches and crackled in the crisp breeze. The sun streamed through the treetops and cast long rectangles of golden light at their feet. But Greta didn't notice. Instead, she imagined the possessive look in Catrina's striking blue eyes when she looked at Jacob. Greta stopped to adjust her woolen hosen where the fabric bunched at her ankle. *Remember, this is not a competition. Jacob is not interested in you.* She sighed. "I just want to get this over with."

"Oh, Greta! For goodness' sake. You sound like you are on the way to the executioner's block."

"I simply cannot put Catrina Witmer out of my mind."

Ruth looked sympathetic. "I imagine not. Just try and remember what you told your students this week—that strength of character trumps beauty every time."

"Easy to say but not so easy to believe!"

They rounded the top of a hill and saw other settlers strolling toward the Gruber cabin. Greta felt a familiar pang of loneliness as she watched couples stroll side by side. A father hoisted a young boy onto his shoulders and then reached for his wife's hand. Greta looked away and tried to ignore the emptiness she felt deep inside.

Greta watched as Jacob stepped through the threshold of the cabin. Her heart caught in her throat as she studied his dark, somber eyes. She swallowed hard and looked away.

The Grubers' son, Christian, met Greta at the door. "I am glad that you came to my house today." He grinned. "I always come to your house."

"And I am very glad to be here, Christian." She crouched down, straightened his waistcoat, and smiled. But when she glanced past him, the smile faded. Catrina sat primly on one of the backless benches, her lovely eyes on Jacob. He felt Catrina's stare and glanced up. Their eyes met and Catrina boldly held the gaze for a few beats, then dropped her eyes modestly.

Greta flinched. *I dare say she would be bold enough to sit down right beside him, if men and women sat on the same side during worship services!* She looked away. *I cannot let myself think ill of Catrina. After all, Jacob is free and she is a good match. And she did ask me if I held any prior claim to his affection.* The realization only made her feel more alone.

After the service, Greta picked at her food and

watched Jacob lean against the wall with his wooden trencher in hand. His eyes looked dark and distant. Catrina caught his gaze from across the room and flashed him a smile. He nodded and looked back at the rabbit stew on his trencher. Greta watched Catrina frown and stare at him. She looked confused. Greta felt her heart skip across her breastbone. *He does not look very interested in Catrina.* She stood up straighter. *How I wish I knew what he was thinking right now!*

Catrina stared at Jacob for a few beats. When he did not look back up, she took a deep breath, squared her shoulders, and turned away. *She is not going to let him ignore her, is she?* Greta watched Catrina walk to the table and pick up a wooden platter covered with a white cloth. She wove her way through the room until she reached Jacob. Her lips broke into an alluring smile.

"I baked something special." Catrina whipped the cloth off the platter. "Cake!" The soft white confection looked delicate and delicious, especially compared to the coarse, unseasoned food on Jacob's plate. "You will have the first slice."

She took his arm and steered him toward the table. "I know how long it has been since you have had cake. You have been in the wilderness for so long—months and months!" Her soft, pale fingers squeezed his arm. "You must be so brave! However have you managed?"

Greta watched from across the room with her mouth agape. "She stole my idea!" Greta grabbed Ruth's sleeve. "Do you see that? That was my idea! I was going to bring cake! That is *my* cake!"

"It is not exactly *your* cake, dear."

"It should have been! I braved wasps to bake that man a cake. WASPS!"

"Shhh. Do not shout, dear. It makes you sound like a heathen. Anyway, I thought you said that you were making that cake for the children."

"*Ja.* For the children." Her shoulders sagged in defeat. "I have one hope left."

"What is that?"

"That her cake tastes like chalk."

"That sounds a bit unkind, does it not?"

Greta gave an exaggerated sigh. "I did not say that I *want* it to taste like chalk. Just that my only *hope* is that it does."

Ruth grunted.

Catrina made a show of cutting the cake. She looked around the room to make sure that everyone watched as she placed a fat slice on Jacob's wooden trencher. He picked up a generous bite and popped it in his mouth. Greta held her breath as she waited for his reaction.

Jacob chewed. Seconds ticked by. Then he shook his head. He grinned. "That just might be the best thing I have ever tasted." Catrina smiled and looked down in a show of modesty.

The children shouted and gathered around Catrina. They pulled at her skirts and reached for the sugary treat. She grinned and patted them on the heads. "Who wants cake?"

"We do!" they shrieked in unison, and jumped up and down.

"Even the children like her better," Greta whispered to Ruth.

"Oh, Greta, enough."

Catrina passed out slices of cake to all of the settlement's youngsters. The entire room came alive with energy and unexpected excitement. Except for Greta's corner. She watched Jacob enjoy his slice of cake with a look of shock on her face. *How did my plan fail so, and hers became such a success?!* She swallowed and tried to push away her competitive thoughts. *Ach, I cannot blame her for her skills. She has bested me. I just wish I did not feel so small and meager!*

Little Anna reached up and tugged on Catrina's sleeve. "Greta says that there is not any sugar. How did you get sugar? And white flour? Are you a princess?"

Catrina put her hands to her cheeks. "A princess, goodness no." She glanced at Jacob to see if he was paying attention, then looked back to Anna. "I am a Plain woman, who just wants to make others happy. We brought supplies from Philadelphia with us— sugar, white flour, coffee, and chickens. Oh, and nails." She turned to Jacob. "You must take some nails, and some hens as well—it is the least that we can do to thank you for all of your help." Jacob nodded but did not reply. He was too busy chewing his cake.

Anna wrinkled her nose. "I do not care about coffee and nails. But I will take the sugar and white flour!"

Greta's stomach twisted. *All of his help? How much time has Jacob been spending with her?* She felt hot and flustered. The voices in the room became too loud. Each chuckle and giggle felt like a hammer on her temple. The room began to shift in front of her. *It is too much. It is all too much. I have to get out of this room.*

She pushed her way out of the corner and hurried to the door. *I must have fresh air. I simply must get away from here!*

Jacob saw Greta's face turn pale as frost on a windowpane. He watched her wobble and nearly fall as she hurried past the families eating cake and laughing. *What ails her?* His brow creased in concern as he set his trencher on the table and watched her fling open the cabin door. *Has she taken ill? She may need help.* Jacob started toward the door when Abraham slapped him on the back and startled him from his thoughts. "Good to see you enjoying yourself, Jacob. Mighty fine cake, *ja?*"

"What? Oh, *ja.*" Jacob's eyes remained on the empty doorway.

"How is the winter wheat coming? Put in a good crop this year?"

Jacob ran his fingers through his hair. His heart beat harder as each second slipped past. "Yeah. Just, uh, just allow me a moment. I will be back." He bolted for the door.

Catrina watched him push through the crowd with narrowed eyes. She reached for his arm as he rushed past her. "Oh, Jacob. Wait." She flashed a dazzling smile. "I have been meaning to ask you—"

"Uh, another time. I need to step out for just a—"

"This will only take a moment." She threw up her hands. "We just cannot figure out the best place to build the root cellar. Can you give us some advice? Grandmother thinks—"

"Another time."

"Oh, but here is Grandmother now." Catrina

caught Frena Witmer by the sleeve as she wandered by. "Jacob knows exactly what to do about the root cellar, Grandmother." She motioned toward Jacob. "Please, continue. We do welcome your advice." Jacob glanced toward the door.

Frena beamed. "You have been a tremendous help, Jacob. And here you are, ready to give more advice. My husband thinks that we should build the root cellar into a hill that is too far from the house." She shook her head. "I do not fancy long walks every time I need to fetch something from our food stores."

"*Ja*." Jacob forced his attention away from the doorway and to the old woman who depended on him for help. He knew that he had become too entangled in the conversation to escape now. He sighed and suggested the best location for the cool storage building. But as he spoke his thoughts stayed on the young woman who had slipped out the door.

Greta gulped big breaths of fresh air. The world stopped spinning as she stood alone in the silent clearing. She put a hand over her heart and felt the beat settle back to normal. *I must have become overheated with all the people packed together like herring in a barrel and the fire burning in the hearth.* But deep inside, she knew the truth. The thought of Jacob falling in love with Catrina had overwhelmed her with a wave of panic. She squeezed her eyes closed. "I must learn to go on without him. I cannot hope for his affection. It is over between us. No, in truth, it never even began!"

But as she said the words, she felt a cry from deep within that urged her not to give up. She shook her head. *I will give him one chance. One last chance to show me that he cares.* She closed her eyes and swallowed. *If he comes after me, then I will know. He must have seen me take ill and stumble outside. If he cares, then he will follow to check on my health.* She kept her eyes squeezed shut and counted. *One. Two. Three. Four. Five.* She took a deep breath, opened her eyes, and turned back toward the cabin. Her heart caught in her chest. She needed him to be there.

He wasn't.

Greta walked away, into the quiet isolation of the forest. She felt as if she were the only person left in the world as she cut through the unending wilderness of the Pennsylvania backcountry. Pines and oaks stretched high above her and blocked out the low, late autumn sun. She pulled her cloak closer and shivered as she accepted that she was on her own.

Jacob managed to slip away from the Witmers and rush outside. The world felt strangely quiet after the chatter and movement inside the cramped cabin. He stood still in the silence for a long moment, watching his breath form clouds in the cold air. A rabbit bounded through the wild grasses that fought to overtake the clearing. But other than that, he found no sign of life beyond the gentle rasp of his own breath.

He was too late.

Jacob let out a long, slow sigh. *It is just as well, I suppose. What was I thinking, trying to run after her like a fool? She holds no affection for me and does not want my help. I must respect her wishes.*

Chapter Sixteen

Greta was strolling toward the creek, the yoke on her shoulders, when she saw Jacob heading toward her on the footpath. He raised a hand in greeting and she offered a reserved, but polite, nod. *Do not make a fool of yourself. Remember that his eyes are on another.* She felt a pang as he strode through the tangle of wild grass that sprouted across the cleared land. *He is so handsome and sure of himself.* She sighed and headed down to the riverbed.

"Greta!"

Greta turned back around, careful to keep her expression even. "*Ja?*"

Jacob held up a stout turkey and picked up his pace. Greta fidgeted with the bucket and wondered what to say as he cut the distance between them.

"For the Widow Yoder." He cleared his throat and looked away. "And for you."

Greta forced a polite expression. *I am always an afterthought to him.* "*Ja.* I am sure that she will be very pleased."

"Good."

They stared at each other for a moment as each

waited for the other to break the awkward silence. Greta reached for the turkey. "Well, I will go ahead and take it to her."

"*Ja.*"

Greta stalked away before her resolve faltered and she revealed her feelings for the handsome widower. She made sure to maintain a straight, regal posture to demonstrate her confidence and contentment. But her stomach churned and her mind urged her to go back. *No! You have more self-respect than that, Greta Scholtz. Jacob has made his intentions clear.* She looked at the sack in her hands. *The fact that he cares so much for widows only makes it worse. He is a good man, even though he can be so distant and reserved.* She thought about his aloof demeanor and the way it drove her away at first. She shook her head. *I understand him so much better now. He had to let go of the pain of the past.* She tightened her lips. *And if he has, I suppose that he may find contentment with Catrina.*

Greta wondered if Jacob watched her as she strode across the clearing. *No. Do not be silly. Why would his eyes follow you when he has someone of real beauty to admire?* Greta felt hot tears forming behind her eyes and she fought to push them back. *If only we had had more time before she arrived. I had just started to get through to him. And now it is too late. . . .*

Ruth beamed when Greta strode in with the turkey. Greta wiped her eyes and forced a smile.

"A gift for you from Jacob Miller."

Ruth raised an eyebrow. "For me?"

"*Ja.* That is what he said."

"Hmmm." Ruth studied Greta's demeanor.

"Did you invite him in for dinner? That would be a reasonable way of saying thank you."

Greta grabbed the straw broom to keep her hands busy. "He did not want to come."

Ruth frowned. She shrugged and lowered herself onto the three-legged stool by the hearth. "I worried about him for months, you know. Ever since he lost his wife and son." She began to pluck the soft, dark feathers from the bird. "I really believed that you had broken through to him. I thought that you two were meant to be." She glanced up at Greta. "He said he did not want to come to dinner? He said those words?"

"Not exactly. He did not need to."

"What did he say, exactly?"

Greta shrugged. "It does not matter. He has made his intentions clear. Or lack of intentions, I should say." She swept the floor forcefully. "And I will not make a fool of myself by running after him like a lovesick puppy."

"Is that your pride speaking?" Ruth raised an eyebrow. "I have warned you about that already."

"It is my self-respect."

"In a case like this there is a fine line between the two."

"Ruth, I have seen him with Catrina. Any possibility for us is over. Please do not tempt my hopes. It hurts too much."

Ruth frowned. She started to speak but closed her mouth again. She sighed and nodded. "All right. But can we at least enjoy some roast turkey?"

Greta laughed. "Now that is something that we can agree on."

* * *

The days passed slowly as Greta brooded over Jacob and went through the motions of her daily tasks. The bright spot in each day was when her students arrived, eager to learn. One afternoon, Eliza took Greta's hand and squeezed it. "I love your school, Greta." Greta thought her heart would burst. She felt a lump form in her throat and looked away before the girl could see the moisture in her eyes.

Greta wiped her eyes and patted the little girl's hand. "And I love teaching you." *I have a purpose in my life and people who care about me. I must accept that I do not need Jacob Miller.*

"When I am around you, I do not feel so sad."

Greta leaned closer. "Do you feel sad a lot?"

Eliza nodded. "I miss Mama and Papa."

"*Ja.* How could you not?" Greta scooped Eliza into her arms and hugged her. "Do you want to know something?"

"What?"

"I miss my papa too."

"What about your mother?"

"She died when I was young. I do not remember her."

Eliza snuggled closer. Greta smoothed the child's prayer *kappe.* "But, *der Herr* has given us other people to love, so that we can go on living and know that we are not alone."

Eliza pulled back and looked Greta in the eye. "Like you?"

Greta beamed. "*Ja.* Like me. I love you very much."

"And Jacob? He loves you, *ja?*"

Greta's face fell. "Oh. Well. I don't—" She cleared

her throat. "My goodness, the time is getting away from us. We had better get started with the lesson."

"But Greta, why is there no wedding planned? Everyone used to say that you and Jacob would marry."

Greta hesitated. She cleared her throat again. "I guess Catrina is the better match." The words felt sticky and raw in her mouth.

Anna stared at Greta with solemn eyes. "Are they a perfect match? Mama says that we all should wait until we find *der Herr*'s perfect match for us."

"Jacob and Catrina, a perfect match?"

"*Ja.*"

"I think . . . I think we should open the *Martyrs Mirror* and see if you can read the first paragraph."

Greta tried to put all of her focus on the children's lesson as they took turns sounding out passages from the Bible. The young schoolteacher managed to keep a polite smile on her face and nod at Peter's progress. But she could not stop herself from repeating Eliza's words over and over again in her head. *"He loves you,* ja*?"*

Someone knocked on the door and Greta's eyes flew to the threshold. She felt her stomach tighten with the hope that it might be Jacob. *Do not be foolish.* Greta swallowed and smoothed her heavy skirts. "Please, come in."

The door swung open with a slow creak. Greta told herself not to hope as she looked up. But there he stood. His tall frame and magnetic gaze filled the threshold.

"Jacob! What a surprise." Greta grinned and started to get up from her place by the hearth. Jacob nodded but looked uncomfortable. And then Catrina Witmer swept into the cabin. Greta felt her entire body deflate.

"Greta, darling!" Catrina flounced over to Greta. Her raven-black hair was carefully combed and tucked beneath her prayer *kappe*, her apron and bodice were perfectly ironed, and her complexion looked completely unblemished.

Everything about her is perfect. "Catrina. What a . . . pleasant surprise."

"*Ja.*" She hurried to Greta, kissed her on both cheeks, and then glanced around the room. "Oh! This must be the school that I have heard so much about. I do hope that we are not disturbing you."

"No." Greta managed a stiff smile. "No."

Catrina clapped. "*Wunderbar!*"

Greta flinched at the outburst. "To what do we owe this pleasure?"

"Why, I have not seen you in ages! I said to Jacob that we simply must call on you. It is as though you want to stay hidden away in this little cabin! Jacob has been to dinner so many times and the Grubers hosted a singing, but you have been nowhere to be found. Do tell me that you are well."

"*Ja.* Very well, thank you."

"You look a bit pale and thin, dear." Catrina frowned and studied Greta. "But I have just the thing to cheer you." She flashed her signature smile. "I was going through some of the things that I brought out here. You see, I just have too much. Having so many shifts and bodices and stays and woolen hosen, it just feels so . . . worldly." She lowered her lashes. "You must understand, I have not always been Amish and I have many lovely things from my life before. Remember, my grandparents converted after my mother was grown, so I was not raised in the faith. But, when I heard that they were moving here, to a wild, new land, I knew that I had to come. I knew that I was meant for something more."

"It must be a challenge to grow accustomed to our Plain ways."

"*Ja.* But, as I was saying . . ." Her eyes slid over to Jacob. "Jacob was at our farm today—he has been such a dear, you know, so helpful—and I thought, what perfect timing."

"Perfect timing?"

"*Ja.* For Jacob to help me carry these things to you."

"To me?"

"Why, who else? The thought of you and Widow Yoder here all alone! It must be simply dreadful. You must barely get by, surviving on charity. My parents have done very well in Philadelphia, you see. It only seems right to share when everything that you have is so very . . . shabby." She ran her eyes down Greta's figure and shook her head. "All of that linsey-woolsey. Such cheap, coarse fabric."

"Oh. Well, I do have my school. I earn—"

"That's right, dear." She motioned to the large basket that Jacob held in his hands. "I brought you some of my old bodices and shifts. The plainest ones, of course. I know that is what you want." Catrina's face looked pleasant and expectant. "And white linen for new neck cloths and prayer *kappes*. I could not help but notice how very worn and stained yours are. You poor dear."

Jacob frowned. He started to speak, but Greta nodded curtly and muttered a polite "thank you" before he could intervene.

"*Wunderbar.*" Catrina flashed a gorgeous smile and

looked up at Jacob. "We really must be on our way. Grandmother will be expecting us both for dinner." Jacob glanced at Greta, but she did not notice. She did not want to see the happy couple discuss their dinner plans so she kept her eyes on the bolt of cloth. Jacob's gaze stayed on the soft curve of her cheek and the splash of freckles across her nose.

Greta pushed the fabric aside and stood up. She straightened her skirts and raised her chin. "Good day. I must get back to my students." She picked up the *Ausbund* and pointed to a word. "Christian, can you tell me what this says?"

Jacob's eyes lingered on Greta for another long moment. He watched the children's eyes light up as she spoke and felt a gentle warmth fill his chest as he observed the simple interaction. *Just look up at me, Greta. Just give me a sign that you want me here, in your cabin. In your life.*

Greta could feel Jacob's eyes on her. Humiliated by Catrina's show of charity, she pushed down her desire to return his steady gaze and threw herself into the lesson.

Jacob frowned. *She is not going to look at me. She is making a point to ignore me.*

"Come along, Jacob. We really must be going."

"Wait!" Anna jumped up. "Did you bring another cake?" She grabbed Catrina's skirt and tugged the fabric. "Please say that you did!" Catrina stiffened and pried the girl's finger from the fabric. "Sticky fingers, dear." She wrinkled her nose. "You mustn't touch."

Then she forced a strained smile. "I will bake another cake soon."

"Good." Anna tilted her head and frowned. "Because we thought that we would have cake at the wedding. And now we will not."

"The wedding?" Catrina smoothed the front of her blouse and dusted off her skirt.

"*Ja.* Jacob and Greta."

"Oh?" Catrina's eyes widened. Greta nearly gasped. She wanted to sink into the dirt floor.

"Oh, *ja.* Everyone knew that they would be married."

"Anna—" Jacob stepped forward and motioned at the girl to hush. Anna shrugged. "But then Greta said that Catrina is a perfect match for Jacob and that they will be the ones to marry."

Catrina broke into a relieved grin. She flashed Greta a grateful look.

"Oh. No. I did not say that exactly. I mean . . . Oh . . ."

Jacob frowned. *She believes that Catrina is the better match?* His stomach tightened. *Sure, Catrina is beautiful, but she does not have Greta's spirit. She does not linger in my mind or stir my heart as Greta does. And yet, Greta hopes that I marry another!* He stared at her for a long, painful moment, then gave a curt nod and turned on his heels.

Catrina waved to the children, then blew Greta a kiss. "Good-bye, Greta dear. I am so very glad that we found you well. Do pay us a visit soon." She brimmed with joy and natural poise as she followed Jacob out the door.

* * *

Greta felt so flustered that she dismissed the children early. She shut the door behind them, leaned against it, closed her eyes, and let out a long, deep breath.

"Well, that was an interesting visit." Ruth walked over to the bundle of fabric and raised an eyebrow.

Greta opened her eyes and shook her head. "My goodness! I have never been so hurt by an act of kindness before!" She pressed her hands to her face. "And why did Anna say that! I thought I would die."

Ruth shrugged. "Children say the funniest things. Everyone knows not to take their words too seriously. Not when they are talking about their teacher's marriage plans, anyway."

"I hope that you are right."

Ruth frowned and ran her fingers along a bolt of white fabric from Catrina's basket. "Catrina meant well. She has no idea that you care for Jacob." She pushed the fabric away. "She could not know how embarrassed you would feel in front of him."

"No, I suppose not." Greta picked through the basket. "These are very fine. I wonder why she forsook the comforts of a well-to-do home in Philadelphia for the hardships of the wilderness and a Plain life."

"Clearly, she is searching for something more meaningful than a fancy life in the city could bring."

"*Ja.* I just hope that something is not Jacob Miller!"

Chapter Seventeen

Greta leaned into the fireplace and collected ashes to make lye soap. Ruth poured a bucket of water into the kettle so that they could boil the ashes after Greta gathered them. "Have you heard the Grubers' good news?"

"No."

"They will have a new child come spring."

"What a blessing. My, what a full house they will have!" Greta smiled for the growing family, but she felt a sadness settle inside of her. *Will I ever know the joy of having my own family?* She tried to push the emptiness away. *Thou shalt not covet!* "I am happy for them."

"I know it is hard, Greta."

"Hard? Whatever do you mean?"

"Ach! Do not pretend, child. Just when you admitted your feelings for Jacob, Catrina pulled him away. I know that you long for a family of your own. Your own children, your own hearth and husband." Ruth shook her head and set the water bucket aside. "You cannot live alone with an old woman forever."

Greta frowned. "You should not say such things. I do not want to leave you."

Ruth patted Greta's shoulder. "Do not worry about me. You cannot stay here forever, wasting your youth and hopes."

Greta laughed. "Who do you have in mind? The Widower Hertzberger? He is eligible—and only sixty-five years old!"

"Do not give up hope so easily."

"Well, I certainly do not see how this is going to work out."

Ruth smiled and wiped a ring of water off the hearthstone. "We can never see *der Herr*'s plan before it unfolds. But He has a way of making things work out in ways that we cannot predict."

Greta backed out of the fireplace and brushed the soot off her hands. "I just cannot imagine how I will ever find love." She shook her head. "I know that many women marry out of practicality. I realize that I could not survive in the backcountry alone. But with the support of our settlement . . . well, we are doing all right. So I refuse to marry a man that I do not love. I would rather wait forever than compromise."

Ruth chuckled. "At the moment there is no one for you to marry even if you were willing to compromise." She raised an eyebrow. "That is, unless you *are* interested in the Widower Hertzberger."

Greta put a hand over her face and groaned. "Oh, Ruth."

"You just put soot all over your forehead, dear."

Greta sighed and wiped her face with the corner of her apron. "Well, there is no use crying over spilt milk. Jacob is no longer interested and that is that."

Ruth stopped and looked Greta in the eye. "How can you be so sure of that?"

"Because I have been told!"

"By Jacob?"

"No. Of course not. We have not spoken of such things."

Ruth raised an eyebrow.

Greta pushed the bucket of ashes against the wall. "Why would you doubt what the Grubers said? It was as good as from Jacob's own mouth."

"But it was not."

"The Grubers are honest folk."

"Of course they are. But misunderstandings can develop when information is passed from one to another."

"Jacob has given me no reason to believe otherwise."

"The two of you were growing close until Jonah told you that Jacob held no affection for you. And, Jacob has never seemed the type to choose beauty over character." Ruth picked up an armful of kindling and arranged it inside the newly swept fireplace. "But he strikes me as having too much pride." She glanced at Greta with a stern look. "Like you." Greta squirmed under Ruth's gaze. "Both of you are unwilling to just admit the truth to each other. I do wonder what would happen if you just marched up to him and told him how you really feel."

"Well, that would be a bold move! I should think that would be quite unseemly for a Plain woman."

Ruth shrugged. "Perhaps. But letting the man you love slip through your fingers would be worse."

Greta pursed her lips and added a log to the stack of kindling.

"I never said that I loved him."

"You did not have to."

Greta stopped. *Do I love him? I know that he makes me laugh. I know that he ignites something inside of me. I know that I think of him day and night. And I know that I cannot bear to spend the rest of my life with anyone but him.* Greta sat back onto the dirt floor. The revelation struck her like a barrage of rain from a sudden storm.

"You did not realize that it is more than just affection."

Greta closed her eyes. "I did not want it to be. Not when I have no hope for a marriage."

Ruth put a warm hand on Greta's shoulder. "He was a shell of a man after losing his family. He has changed these past weeks. You changed him." She shook her head. "And now he is alone. He might close his heart forever now."

"But he is not alone! He is with Catrina every time I see him."

"But he is still alone in here." Ruth tapped her heart. "She does not fill that void in him."

Greta swallowed and looked Ruth in the eye. "And you think that I do?"

Ruth nodded, her face serious. "*Ja. Ja*, I do."

"But what if you are wrong? What if I pour my feelings out to him and he rejects me? What if he really does prefer Catrina?" Greta looked away. "She is beautiful. And perfect in every way."

"Only on the outside."

"That is what people see."

"Not people of character."

"Is Jacob a person of character?"

"Would you love him if he were not?"

Greta sucked in her breath. Maybe there was a chance. Maybe Jacob was not as taken by Catrina as she thought.

"There is only one way to find out." Ruth gave her a serious look. "Let him know how you feel."

Greta shook her head. "I cannot. It is too embarrassing. Just look at me and look at her. I will make a fool of myself."

Ruth clucked her tongue. "There you go with your pride again."

"I prefer to call it self-respect."

"Do not mince words, Greta Scholtz. You just might let true love slip right through your fingers!"

"If he loves me he will come to me instead of running off with Catrina."

"Not if he thinks that you have no affection for him."

"Humph."

"Humph."

Each woman crossed her arms and stared at the other.

"Just think about it. That is all I ask."

Greta threw up her hands. "Fine! You have worn me down! I will think about it. But I am not making any promises!"

Ruth shrugged. "You better think fast because you will see Jacob on the morrow."

"Why?"

"The settlement is going to build an addition onto the Grubers' cabin. With the baby on the way, they need the space."

Greta scowled. "I will think about that tomorrow. For now, let's get this ash on to boil." She wiped the sweat from her forehead. "It will take the rest of the day to make the soap, so we better get started."

Ruth clucked her tongue. "You can avoid thinking about Jacob today. But you cannot avoid seeing him tomorrow."

Ruth and Greta ate a cold breakfast so that they could get an early start to the Gruber farm. But Greta brooded and took her time even though they were in a hurry. She broke the crust of ice over the water bucket and washed her face in silence. Her fingers moved slowly as she patted her cheeks dry and tied on a crisp, white prayer *kappe*.

"Do not dawdle, Greta. You cannot put off seeing the two of them together forever."

Greta sighed and fastened her shoes. "I am not dawdling."

"Then let's go. The sun is nearly up."

Greta followed Ruth out the door and braced herself for what lay ahead. *I cannot bear to see the two of them together.* She clenched her jaw. *If only I had said something earlier. Before it was too late.*

"It is not too late to let Jacob know how you feel, you know."

"We have already been over this."

"*Ja.* And you agreed to tell him how you feel."

"Ruth! I never agreed to that."

Ruth laughed. "It was worth a try."

"You cannot trick me into making a fool of myself."

"Ach. Young people today make everything so complicated."

"Oh, Ruth. I will read the situation when I see him. And if he gives me any sign of encouragement . . ."

"And if he does not?"

"I cannot compete with Catrina. I will not humiliate myself trying."

"I have already told you that character beats beauty every time."

Greta sighed. "Let's just hope that Jacob Miller agrees."

Christian and the Fisher twins ran to meet Greta as soon as she and Ruth walked into the clearing in front of the Gruber cabin.

"Greta! Have you come to help make our house bigger?"

"*Ja.*"

"I am going to have a new baby brother, you know."

"Or sister."

"*Ja.* But I am hoping for a brother." Christian grinned and dashed to the cluster of men on the far side of the cabin. They stood with tools in their hands as they measured and planned, stroked their beards, and nodded.

Eliza and Peter grabbed Greta's hands. "Greta?"

"*Ja?*"

"Will there still be room for us here, when Mrs. Gruber has another baby?" Peter's big, round eyes widened with concern.

Eliza pulled on Greta's hand. "Mrs. Gruber is already so busy. How will she take care of us when she has one more of her own?" The little girl looked down and frowned. "We do not want to be a burden."

"Oh, Eliza, you could never be a burden!" Greta

crouched down and hugged both children to her chest. "Neither one of you could ever be a burden."

"But Mrs. Gruber already has six children. With the new baby that will make seven." Eliza's lip trembled. "Even with the new addition, there will not be room for us."

Peter tightened his grip on Greta. "Can we come live with you? You have enough room for us. And we promise to help. We could fetch the firewood and water."

"Oh, Peter. I would love for you to live with me. I would love that very much."

Eliza drew back and stared at Greta. "So we can come?" Her frown transformed into a brilliant grin. "Do you want us to live with you? Do you really?"

Greta's heart melted at the children's need for love and a permanent home of their own. *But how can I be a mother to them when I can barely put enough food on the table for Ruth and me?*

"I cannot say what will be. I will have to speak with the elders." She straightened Eliza's prayer *kappe* and hugged the girl again. She kissed Peter on the top of his head, then fastened a hook and eye on his waistcoat that had come undone. "I do want you to come. I just do not know if it will work out."

"Please try, Greta."

Peter's big brown eyes stared into hers. "*Ja.* Please try."

Greta took a deep breath. "I will try. But I cannot promise anything." She forced an optimistic smile. "Now, why don't you see what the menfolk need? I am sure there is something that you can fetch for them."

The children nodded and scampered away. Their

eager voices carried back to Greta as she watched their small feet pound through the tall grass. Ruth frowned. "You should not get their hopes up, Greta. They need more than we can provide."

Greta pursed her lips. "We will see."

Something caught Ruth's attention and she cut her eyes toward the cabin, then cleared her throat and looked away. Greta turned around to see what Ruth had seen. Catrina walked confidently beside Jacob, a soft, slender hand resting on his arm. Greta let out a long breath.

"I have seen all that I need to see."

Ruth changed the subject. "I suppose we ought to get to work. Let's go see what we can do to help."

Greta nodded and tried to set her mind on other things. Soon the two women were leaning over Barbara Gruber's hearth, helping her prepare a hearty meal for the men. They could hear the bang of hammers and the screech of handsaws as they scrubbed and quartered root vegetables. Barbara skirted an obstacle course of toddlers as she stoked the fire and sliced salt pork to season the stew.

Greta liked the feeling of working side by side with her friends. She relished the fact that the entire settlement came together to help a growing family. *It is our way.* Soon the smell of simmering meat wafted through the cabin and mixed with the earthy scent of woodsmoke. A cold wind blew outside, but in the snug one-room cabin, the women felt cozy and warm.

Barbara stirred the cauldron and ladled out a taste. She nodded and set down the spoon. "That will do just fine." She glanced out the window to check the position of the sun.

"We still have some time until lunch. Why don't we make a treat for the men?"

Ruth cocked her head. "What do you have up your sleeve?"

Barbara beamed. "Coffee!"

Greta clapped her hands. "How did you ever?"

"We have been saving the last of the beans. I think this is the perfect time to use them. What better way to thank everyone for their hard work?"

The women heated the cast-iron spider over the coals and poured the last of Barbara's precious coffee beans across it. Barbara stirred the beans as they chatted and laughed, their faces aglow with the thrill of surprise. After the beans roasted, Greta ground them in the Grubers' little coffee grinder while Barbara pulled out a pallet so that the youngest children could nap.

Ruth leaned over and whispered in Greta's ear, "You should be the one to take Jacob his cup." Greta shook her head. But she imagined Jacob's reaction when she handed him a cup of rich, steaming coffee. He probably has not had coffee in months. Years, maybe. She smiled as she remembered the fashionable coffeehouses that lined Germany's bustling streets. She had never been inside one of those trendy cafés—that would have been far too worldly for a Plain woman living a simple farming life. But the smell of coffee still made her feel as if they were overcoming the wilderness by bringing a little bit of Old World sophistication and luxury to the bleak backcountry.

Greta looked to make sure that no one could hear and whispered back to Ruth. "That seems a bold move, especially since we just saw Catrina on his arm."

Ruth shrugged. "What do you have to lose, Greta? He might welcome your company. And if he does not, there is no loss of face. It is perfectly reasonable for you to pass out the coffee to him. You must pass it out to all the men. It is not forward of you." Ruth raised her eyes to see if anyone else was in earshot. "Just try, Greta. You may be surprised by his reception. And you would have an opportunity to tell him how you really feel."

Greta frowned as she considered. *It would make a positive impression.* Greta shook the coffee grounds out of the grinder and into a linen bag, then dropped the bag in boiling water to steep. *Almost ready.* She imagined passing the warm drink into Jacob's hands. Greta could see his face light up with surprise and she made up her mind. *I will do it! And maybe, just maybe he will notice me again.*

Greta watched the boiling water until it turned a rich brown. "It looks ready!" She ladled a serving into a pewter cup and hurried outside, careful not to slosh the hot liquid over the top. Her stomach jumped at the thought of Jacob's smile when she surprised him. *Slow down, Greta. Do not spill it!* She forced herself to slow her pace as she rounded the corner of the cabin.

Jacob stood on the far side of a pile of lumber, a mallet in his hand. She studied his strong, sharp jaw and brooding eyes as she cut the distance between them. *He does not see me.* Greta started to shout a greeting when she felt a gentle pressure on her arm. She looked down and saw a soft white hand, unblemished from work or sun.

"Oh, Greta!" Catrina smiled and moved her hand from Greta's arm to the pewter cup. "Please let me! Jacob will be overjoyed."

"Oh, no, I—" Greta tried to hold on to the cup, but Catrina pulled it toward her.

"Thank you!"

The coffee sloshed across the lip of the cup. Greta gasped and let go. *Better to let her have it than to spill it—there is barely enough to go around.*

"Aren't you a dear? The men have not had coffee in ages." Catrina turned and marched over to Jacob before Greta could protest.

"Jacob?" Catrina gazed at him with beguiling eyes. "I have refreshments."

"Huh?" He stopped working and looked up. "Oh. *Danke.*" He wiped his brow and took the cup.

"Careful! It is hot."

"Hot? What is it?" He glanced down, raised his eyebrows, and grinned. "How did you ever manage . . . ? Catrina, you do know how to work wonders. I have not had a cup of coffee in . . ." He shook his head and blew across the surface of the liquid. "I do not know how long it has been."

Catrina giggled. "I did not do it all on my own, but I do hope you like it."

Jacob smiled. "I certainly do."

Greta watched with her mouth agape. *Well, I never!* She clenched her fists as she listened to Catrina's feminine giggles and the murmured responses of Jacob's deep, warm voice. When Jacob broke out into a grin—his eyes still locked on Catrina's—Greta knew that she had had enough. She turned on her heels and stalked back inside the cabin, muttering to herself the entire way.

Greta refused to let the other women see her distress. She turned her face toward the fire and filled the pewter cups with coffee. Her hands trembled as she worked and the cups clinked against the cast-iron cauldron. Greta closed her eyes and swallowed hard. *Do not let them get to you.* She opened her eyes and pushed back her emotions. "Barbara? Are these all of the cups that you have?"

"*Ja.* We only have four. You will have to pass out the coffee in rounds."

Greta nodded and set off with a cup in each hand. Her expression looked more fit for a funeral than a work party. She kept her face down each time she marched back and forth from the hearth and made sure not to let her eyes wander toward Jacob. *I will not let him see me pining after him! If he wants to go googly-eyed over another woman then that is fine with me!* But Greta could still feel the lump in her throat and her eyes burned from holding back tears.

Jacob noticed Greta as she strode across the clearing with pewter cups in hand. Everywhere she went, faces lit up and spirits lifted at the unexpected treat. But Greta did not notice. Her expression remained blank and unreadable. Jacob followed her with his eyes. He studied her determined posture and the calluses on her hands. *She is so dedicated to her work. She is always serving, always thinking of others.* He waited for her to glance his way, to give him some small sign that she noticed him too.

She never looked his way. He sighed and shrugged his shoulders. *I cannot change her heart. It is time to let that dream die, no matter how much affection I have for her.*

But there was another woman who watched him. Catrina caught his eye from across the clearing and looked away coyly. Jacob did not smile, but he met her gaze with a thoughtful stare. *I do not care for Catrina as I do for Greta, but I need to move on from the past and forge a new life. I cannot let myself slip back into solitude and grief. And here is a beautiful young woman, ready to help me feel whole again. She could be a good partner. Couldn't she?* His stomach felt heavy, as though he had swallowed a stone. He knew that he could never feel true love for Catrina Witmer. *But I cannot bear the thought of another long, hard winter, cold and alone in my isolated cabin, pining for both Marta and Greta.*

Chapter Eighteen

Greta threw herself into her work. She scrubbed harder, swept faster, and taught with more enthusiasm. On baking day she punched the dough with all of her strength. The warm, elastic flour sank beneath her fists. But no matter how hard she hit, Greta could not let go of her hurt and regret. Her thoughts returned to the moment when Catrina grabbed the coffee cup from her hand and stole her chance to connect with Jacob. She punched the dough even harder.

Ruth raised an eyebrow. "Well, you certainly seem to be winning the fight against that dough." Greta squeezed her eyes shut. Her entire body felt tense. *Lord, help me not to hold a grudge! Help me to be happy for them.*

"You know, dear, the Lord has a way of working things out."

Greta let out a long breath and opened her eyes. "*Ja.* Jacob is learning to let someone back in his heart. That is a good thing." She pushed her palms into the dough. "I must be happy for them."

Ruth paused and chose her words carefully. "*Ja*, it is good that Jacob is learning to love again. But, I am not so sure that Catrina is the one who he loves."

Greta shrugged and sank her fist into the dough. "Looks clear enough to me."

"*Ja*. Well, as I have said, the Lord has a way of working things out in ways we do not see and cannot expect."

"I did not see Catrina coming, that is for sure."

"That is not what I meant."

Greta shrugged again. "That is what I see."

Ruth patted her shoulder. "Do not trust in what you can see. Trust in what *der Herr* can do without your seeing."

Greta nodded and willed herself to believe, even as her heart cried out that all was lost.

"You have taken your feelings out on that dough long enough, haven't you?"

Greta sighed, folded the dough into a clean, white cloth, and headed to the bake-oven.

Thoughts of Jacob and Catrina swirled through her mind as she walked through the clear, crisp air. Cold had settled across the backcountry like feathers of a plucked goose that drifted down and settled against the earth. The barren winter fields echoed the stark isolation that she felt within her heart.

Greta contemplated her rival's stunning smile, innocent expression, and flawless beauty. Greta sighed and kicked a stone. She watched it skid across the path and into the woods. *I know that I cannot compete with her beauty or her competency in the kitchen. If der Herr has blessed her with beauty, so be it. He has blessed me with other things. And if Jacob prefers beauty . . . well, then he is not the man I thought he was.* She raised her chin.

So what if she is charming and a talented cook? I have gifts too. And I will share them with whomever der Herr sends my way. She thought of the children and felt a renewed sense of purpose. *They need me. And I have more to offer them than a pretty face or a freshly baked cake.*

When she reached the bake-oven, another woman blocked the entrance, her back to Greta. The woman's bodice and neck cloth looked perfectly ironed, her prayer *kappe* neatly starched, and her apron bright white. There was only one woman in the settlement who managed to keep such a neat appearance. Greta noticed her own stained apron, wrinkled skirt, and limp prayer *kappe. How does she manage it? How on earth does she manage to stay so perfect?!* Greta felt her stomach tighten, but she refused to give in to her emotions.

"Good day, Catrina. I hope you are well."

The woman turned around and flashed a dazzling grin.

"Greta dear, how are you?" Her eyes ran down Greta's worn bodice, then back up again. "Why ever are you still in that old thing? Have you not sewed a new shift and neck cloth yet?"

"No. I am much too busy of late. Perhaps after I air the linens and gather kindling tomorrow. Although . . ."

"Although what, dear?"

"It is just that I am not sure I feel comfortable. I do appreciate your generosity, but I fear some of those fabrics are too lovely for me. The rich textures and the quality of the weave . . . they seem too luxurious."

"Too luxurious? Greta dear, you have been in the wilderness too long. Why, you should see what they are wearing in Philadelphia—not to mention London and Paris." She flicked her hand. "I would hardly call the fabrics I gave you luxurious."

"*Ja.*" Greta frowned and tried to find words that sounded both polite and firm. "But we do not compare ourselves to worldly fashions or worldly standards. Even the smallest bit of ornamentation is too much for us. We want to be Plain." She put her hand over her chest. "When we are Plain, the beauty of our hearts shows through. That is the only beauty that is real or lasting."

"Is that how you really feel?" Catrina looked at her with wide, questioning eyes.

"*Ja,* it is."

Catrina looked surprised. Her mouth opened to speak, but she closed it again when Jacob emerged from the woods. Greta felt flustered. She focused on unwrapping the dough that she carried in her basket. "Are you finished with the bake-oven?"

"*Ja.* And the temperature should still be good for baking. No need to build a new fire." Catrina picked up the wooden paddle, slid it in the oven, and pulled out a perfect loaf of bread. "Ah, just right."

Ja. *Of course it is.*

"You know, I would be happy to help you with your baking. I hear that you have a habit of burning bread." Catrina's face looked genuine, but Greta could not see past her hurt. She clenched her jaw. She counted to ten. "No, thank you, Catrina. I am sure that I can manage."

"As you wish." Catrina turned away from Greta and waved at Jacob as he walked toward them. She held up the loaf of bread, then tucked it in her basket and strode toward him. Greta crouched over the oven and refused to watch Catrina slink away with the handsome widower.

Catrina slipped her arm into Jacob's as soon as she passed him on the path. "Won't you carry my basket? All of this freshly baked bread is getting heavy." She moved the cloth aside and let the warm, nutty aroma reach Jacob's nose. "You may have some if you escort me home. And preserves as well. Grandmother brought a jar of mayhaw jelly with us that she canned last year. Do say that you will join us for some refreshment."

"Oh, well . . ." He glanced past Catrina and hoped to catch Greta's eye. But Greta refused to turn around. *I know that she saw me coming this way. Now she will not even say hello? She will not even wave?* He clenched his jaw. *Does she not even want to be my friend?*

"Do say you will join us, Jacob."

Jacob felt the soft touch of Catrina's delicate fingers on his arm. He sighed. "*Ja.* Sure. Let us walk and enjoy a nice meal."

"Yes, let's." Catrina smiled sweetly, but her touch felt distant. He remembered the way Greta held on to him when he carried her home after she twisted her ankle. Her grip had felt warm and full of life.

"Jacob?"

Jacob nodded. "*Ja.*"

"Whatever is distracting you? My cabin is this way." She tugged on his arm. "I will have to bake you a pie soon," Catrina murmured as she led him away. "You would like that, wouldn't you?"

"*Ja,* sure." Jacob glanced back again. He caught a glimpse of Greta's profile outlined by the low afternoon sun. The silhouette looked simple and honest: straight lines of a homespun skirt and bodice and the curve of her bound chestnut-colored hair. He sensed a gentle purpose in her movements, a beauty that he felt as well as saw.

Greta did not turn her head to look at him. Jacob cleared his throat and looked back to Catrina. She tightened her grip on his arm and peered up at him through thick black lashes. The alluring young lady tried to pull him into a conversation by gushing over his carpentry skills. Her chatter and giggles provided a comfortable distraction and he let himself slip into a mindless rhythm as he strolled through the long afternoon shadows with a beautiful woman on his arm. And yet, he could not ignore the quiet tug on his heart. An image of a woman standing alone in the setting sun burned inside his mind.

Greta felt satisfied that she had resisted every urge to look Jacob's way. *I have more self-respect than that.* Everything in her had screamed to look toward him, to catch his eye and communicate how she felt with a truthful, burning look. *But not when Catrina Witmer is on his arm.*

"Ah, Greta. How do you do?"

Greta jumped.

Amos grinned. "I am sorry that I startled you."

Greta shook her head. "Not at all. I am fine, Amos. How are you?"

"I am very well. Very well, indeed!"

"You are certainly in a fine mood."

"*Ja.* I was just thinking how good it is to see our Jacob escorting a young woman home. Why, just a few weeks ago I thought we would never reach him. But look at this!" He shook his head and grinned wider. "It looks like Jacob's heart has finally healed."

Greta swallowed and checked the oven temperature with her hand so that Amos could not see the expression on her face.

"You know, Greta, I really did think that you two were a perfect match. But you were right, I suppose. You insisted all along that it was not meant to be. And now, just look at how well everything has turned out." He patted Greta's arm. "Now, I do give you credit, child. You were a good influence on him even though you were not interested in a relationship."

Greta straightened up. "What do you mean?"

"Just look at the difference in him. His heart is with Catrina, but you were the one who reached him so that he could find love again. You reopened his damaged heart."

"Me?"

"*Ja*. Who else?"

"Oh, I just . . . I don't know . . ." Greta picked at the ties on her prayer *kappe*. Amos's words made her feel uneasy. "What makes you say that?"

"Is it not obvious? He was despondent until you arrived. We all watched you draw him out of his shell." Amos shrugged. "That is why we all thought that you were meant to be together. We all saw how he reacted to you."

Greta shook her head. "That is what the Widow Yoder says. But, Amos, how could any of you think that? He has chosen Catrina!"

"*Ja*, and it is wonderful good, is it not?"

Wonderful good?! Amos's enthusiasm felt like a cheese grater scraping against Greta's heart.

Amos motioned down the path. Jacob and Catrina looked very small in the distance, arms still linked. "Thanks to you. Without your help, I do not know if Jacob would have ever loved again."

"Mmmm." Greta tried to sound enthusiastic, but all she could manage was a murmur. *I brought them together? Great. Just great.*

Amos looked down at Greta. "And how are you, now that no one is pressuring you to marry the wrong man?"

"Oh, I am fine. Completely fine." She forced a smile. "I feel splendid. Absolutely splendid."

"*Wunderbar!*"

Greta stood frozen with the fake smile plastered on her face and wished she could disappear. She took a long, deep breath and made a promise to herself. *I will put my efforts into the gifts* der Herr *has given me. I may not have Catrina's worldly beauty, but I have other attributes that are more lasting—and more valuable.*

"Actually, Amos, I have been thinking." She swallowed and considered how to word her request.

"*Ja?*"

Greta squared her shoulders and plunged ahead. "It is clear that the Grubers have their hands full. They cannot keep the Fisher twins forever. Even with the new addition, the cabin is too small for their growing family. And Mrs. Gruber is exhausted. With another little one on the way, she needs more rest."

"*Ja.* True enough."

"Well, I thought that perhaps Peter and Eliza could stay with the Widow Yoder and me." Greta's stomach tightened with need. *Let this work out. I want to be there for those children. I want to use the gifts that* der Herr *has given me.*

Amos tugged at his beard. "I should talk this over with Abraham. I have no doubt that you would make a wonderful foster mother."

"But you wonder how we would put enough food on the table for them."

Amos spread out his hands. "Well, *ja.*"

"I earn a little through teaching, as you know. We will manage. And the settlement will be generous, I am sure. That is our way."

"*Ja.* That is our way." Amos tugged at his beard again. "Well, it probably makes more sense for Jacob and Catrina to take them in, assuming they marry. And why wouldn't they?"

"Indeed." Greta looked down. "Why wouldn't they?"

"But, until then . . ." He shrugged. "Let me speak it over with Abraham."

Greta felt a newfound strength as she walked home with her freshly baked bread. The crust had burned black, as always, but even that could not dampen her optimism.

Ruth looked up with surprise when Greta swept through the door. "Aren't you looking happy? What has you in such a good mood? Let me guess. You finally managed not to burn the bread!" Ruth clapped her hands in anticipation. "Let's have a slice right now."

"Um. No."

"Oh." Ruth sagged against the backless bench. "Then what?"

Greta set the basket down by the hearth and warmed her hands. "I spoke to Amos today and he thinks that it is a good idea for Peter and Eliza to live with us, at least for a while."

Ruth's face brightened again. "That *is* good news."

"*Ja.*" Greta glanced at Ruth. "You do not mind, do you? It will not be too much for you?"

Ruth waved her hand. "No. A child is always a blessing." She looked away. "I was never blessed with one of my own, you know. It will do me good to see children at my own hearth. They will be the grandchildren that I never had."

Greta grabbed the broom. "I am so glad that we are of one mind on this." She swept the hard-packed floor in quick, firm motions. "I am going to get this place ready!" She grinned. "Won't they be happy when they hear? They have been asking to live with us for some time, you know."

"*Ja,* I know." Ruth eyed her young friend. "I cannot help but notice a shift in your mood. You are feeling better?"

"I just know that I cannot compete with Catrina on her terms. I have to be myself. And if that is not enough, then Jacob was never the right man for me. I do not have her beauty, but I have other attributes. Like teaching and taking in the twins."

"Those gifts are more important than the gift of outward beauty." Ruth patted Greta's arm. "And I am sure that everyone in our settlement would agree. We all strive to be Plain here."

Greta frowned. *Not everyone.* She shook her head and dismissed the thought. She refused to let Catrina spoil her newfound peace.

Chapter Nineteen

Jacob stood up, stretched his back, and surveyed the new chicken coop. "All finished."

Catrina's grandfather set down his hammer and shook Jacob's hand. "Thanks for the help."

Catrina appeared as if on cue. "Jacob, you must stay for dinner."

Jacob shook his head. "I appreciate the offer, Catrina, but I best be getting on."

Georg Witmer nodded and headed toward the cabin while Catrina lingered by Jacob's side. "What would we do without you? The foxes took three chickens this week."

Jacob eyed the new chicken coop as he packed away his tools. "Looks sturdy enough. I think it will do."

"I am sure it will do very well. You are an excellent carpenter."

Jacob shrugged and deflected the compliment. "'Tis nothing."

Catrina smiled. "I will have to bake you a cake.

We will have plenty of eggs for one, now that the chickens have a safe place to lay."

"I would not complain if you did." He glanced at the sun's position in the sky and nodded to Catrina. "I best make haste. I have my own farm to tend."

"Must you?"

"I am sure that you have your own chores to take care of, as well."

Catrina shrugged. "It is not baking day."

"Surely there is much more to do around here than bake."

Catrina shrugged again, then smiled. "Do say that you will stay for dinner."

Jacob shook his head. "I have the stock to feed."

Catrina sighed and pushed her lip into a pouty expression. "Please?"

Jacob sighed and glanced at the sun again. He frowned. "Okay. But I cannot stay long."

Her face brightened and she clapped her hands. "We already have a venison stew simmering in the cauldron. It should be ready by now."

Jacob's stomach growled and he realized how hungry he was. "That sounds perfect."

The rich smell of roasted game welcomed them as they walked through the cabin door.

"Jacob will stay for dinner, Grandmother."

"We are glad to have you," the elderly woman replied as she took Jacob's coat and hung it on a peg. "It is the least we can do for you after the work that you put in for us today."

"I am happy to help. And your husband is good company. He is handy with a hammer and nail."

Georg shrugged. "I am not an adventurer, Jacob. I know how to put a hammer to a nail, but this is a strange, inhospitable land. It is good to have men like you to show us how to survive."

"The Rhine River Valley is easy to farm, compared to the endless forests here." Jacob shook his head. "I have done little but clear land for the past twelve months."

"It is a wild, lonely place, compared to home," Catrina remarked as she sat down at the table. Her grandmother set the table and ladled out servings of stew as the young woman rested her chin on her hands and stared into the fire.

"My granddaughter is accustomed to the lively streets of Philadelphia, you see. She is not at home here. She is still learning our ways." Jacob watched Frena pass out the food as her granddaughter sat with her soft white fingers folded like a delicate china doll. "My husband and I found the Amish faith after our children were grown and we all moved to the New World. They did not convert when we did, so Catrina was not raised Amish."

"I grew up in my father's general store, surrounded by all sorts of lovely things. Lace, and furs, and candy." Catrina's expression perked up as she remembered the luxuries that once defined her life. "We never ran out of things like coffee or sugar. And I had new bodices and hosen whenever I wanted." She sighed. "I even had a housekeeper."

"What brought you here, Miss Witmer? It is a very different world that you have taken on."

Catrina shrugged. "I have never experienced anything except the life of a shopkeeper's daughter." She looked down. "But I have always felt as if something were missing, even with all of those luxuries." She sighed and traced a pattern in the tabletop's wood grain. "I suppose I believe that there is more to life than that."

Jacob nodded. "Then you have come to the right place."

Frena put a jug of water on the table and sat down with the others. "It is a joy to have her along, but it has been quite a strain on her."

Catrina waved her hand and smiled. "With friends like Jacob to help, I am learning how to fit in just fine."

Jacob cleared his throat and shifted in his seat. "Do you not miss the city, Catrina?"

"*Ja.* I miss it very much."

"Will you return?"

She gazed into his eyes. "That depends on if I feel there is a reason to stay, Jacob."

"The ability to worship freely as Amish—is that not a reason to stay, Catrina?"

Catrina looked away. "Naturally." But her tone sounded flat and halfhearted.

Georg frowned at his granddaughter. "Do not worry, Jacob. She will learn our ways."

Frena nodded. "She just needs the right partner to help her find her path."

Catrina's soft hands and sparkling laughter lingered in Jacob's mind as he walked home after dinner. *But is there a Plain heart behind that enchanting smile?* He sighed as his thoughts drifted to another woman, one who's lively green eyes sparked with depth and understanding.

"Good evening, Jacob." Amos and Abraham paused on the path in front of him.

Jacob looked up. "I did not notice you two. Good evening."

Abraham nodded. "*Ja.* You seem deep in thought." The two elders waited for a response, but Jacob did not disclose what was on his mind.

"I see you are headed away from the Witmer farm." Amos pointed his chin in that direction. "Paying Catrina another visit?"

Jacob frowned. *I am not going to be able to avoid this topic of conversation, am I?* "I helped her grandfather build a chicken coop."

Abraham nodded. "Always doing your part."

Jacob shrugged. "Just doing what is expected of us."

Amos grinned. "But not all of us have a pretty young lady waiting with a nice dinner, after our work is done."

Jacob shrugged again. Abraham slapped him on the back. "You cannot hide your courtship from us! You think we have not noticed that the two of you make a fine match?"

"Well, I don't know if I would call it a match . . ." Jacob rubbed the back of his neck. "At least not yet. I do have to admit that it is moving in that direction. . . ."

Amos waved him off. "Bah! I realize that we missed the mark with Greta, but you cannot deny that you and Miss Witmer are meant for each other!"

"It is a relief to see you find your way." Abraham stabbed the air with his pointer finger. "We have noticed quite a change in you, Jacob!"

"Oh?"

"You have come out of your shell. Have you not noticed?" Amos spread out his hands. "We see you smiling, talking. You seem as if you are getting back to yourself again."

"*Ja.*" Jacob removed his black beaver-felt hat and ran his fingers through his hair. "I don't know."

"We know. We see the change."

Jacob sighed and replaced his hat. "I appreciate your concern, but—"

"Come now, Jacob. We are a community here. You cannot hide from us!" Abraham slapped his back again. Jacob flinched. "*Ja.* I can see that."

"So, can we expect a wedding soon? We want to see you settled." Amos put his hand on Jacob's shoulder. "Man was not meant to be alone. It is time to put away the past and move into the future."

Jacob sighed. "*Ja.* I can see that now. But I don't know. . . ."

Amos's head bobbed up and down. "*Ja! Ja!* I am glad that things are moving forward!" He motioned in the direction of the Witmer cabin. "With you and Catrina, that is. It sure seems funny now that we all had Greta pegged as your future bride." Amos shrugged. "Of course now it is clear that we were all wrong on that account. I just spoke to Greta about you yesterday, as a matter of fact." Jacob felt his stomach tighten. "*Ja,*" Amos continued. "She is a dear sister. A hard worker and an eager servant."

"What did she say about Jacob?" Abraham asked. "Just a few weeks ago we were pushing a marriage between them. How does she feel about that now?"

Jacob's stomach churned as he waited for the answer.

"She agreed that it was the wrong path."

Jacob shifted his weight from one foot to the other.

Why am I so disappointed? What did I expect her to say? I have already heard this from Jonah.

Abraham stroked his beard. "She would be surprised to hear what an impact she had on Jacob, I believe."

"*Ja.* She was. When I told her—"

Jacob put up a hand. "Wait a minute. You two are discussing me as if I am not here. What makes you think that she had an impact on me?"

Abraham cocked his head. "Is it not obvious, Jacob?"

Jacob frowned in reply.

"She is the reason you are able to let Catrina into your life!" Amos threw up his hands. "Can you not see that?"

"*Ja.*" Abraham nodded. "Your heart did not soften on its own."

Jacob frowned. "I do not know about that."

Both elders shot Jacob a dismissive look. "She did not see it either." Amos grinned. "Funny how things go."

"Hilarious."

"*Ja.* But she has moved on now," Amos said.

Abraham smiled. "She has come a long way since her arrival, little more than a fortnight ago. I remember that she struggled at first. But she has risen to the challenge."

"*Ja,*" Amos agreed. "She is taking in the Fisher twins. She has found a good future without you, Jacob. A relief, I know. A man like you could leave a trail of broken hearts if he were not careful! But you are free to pursue the lovely Catrina!" Amos slapped Jacob's back and chuckled.

Then why am I the one who feels brokenhearted?

Jacob could not listen to one more word about Greta Scholtz. He murmured a quick good-bye and headed down the path, but thoughts of the young schoolteacher invaded his mind. He remembered how incompetent she looked when she fell on her backside the first day they met. She had not seemed cut out for backcountry life. Not one bit.

And yet, she persevered. She fought to succeed. Jacob swallowed hard. *Will Catrina fight as hard as Greta did to fit in here?* He remembered how Catrina sat at the table as dainty as a porcelain doll, while her elderly grandmother waited on them all during supper. *Will she take on a servant's heart? Would she become a second mother to the settlement's children as Greta has?*

Jacob frowned and wrapped his coat closer, but the cold night air still cut through him. *Why am I even comparing them? Greta is not even interested in me.* He shook his head. *Only a fool chases a dream that cannot be his.*

Chapter Twenty

Rainwater found its way through Jacob's shingles once again and he trudged onto the roof to make repairs. *Truth be told, I spend more time on my roof than under it!* Jacob did not want to admit what distracted him from the task at hand. But his eyes kept wandering to his neighbor's land to scan the landscape for Greta. Water from the recent rains formed narrow streams that sparkled across the old woman's field and drained into the creek at the base of the hill.

He shook his head and trained his eyes on a cracked shingle. *She is not the woman for whom you should be looking.*

"Jacob!" Jacob recognized Catrina's voice. He raised his eyebrows. *It is as if she read my mind.*

"I am on the roof, making good use of those nails your grandfather gave me."

"Do be careful!"

"Do not worry about me."

"I won't. I am much too busy worrying about this mud. My shoes are covered in it." The tone of her voice sharpened. "However will I get it all off?"

"Mud comes with the territory. Best get used to it."
She did not answer so Jacob scooted to the edge of
the roof and looked down. Catrina ignored him and
scraped her shoes against the edge of the porch.

"You are putting mud on my porch, you know."

"There was already mud on your porch. There is
mud everywhere. This whole place is filled with mud.
Mud, mud, mud." She scraped her shoes harder.
"And I HATE mud."

Jacob shrugged. "You may as well relax and go
with it."

"We did not have this problem in Philadelphia."
Catrina pulled out a handkerchief and dabbed the
sides of the leather shoes. "We had cobblestone
streets."

"You will not see that here anytime soon. If ever."

Catrina pursed her lips and kept wiping her shoes.
Jacob shook his head and turned his attention back
to the roof. The sun felt warm on the back of his
neck and he whistled a cheerful tune as he ham-
mered a nail.

"Jacob, do come down."

"I need to patch up the roof. Awful lot of water
getting in."

Catrina held up a basket. "Grandmother wants me
to give you these eggs. We heard that the foxes took
the hens we gave you." She swatted at a bug and
scowled.

Jacob nodded. "*Ja.* There is only one left."

"What a dreadful place this is. Full of foxes and
wolves and bears." She swatted at the bug again. "I
put a slice of pie in the basket too. Come down and
share it with me."

"I will be down as soon as I get this shingle in place."

"No, come down now. I came all the way here in the mud." Jacob glanced down at her and frowned. He did not like the demanding tone in her voice. She responded with her best grin. "All work and no play makes Jack a dull boy." Her tone turned honey-smooth.

Jacob sighed. "All right, all right. I'm coming down." He caught himself glancing over at Widow Yoder's pastureland before he scrambled down the ladder. *Put Greta out of your mind. There is someone here, right now, who is actually interested in you.*

Catrina complimented his work as she pulled the cloth off the basket.

"So what kind of pie do you have in there?"

"Dried apple."

"My favorite."

"Good. Now, eat up. Grandmother is expecting me to return right away." He had no trouble following her orders and the pie disappeared in minutes. Jacob licked the crumbly, greasy crust from his fingers and sighed. "That hit the spot." He tipped his hat and hurried back up the ladder. "Be sure to thank your grandmother for the eggs."

"*Ja*. I will put them in the springhouse for you and be on my way."

"*Danke*, Catrina."

Jacob noticed a lonely figure wander through the neighboring field as he picked up his hammer. Greta's full skirts whipped in the wind and a stray curl fell from her prayer *kappe*. He paused and studied the peaceful, confident gait. Jacob knew that his eyes lingered too long. He cleared his throat, grabbed a nail, and forced his gaze back to the roof.

A rich, sweet melody carried on the breeze. The song tickled Jacob's ears and tempted him to look back toward Greta. He recognized the tune and smiled; it was his favorite song from the *Ausbund*. His eyes followed the young woman as she picked her way across the muddy clearing.

Greta felt someone watching her. She glanced up, and scanned the tree line and the field before she noticed Jacob perched on his roof. Their eyes met. She stopped singing and looked away.

Jacob turned back to the broken shingles.

"Jacob!" Catrina's shrill voice carried across the yard.

"*Ja?*"

"I am leaving the eggs beside the path."

Jacob frowned and peered over the edge of the roof. Catrina stood with her hands on her hips as she studied the mud puddle that blocked her path to the springhouse. "If you leave the eggs there, the fox might run off with them. The springhouse is just a few feet farther down the path. Can't you put them away?"

Catrina shook her head. "You will have to do it when you come down. I cannot possibly get through that puddle." She set the basket down. "Do you not remember that I just cleaned my shoes?"

"*Ja.* I remember that you scraped the mud onto my front porch."

"What was that, Jacob? I did not quite hear you."

"Nothing, Catrina."

"Indeed." She raised her chin, smoothed her prayer *kappe*, and checked that each strand of hair remained in place. Catrina turned to leave, but a hen exploded from the brush beside the path. She gasped and jumped out of the way. A flash of orange shot out of the woods and lunged toward the panicked bird.

"Catrina! The fox! Stop him!" Jacob scrambled across the roof to save his last hen.

Catrina froze in place, pressed her hands against her cheeks, and watched the fox chase the terrified bird.

"Stop that fox!" Jacob shouted again.

"Oh! I could not possibly! It looks as if it might bite. And the mud, Jacob. THE MUD!"

Jacob felt a surge of frustration as he stumbled over the top of the ladder. He knew that he could not get there in time. *And she is standing right there!*

"I will save it!" Greta shouted from the edge of Widow Yoder's field. "I can get there!"

Greta took off as fast as her feet could fly. She waved her hands and shouted as she sloshed though mud and jumped across narrow streams of rain runoff. She tumbled over the fence and kept hollering, "Get out of here! Go!" The fox ignored Greta's shouts until she reached Jacob's yard. Then the animal's dark eyes cut to her. He took off like an arrow and disappeared into the brush.

Greta scooped up the hen and gave her a quick once-over. The bird's beady eyes flashed with indignation. "A little worse for wear, but she will make it." Greta let the hen go and it raced for the safety of the chicken coop.

Jacob reached the scene of the crime a few seconds later. "Thank you, Greta. You saved my breakfast."

Greta shrugged and brushed a chicken feather from her apron. "It is nothing. It is what neighbors do."

Jacob shook his head. "You were fantastic. You came out of nowhere and—"

"Jacob!" Catrina waved to Jacob from the dry ground above the springhouse. "Won't you give me a hand?"

He turned around. "*Ja.* Give me a second." Jacob turned back to Greta, but she was already headed away. He watched her trudge through the mud and noticed the dirty water that darkened her skirts all the way up to her knees. Yet she did not complain or ask for thanks.

"Jacob! Please come!"

Jacob sighed and returned his attention to Catrina. She waited on the high ground with her skirts hitched up above the mud.

"How can I help you, Catrina?"

"I need you to escort me to the main path."

"You managed to make it down from the path. Can you not make it back?"

"That was before a wild animal attacked me."

"That fox was not after you, Catrina. He just wanted a nice chicken dinner."

"Well, between the wild beasts and the mud, I dare not move." She extended a soft, pale arm. "Take my hand. I feel as if I might faint if you do not lead me out of here."

Jacob stole a glance over his shoulder. Greta looked small in the distance as she strode through the wild grasses with her head held high. He thought he heard a faint song that carried on the breeze. The familiar tune stirred something deep within him.

"Jacob." Catrina wiggled the fingers of her outstretched hand. "I am waiting."

Jacob looked back to her. "*Ja, ja.* I am coming to rescue you from your horrific peril."

Catrina poked out her bottom lip. "You must not make fun of me, Jacob."

"No. I apologize." He gave her a good-natured grin and took her arm. "All is well."

"That fox terrified me. Who knows what might have happened?"

"Nothing happened."

Catrina shrugged and lifted her chin. "Not this time, anyway."

"Foxes do not hurt people."

"Unless they are rabid."

"And this one was not."

Catrina smiled and reached for Jacob's hand. "Why are we quarreling? Would you not rather pass the time in pleasant conversation?" She stared into his eyes and batted her thick black lashes.

Jacob sighed. "Let's get you to dry ground."

Catrina's face lit up in a lovely grin. "You are a perfect gentleman, Jacob Miller."

Greta did not see Jacob again for several days. She occupied herself with an endless list of chores to take advantage of a warm spell. Linens had to be aired, meat salted and sent to the smokehouse, muddied clothing boiled and scrubbed clean. The harder she worked the less time she had to think about Jacob Miller and the beautiful young woman who clung to his arm.

Greta did steal glances toward his farm whenever she cut across the field to fetch water. But she never caught a glimpse of his strong, silent silhouette. *Where is he? He ought to be hunting or harvesting.*

She shrugged off his absence and reminded herself that he was of no concern to her. And, when she saw Catrina sashay across his front yard one afternoon with a basket in hand, Greta vowed to never look in the direction of his farm again.

When Greta returned to the cabin with two buckets of water, Abraham and Amos waited by the hearth.

"There is still a nip in the air," Amos remarked as he held his palms toward the crackling fire.

"*Ja.*" Greta set the buckets down and stretched her back. *I hope they have good news for me!* She told herself to be patient as she pulled off her cloak and hung it on the peg.

"It is a pleasant surprise to see you this morning. Would you stay for breakfast?"

"No." Mr. Riehl shook his head. "We just stopped by to let you know that the Fisher twins will come to live with you."

Greta's face brightened and she clasped her hands together. "*Wunderbar!*"

Ruth smiled as she stirred a bowl of corn cake batter.

"*Ja.*" Amos grinned. "We are sure that you will make a good foster mother."

"When will they move in?" Greta's thoughts flew in a thousand different directions as she thought of all the things that needed to be done.

The two elders looked at each other and shrugged. "This afternoon. If that suits you."

"This afternoon!" Greta pressed her hands to her cheeks. "So much to do in so little time."

"We can tell them to wait."

"No! Tell them to come as soon as they can!"

Greta raced around the cabin in a panic. Ruth

shook her head and smiled. "You are going to run yourself ragged."

Greta frowned and finished scrubbing the hearth. Then she moved to the window and pulled out the tacks that held the oilcloth in place.

"Sit and have a glass of water." Ruth ladled a drink from the water bucket. Greta shook her head. "The oilcloth needs to come down until the cold returns. It is warm enough to melt the grease in the cloth, and you know what a mess that can make."

Ruth clucked her tongue and set the pewter cup back on the shelf. "The children will love you, Greta, regardless of the state of the cabin."

Greta swallowed. "Do you really think so?"

"*Ja*. Of course. They already do."

Greta pulled out another tack. "They will have to eat burnt bread."

Ruth shrugged. "So you cannot bake. You have more important talents."

"Truly?"

"Truly. Just look at how much you love the children, and how well you have taught them. They are reading entire passages of the Bible now." Ruth pointed a finger at Greta. "None of them could do that a few weeks ago."

There was a knock at the door.

"They are here!" Greta smoothed her skirts and straightened her prayer *kappe*.

"Greta, there is no need to be so nervous. They have been coming here every day."

"I know. I just want everything to be perfect for them. And I know that I will never live up to that standard."

Ruth waved her hand. "Nobody's perfect."

Really? Catrina's flawless skin and immaculate white apron came to mind. She pushed the image away and opened the door.

"Greta!" Eliza and Peter flew into her arms. "Are we really going to stay with you?"

"*Ja.* You really are." As she held them close she realized that Ruth was right. They would not care if she burned the bread or overcooked the stew or wore a stained apron. All they wanted was to be loved. And she had plenty of that to give.

Chapter Twenty-One

The twins settled in right away. Within a few days it felt as if they had always been there—except that everything felt brighter, happier, and more exciting. For the first time in her life, Greta even looked forward to cooking because Peter and Eliza liked to help. Peter would watch her work with a serious expression on his small face, ready to hand her a pot or cooking utensil. Eliza would roll up her sleeves and kneel beside the fire. She would stir and taste, then give a solemn nod when Greta pulled the cauldron off the fire.

The first baking day the twins helped as always—and ended up covered with flour. Greta could only see their eyes as they stared up at her and blinked to keep out the white powder. She stared at the mayhem and almost scolded her messy charges, but could not help laughing instead.

"My goodness! How did this ever happen?!" Greta shooed them toward the door. "Outside, both of you. We will have to wash it off." She started with Peter, but when she tried to rinse the flour off of him with a bucket of water, the powder transformed into a sticky paste. Greta put her hands to her cheeks and groaned. "I should have thought of that." The harder she scrubbed the more the paste stuck to his skin.

"Yuck!" Peter ran away from the wash bucket. "Too gooey!"

"Peter, wait! Come back!" Greta took off after him with the wet washrag in hand. Eliza followed, a trail of flour billowing behind her. Peter dashed across the backyard and through the field. He laughed and shouted as he dodged mud puddles and chickens. Greta giggled as she leapt a ditch and raced after them. The wind whipped against her skirts and hair and made her feel alive.

Eliza whizzed past. "You can't catch me either!"

Greta grinned and picked up speed. "I will get you both!" Eliza cut to the right and Greta turned her head to watch where the girl went, but kept running forward, toward Peter. Greta whipped her head back around just in time to see Jacob's tall, muscular body blocking her path. She gasped and stumbled to a halt.

"Oh! Oh, my."

Jacob smiled indulgently. "I am not sure I should ask. . . ." Peter zipped by and screamed. His body was still covered in a sticky coating of flour. Jacob raised an eyebrow.

"Oh!" Greta covered her face with her hands, humiliated. When she moved them away she noticed that her palms were covered in flour. "Oh, no!"

Jacob's smile widened to a grin. "That's right, Greta, you are covered in flour too."

"I did not realize." She bit her lip and brushed her blouse. *I wish I could sink into the ground right now! Of all the people to see me like this!* Peter raced past again, still screaming. Eliza followed close behind, shrieking and laughing. "We are not always this strange. Honestly."

Jacob shrugged. "Looks like they are happy, anyway."

Greta nodded. "*Ja.*"

Jacob looked down at her, the grin on his face softening his hard features. They stood quietly for a moment, unsure of what to say. Jacob broke the silence with a loud, sickly cough.

Greta frowned. "That sounds bad. Are you all right?"

"I will be fine. Been a little under the weather is all."

"I noticed that you have not been out for the hunt or the harvest."

"You noticed that, huh?"

"*Ja.* I mean, no. I mean, not that I was watching your farm or anything. I just happened to see, or not see, when I got water . . ." Greta cleared her throat and adjusted her prayer *kappe.* She could feel her cheeks turning red. Jacob watched with an amused expression on his face.

"I have gotten some of it done. Not as much as I'd like, but there is still time yet."

"I did not know that you were ill. I would have offered to help. Especially after all that you did for us when I sprained my ankle."

"It was nothing." He rubbed the back of his neck and looked away. "Anyway, Catrina came by with food."

"*Ja.* I noticed that, too." Greta gasped. "I mean,

not that I was watching." She shook her head. "Like I said. I just noticed that . . . Never mind."

"Jacob!" Catrina's shrill voice carried across Jacob's backyard.

"Sounds like her grandmother has sent me another basket of food." He turned around and gave the beautiful young woman a polite nod.

"Oh. Well. How nice of her." Greta's stomach sank. She remembered her unkempt appearance and tried to smooth out her skirts. The motion spread the flour onto more of the fabric.

"Don't worry, Greta, a little flour never hurt anyone."

Greta smiled. "No, I suppose not."

Catrina waved dramatically and held up the basket. "Jacob, you should be resting. I have your supper." She raised the hem of her skirts to avoid the mud and carefully picked her way toward them. "You must be feeling better, *ja*?" She glanced at Greta dismissively, then did a double take. "My goodness, whatever happened to you?"

Greta shrugged and gave a half smile. "Just enjoying baking day."

"Hmmm. Yes. Well, I am sure you are." Catrina put her arm in Jacob's. "You ought to get out of the cold air, Jacob. It is not good for your recovery."

The twins noticed that Greta had stopped chasing them and circled back to the adults. Peter whooped and careened into Greta. She hugged the boy despite the sticky paste covering his body. "I told you that I would catch you!"

"You did not catch me!" Peter protested. "*I* caught *you*!"

Jacob's heart warmed as he watched Greta laugh

and pull the child closer. He leaned forward and tousled Peter's hair. The little boy turned to hug him and Catrina, but she shrank back. "No! You are all gooey! What is that? What have you done to yourself?"

Greta laughed and pulled Peter back into her arms. "It is just flour and water."

Catrina wrinkled her nose and tried to catch Jacob's eye, but his gaze stayed on Greta. Catrina tugged at his arm. "Come, Jacob. There is an unhealthy chill in the air."

The next morning Greta did not see Jacob working outside when she went to fetch water. She shielded her eyes from the sun with the edge of her hand and scanned the fields. Greta wondered if his health had taken a turn for the worse. She frowned, slid the yoke from her shoulders, and cut across the field to Jacob's land.

"Jacob? Are you about?" She marched to the cabin and knocked hard on the stout oak door. "Hello? Jacob?" He responded with an explosive cough. She knocked again. "Jacob?"

"Come in."

She pushed open the door and saw Jacob crouched by the hearth. His eyes looked glassy and his skin was slick with sweat.

"Jacob! You are terribly unwell!"

"*Ja.*" He broke into another coughing fit.

"You must lie down. Let me tend the fire."

"I am so cold." He shivered and leaned closer to the flames. Greta rushed to him and placed her palm on his forehead. She gasped and jerked her hand away. "You are burning up!" Greta grabbed a quilt off the foot of his bedstead and draped the heavy fabric over his shoulders. "There. That will help." She pulled the quilt tight around his chin, then stooped to pick up a log. She dropped it on the flames and pulled her hand back to avoid the shower of sparks that flew upward from the coals.

"So cold."

Greta wondered if Jacob even realized that she was there. "It will be warmer soon." She picked up the poker and jabbed the log until the flames licked against the edge of the hearth. Greta set the poker aside and wiped her forehead. *What now?*

A knock on the door interrupted her question.

"*Ja.* Come in."

The door creaked open and Catrina swept into the room, followed by her grandmother. The young woman looked surprised. "Oh. Greta. Whatever are you doing here?"

"I came to check on Jacob. Seems that he has taken a turn for the worse."

Catrina's grandmother clucked her tongue and felt Jacob's forehead. "*Ja.* He is burning up." She observed him for a moment and nodded. "He is delirious, I imagine."

Catrina smoothed her prayer *kappe* and watched her grandmother dip a rag in the water bucket. "We were afraid of this." Mrs. Witmer wrung out the rag and pressed it to Jacob's forehead.

"He should not have been outside yesterday." Catrina gave Greta a sharp look. "You should not have kept him out there. When I got there I insisted that he go back inside right away."

"I did not even know that he was ill."

Catrina raised an eyebrow. "No. You wouldn't have, would you?"

Greta opened her mouth and then closed it again. She did not know how to respond.

"My grandmother and I have been taking care of Jacob all week. You have not been here."

"I have not been here because . . . because . . ."

"Because why?"

"Because you and he . . . I thought . . ."

"*Ja.* Jacob has shown his intention to court me." Catrina frowned and looked away. "I am sorry that I snapped at you. It is just that Jacob and I have grown close these last weeks and I cannot bear to see him ailing."

"*Ja.* Of course."

Greta's eyes stung. Catrina had taken Greta's place in Jacob's life completely. She felt pushed aside and unwanted. Greta glanced at Frena Witmer to see if she had heard the conversation. The elderly woman was too busy sponging Jacob's forehead to pay attention and Greta felt relieved that her humiliation went unnoticed.

Catrina turned her back on Greta and flounced to the hearth. "You poor dear." She placed a soft hand on his brow. "It's all right. I am here now." Greta studied the scene with a sinking heart. *There is no place for me here.* She backed out of the room, rushed out the door, and hurried across the clearing with her heart pounding in her ears.

Eliza met Greta at the cabin door. "Where is the water? I thought that you went to the creek."

Greta sighed. "Oh. The water. I forgot all about it."

Eliza gave her a quizzical look and then shrugged. "Don't worry. I will get it."

"I will come too!" Peter jumped up and bounded into the sunshine.

"I left the buckets and yoke in the clearing. You will see it."

Eliza nodded her head and chased after Peter. Greta took a deep breath and shut the door. She leaned her forehead against the rough oak door-frame and closed her eyes.

Ruth looked up from her spinning. "You are in quite a state, I see."

"It is that Catrina Witmer. She seems certain of a match." Greta clenched her teeth. "It is just so hard to watch."

Ruth raised her eyebrows. "She was at Jacob's farm again?"

"*Ja.* She's been there all week, apparently. He's been sick and I did not even know it. Catrina and her grandmother have been taking care of him."

Greta looked down. Her stomach churned. "I have no place there."

"Humph!" Ruth frowned as she spun the drop spindle. "You have been so intimidated by Catrina that you tucked your tail and ran. You practically pushed her right into his arms."

"That is a terrible overstatement!"

"Is it?"

Greta paused. She closed her eyes and rubbed her temples. "All right. I admit it. But you cannot blame me, Ruth. Just look at her!"

The drop spindle kept twirling with a soft whir in Ruth's hands. "Do you really believe that, Greta? As a Plain woman, do you really place greater worth on beauty than character?"

"I do value character over looks." Greta looked down. "Well, I do in theory, anyway." She glanced back up at Ruth with a pleading expression. "But when I have to face it in real life, that is a different story. I feel so inadequate next to her. And it is not just her looks. She is always so well put together; nothing is ever stained or wrinkled. And she can bake a perfect cake. Everything she does is perfect." Greta threw up her hands. "Meanwhile, everything that I bake burns, and I run around with flour all over my face and—"

Ruth put up a hand. "That is quite enough. We all have our insecurities, but we do not have to let them win. You need to hold your head up and know that *der Herr* made you to be exactly who He wants you to be."

"Do you really think that Jacob likes me for who I am?"

"*Ja.* I have told you that from the first day you met him."

Greta frowned. "But what about Catrina?"

"I feel sorry for Catrina, really."

Greta looked surprised. "You do?"

"Of course. She must be terribly insecure. Why else would she rely on her beauty the way she does? Why else would she show off her baking skills and put so much effort into her appearance?"

"Catrina, insecure? Why on earth would *she* be insecure?"

Ruth shrugged. "Who knows? We all have our own problems to deal with. Nobody is perfect—no matter how much it seems otherwise."

Greta laughed. "She did not seem insecure to me

today, when she practically kicked me out of Jacob's cabin! She made it clear that *she* was taking care of him and that I was not needed."

Ruth shrugged. "Whose cabin is it?"

"Jacob's, of course."

Ruth grinned. "Then Catrina has no say in the matter."

"No." Greta spread out her hands in a gesture of helplessness. "But—"

Ruth shook her head. "No buts about it. She's got no claim on Jacob. They are not engaged." She gave Greta a hard stare. "Not yet anyway."

Greta narrowed her eyes. "No, not yet."

Ruth shrugged and turned the drop spindle. "Although it seems only a matter of time, *ja?*"

Greta felt intimidated and conflicted. But truth weighed down her heart like a stone. She knew that she had given up on the love she had for Jacob. *Only a matter of time? What have I done?* She remembered the way her heart leapt when Jacob gazed down at her with a sly twinkle in his eyes. She remembered the way her breath caught in her throat when he scooped her up in his strong, muscular arms and carried her to safety. She remembered the warm, familiar joy she felt when he teased her.

Something sparked deep within her and rose to the surface. Greta sat up straighter. She knew that she wasn't willing to give up on Jacob. Not yet. Not ever. She took a deep breath and let it out. A confident smile spread across her face. "'Tis only a matter of time—unless someone helps Jacob realize that he is on the wrong path."

Ruth smiled. "Might that someone be you?"

Greta squared her shoulders. "*Ja.* Naturally."

"Naturally."

"The only question is how."

"Perhaps you should tell Catrina that you held a claim to his heart before she arrived."

"No." Greta's face tightened. "I cannot. The humiliation would be too great if he chooses her. And besides, I only want Jacob to choose me if he truly loves me. If he prefers Catrina, then he should be free to choose her. I want him to make the decision. I don't want to feel that he settled for second best because Catrina removed herself from the competition."

"Then, it is simple. If you believe that you are meant to be with Jacob Miller, let him know it. He cannot choose you if he does not know that you want to be chosen."

"Declare my affection for him? Why Ruth, you push the boundaries of propriety!" Greta shook her head so hard that a lock of hair escaped her prayer *kappe.* "It would be unseemly. I have already told you that."

"Then don't communicate your feelings with words. Show him. Try talking to him again. Let him get to know you better. Do not run away every time Catrina tries to shoo you away."

"*Ja.* That is the way to reach him, surely. I will show him that I care. And then, if he chooses her over me—after I show him that I have affection for him— that is *his* fault."

Chapter Twenty-Two

Greta marched right back to Jacob's cabin with a new sense of purpose. She strode between the towering pines and into his clearing with her head held high. Greta knocked on the door and took a deep breath. *I will not let Catrina intimidate me this time!*

The flawless young woman opened the door, looked surprised, then frowned. "Greta, dear. I am so sorry, but Jacob needs his rest. This really is not a good time."

"Well, I see that you are here."

"Yes, well, Grandmother and I are nursing Jacob back to health."

"Uh-huh. So am I."

"There really is not anything that you can do."

"Oh, I am sure that there is." Greta pushed her way past Catrina. She rolled up her sleeves and surveyed the room. "Now, where to start . . ."

"You can fetch me a bucket of water." Frena Witmer motioned toward the empty bucket. Greta sighed. She had not planned to haul water from the creek. She had imagined sitting by Jacob's bedside and sponging his forehead as he held her hand. But she pushed the thought aside. *I am not above doing the small things.*

"*Ja.* I can do that."

Catrina smiled. "How thoughtful of you."

Greta nodded and grabbed the bucket. She refused to let Catrina get under her skin.

When Greta returned, Frena Witmer sat by Jacob's bedstead with a cold compress in her hand. He shivered and the rough bedstead, which was built directly into the log wall, creaked from his weight. Catrina lounged by the hearth. She yawned and stirred the cauldron, then set the spoon down and leaned back. Greta slid past her beautiful rival to Jacob's bedside. "Let me give you a break." Frena looked up and smiled. "*Ja.*" She stood up and stretched her back. "His fever is coming down, I think. Keep refreshing the compress with cool water."

"*Ja.*"

Catrina snapped into action when she saw Greta take her grandmother's place. "Oh, Greta. You simply must help me." She rushed to Jacob's bedside and slid onto the narrow bench before Greta could. "Go taste the stew, won't you? Tell me if it needs more seasoning." Greta clenched her jaw. She counted to ten. "*Ja.* I can do that." Catrina smiled and readjusted the compress on Jacob's forehead.

Greta and Frena both settled down by the fire. The old woman stoked the coals every now and then as the minutes passed in awkward silence. Greta glanced over at Jacob, and Catrina made a show of reapplying the cold compress to his forehead. Greta frowned and stirred the cauldron. *Perhaps what Ruth said is true. Why would Catrina need to make a show of her efforts unless she feels insecure of herself?*

She sat and waited until she could not take it anymore. *I need to be useful.* Greta stood up and took a deep breath. *I can find something helpful to do, no matter how much Catrina wants to shut me out!*

"Going home, dear?"

"No. I have an idea."

"An idea?" Catrina cocked her head. "What idea?"

"I think that I have seen wild yarrow near here. I am going to see if I can find it again."

Catrina giggled. "Why would you bring Jacob flowers?"

"Yarrow is good medicine," Frena remarked in an authoritative tone. "We can make it into a tea that will help sweat the fever out."

Catrina stopped giggling. She pursed her lips and adjusted her prayer *kappe*. Greta did not look her way. Instead, she nodded at Frena. "*Ja.* I will be back soon."

Greta strode across the yard with a sense of purpose. She searched the edge of the clearing where the wild grasses grew in a tangled mass. No yarrow. Greta wandered into the Yoder field and scanned the ground. No yarrow. She passed Rose and patted the cow's shoulder. The animal studied Greta with warm black eyes as she chewed her cud.

"Where does the yarrow grow, Rose? You eat it, don't you?" Rose bellowed and twitched her tail. Greta sighed. "I know it is late in the season, but surely some leaves survive still." She worked her way through the settlement's clearings and trails, looking everywhere that the wild herb might grow. She had circled all the way back to Jacob's land when she caught sight of feathery, fernlike leaves across the creek from his farm.

"Found it!" She put her hands on her hips and surveyed the landscape. "I can make it across. I am sure of it." She bit her lip and stepped onto a stone, then leapt onto a second rock. She held out her arms to steady herself, jumped to the next rock, and onto the soft mud of the riverbank. Greta grinned and rushed to a knee-deep patch of yarrow. She yanked handfuls of the healing herb from the wet earth and tucked them into her apron. *I knew I could be useful!* When the cloth could hold no more, Greta stood up, wiped the dirt from her fingers, and hurried back to Jacob's cabin.

Frena beamed when Greta opened her apron and shook the yarrow onto the table. "*Wunderbar!* I wondered if you would find any this late in the season." The elderly woman reached for the kettle. "I will get the water boiling." Greta nodded and sat down. She picked through the weeds and separated the delicate, wispy leaves from their stems. Catrina watched from Jacob's bedside. "I did not know those ugly little plants were good for anything."

Greta shrugged. "You cannot judge a book by its cover."

Catrina frowned and turned back to Jacob. She checked his forehead and rewet the compress as Greta dropped the leaves into the cauldron to steep. *I hope this helps. It has to!* She glanced at Jacob. He tossed and turned beneath the quilt.

Greta waited until the water turned yellow, poured the concoction into Jacob's pewter cup, and brought it to his bedside. Catrina looked up and smiled sweetly. "I can give it to him."

"*Danke,* but I will take care of it. I am sure that you could use the break."

Catrina pursed her lips and did not move from the bench. She looked confused by Greta's presence. Greta sighed and knelt by the bedstead. She studied Jacob's ashen face and then lifted his head.

"Wake up, Jacob. You must drink this."

Jacob twitched and mumbled. Greta cringed when she felt his skin. "You are much too hot." She lifted his head higher. "Really, you must drink some of this. It will sweat out the fever."

Jacob mumbled incoherently. Greta pressed the cup to his lips until he took a sip. "Bitter." Jacob's eyes stayed closed but he shook his head. "Bitter."

"Shhhh. Just take a few sips."

He shook his head again. "Bitter."

Greta frowned and pulled the cup away. "He will not drink it." She thought for a moment and then snapped her fingers. "Catrina, do you have any more sugar?"

"There are just a few spoonfuls left."

"*Wunderbar*! Please, go and fetch it. If we sweeten the tea, then Jacob might drink it."

"Oh, I don't know, Greta. It is almost gone. I was saving it . . . Can you not get him to drink it as it is?"

"Catrina! This is much more important than a cake or a pie!"

"She is right, Catrina." Frena shot her granddaughter a warning look. "Go on, now."

Catrina forced a smile. "*Ja.* I will take care of it."

Greta slid onto the bench as soon as her rival vacated it. She smoothed Jacob's hair from his forehead and watched the gentle rise and fall of his chest. She took in his strong jaw and Roman nose and felt her heart warm as she realized how familiar his features were. She thought about the way his eyes sparkled when he laughed and hardened when he was irritated. She remembered the way he ran his fingers through his hair when he was nervous, and the little half smile he flashed when he knew that he had gotten the better of her.

"Oh, Jacob." She smoothed his hair again. "Won't you wake up?" She sighed and ran the back of her fingers across his cheek. "Please be okay." Jacob's eyelids fluttered and opened. He stared up with glazed eyes. "Jacob!" Greta's voice came out in a ragged whisper. His arm reached up to her. She grabbed his hand with both of hers and squeezed. "You are going to be all right."

"Greta? Is that you?"

"*Ja*, it is me." She felt tears form as Jacob stared into her eyes.

"I have been looking for you."

"I have been here."

"No. I have not been able to find you. I have been looking." Jacob frowned. A look of confusion passed over his face. "Greta? Greta, where are you?"

"Shhhh. Jacob. It is the fever talking. I am right here."

"Greta? Where are you? I cannot find you."

"Shhhh." She pulled his hand to her cheek and held it there. His rough skin burned against her soft face. "I am here." She dropped her voice so that Frena could not hear. "I will always be here." She kept his hand pressed against her cheek and leaned closer. "I promise you, Jacob. I will always be here."

The front door opened and a ray of sunlight fell across the dirt floor. Catrina flounced into the cabin and held up a packet of sugar with a victorious expression on her face. Greta cleared her throat and lowered Jacob's hand. A cold draft blew in from the open door and she tucked the quilt around Jacob's shoulders.

Catrina poured the precious white granules into Jacob's pewter cup, stirred the mixture, and brushed Greta aside.

"Jacob, dear. Have a drink." He fumbled at the cup as Catrina held it awkwardly to his lips. Catrina pouted and readjusted the cup. "This is not working. He does not even know that we are here. He is not going to drink this."

"Let me try."

Catrina shrugged and handed her the cup. "You will not be able to do any better." Greta whispered into Jacob's ear and then ran the back of her hand across his cheek. She remembered the song from the *Ausbund* that Jacob liked to hum as he worked and she began to sing it in a low, soft voice. The smell of woodsmoke and pine gave the room a familiar comfort as Greta's song drifted across Jacob's sickbed. Catrina watched through confused eyes, her smooth forehead creased.

Greta leaned closer to Jacob. *This will work. I know that I can reach him.* His eyelids fluttered, then opened. A muddled smile spread across his pale face. "Greta." He reached for her. "Greta."

"Jacob." She held on to his warm, rough hand for a minute and then reached for the cup. "I need you to drink this. It will make you feel better." She held the cup to his lips and he took a long, slow sip. "Good. Very good." Greta watched his Adam's apple bob and then pressed the cup against his lips again.

"Take another sip." Jacob swallowed once more and she smiled. "You will feel better soon. I am sure of it."

Catrina hovered behind the bench and Greta could feel the woman's blue eyes burning into the back of her head. "How did you do that?" Her voice sounded small and unsure.

Greta shrugged. "It was nothing."

"Nothing?"

Greta recognized a fragile, uncertain look in Catrina's expression. *She cannot understand how someone like me can do anything better than her.* Greta looked down. *I should remember her feelings.*

"Now that he is awake, it is a good time to try and get some of that stew in him."

"*Ja!* That would be good." Catrina's signature smile returned. "I will take care of it." She glanced toward the hearth. "Grandmother, the stew is ready, *ja?*" Mrs. Witmer nodded, dipped the big wooden spoon in the cauldron, and ladled out a serving of broth. "*Ja.* Come and get it." Greta lingered over Jacob while Catrina fetched the bowl. Greta touched his forehead again and gazed at his closed eyes. She remembered how those eyes had opened and looked for her as he called her name.

Greta heard Catrina walk away from the hearth and she slipped off the bench. *I will not fight her for a place by Jacob's sickbed. I have no more claim on him than she does—not yet, anyway! I can help him in other ways.* Greta grabbed her cloak and wrapped the rough wool around her slim shoulders. She escaped out the door and wandered into the overgrown front yard. *Jacob has not been able to tend to his chores. This kitchen garden needs harvesting.* She stood with her hands on her hips and surveyed the patch of dirt that Rose had trampled. *I can take care of this.* She nodded and felt a new sense of purpose. "I know that Catrina will not compete over that job!" Greta laughed, shook her head, and headed to the barn in search of a trowel and wooden bucket.

Greta knelt in the dirt and worked to loosen the stubborn soil with the sharp edge of the trowel, then tossed carrots into the bucket. She liked the satisfying plunk that each one made as it hit the wood. She plucked peas and dropped the pods atop the carrots. When she looked up, the sun hovered low in the sky and shadows fell across the yard with long, cold fingers. She wiped her forehead and stretched her back. "Almost finished getting the peas in." Her body shivered as the sun disappeared below the tree line and a chill overtook the air.

The door to the cabin opened and Catrina stepped onto the porch. "Oh! I did not know that you were still here."

"I thought I could save the last of the vegetables. Jacob has been too ill to harvest his kitchen garden."

"Oh. I . . . I would not have thought of that."

Greta waited for Catrina to criticize her dirt-stained apron and loose strands of hair. She tucked a stray curl under her prayer *kappe* and rose from her knees. Catrina stood in silence and Greta wished that she knew what the woman was thinking.

"How is he?"

"Not well. Grandmother is sending me for more sugar. She said that he needs to drink more of your yarrow tea."

"You did not bring all of the sugar here before?"

"No, I thought . . ." Catrina's face tightened. "I thought that I could save a little bit. For after he wakes up. Then he would appreciate it more." She spread out her hands in a helpless gesture. "He won't even remember this. But if I baked a pie for him after he gets better . . ."

"Then he would know to appreciate it and you would get credit for it. He would like you for it."

Catrina frowned and smoothed her skirts. "I am not sure that is quite what I meant."

"I think it is." Greta shrugged. "The way to a man's heart is through his stomach, after all."

Catrina smiled and looked away. *"Ja."*

Greta started for the cabin door. "I will start another batch of tea."

Catrina's smile disappeared and she rushed to follow Greta inside. "I will ask Grandmother to go for the sugar. I don't think that I can bear to leave him."

Greta looked away. *Is it that she cannot bear to leave him, or is it that she cannot bear to leave him with me? Could she feel threatened by me? Is that possible?*

The bitter scent of yarrow mingled with woodsmoke and burned her nostrils as she entered the cabin.

"Grandmother, I just cannot bear to leave Jacob!" Catrina cut a sidelong glance at Greta and then looked back at the elderly woman. "Will you please fetch the sugar for me? Please?" Catrina clasped her hands together in an exaggerated gesture of supplication. Frena sighed and pushed herself up from the hearth. "I suppose I could use the fresh air." She patted her forehead. "It is getting mighty hot by the fire."

"Oh, thank you, Grandmother! I will take care of Jacob until you return." Catrina rushed to the empty bench by Jacob's bedstead while Greta put another log on the fire.

"Greta?"

"*Ja?*" She did not look up from her work.

"I do not know what to do for him."

"It is all right." Greta stopped and turned to Catrina. She forced a supportive smile. "Just keep the compress cool and keep an eye on his fever."

Catrina frowned. "I have never made yarrow tea before. And I would never have thought to harvest a garden. How do you think of these things?"

Greta shrugged. "It is nothing, really. I just want to help and those are two things that I know how to do."

"I know how to bake. That is what I do best. But that does not help in a situation like this. I feel so helpless."

Greta poured water into the wash bucket. The liquid sloshed and splattered her apron. "Go ahead and put a fresh compress on his forehead while I rinse off this dirt. That will help him." Greta plunged her hands into the cold water and scrubbed beneath her nails.

"Oh! Greta! He is terribly hot!" Catrina pulled her hand away from Jacob's forehead as if she had been burned. Her mouth fell open. Greta leapt up from the hearth so fast that she knocked over the bucket. She caught her balance and dried her hands on her apron as she raced to Jacob's bedside. Greta laid a cool palm across his forehead. She nodded. "This is serious. His fever is much too high. We have to get it down." Jacob thrashed beneath the quilt and murmured words that she could not understand.

"What do we do?" Catrina turned to Greta with wide eyes. "What do we do?"

Greta took a deep breath. "Vinegar. And prayer. Keep praying for him." Greta rushed to the corner of the cabin where Jacob stored dried herbs and cooking supplies. She picked through the jugs, popped off a cork, and sniffed. "There! I knew he would have some." She grabbed the earthen jug, hurried back to Jacob, and snatched the compress from his forehead. Greta poured vinegar over the rag and shoved it back into Catrina's hand. "Wrap his feet in this. It will draw the fever down from his brain."

Catrina drew back the quilt and bound his feet in vinegar while Greta snatched the water bucket from the hearth. She ran back to the bedstead and sloshed water across Jacob's face and chest. Catrina gasped and tried to pull the quilt back over him. "He will catch cold!"

Greta shook her head. "No. Let the water evaporate. It will cool him."

Catrina hovered by the bedstead and wrung her hands. "I do not know what to do."

"It will be all right. We are doing everything that can be done." Greta's hands moved with strength and purpose as she sponged his skin with cool water. Catrina bit her lip and stood in silence. Greta began to sing Jacob's favorite hymn from the *Ausbund*, and the room filled with warmth. Jacob quit thrashing and his lips stopped moving. His hands loosened their sweaty grip on the quilt and he drifted into a peaceful sleep.

Greta felt his forehead again and let out a long, deep breath. "He is out of danger."

Catrina began to cry.

"Don't cry now! The danger is over."

Catrina dabbed at her big blue eyes and sniffled.

"It is just that I could not help. I did not know what to do. But you were so helpful! It came so naturally to you!" Catrina blew her nose into her handkerchief. "I do not understand how you did that."

"We all have different gifts, Catrina. There are plenty of things that you can do that I cannot."

Catrina smiled and raised her head a fraction. "Well, that *is* true." She ran her fingers along the edge of her prayer *kappe* and made sure that every tendril of hair was in place. "There *are* a lot of things that Jacob appreciates about me. I was sure that he was about to propose before he got sick."

Chapter Twenty-Three

The days and nights blurred together as Greta, Catrina, and Frena nursed Jacob back to health. Greta warned Ruth to keep the twins away from the fever and the old woman watched over them until their foster mother could return. Catrina continued to coax Greta away from Jacob's bedside. But her manner changed. She tried to imitate Greta's gentle bedside demeanor and soft singing. Jacob did not respond to Catrina's voice or touch. He remained locked in his own fevered world.

Greta steeped the last of the yarrow and watched Catrina fumble with the cold compress. Greta's fingers ached to smooth Jacob's brow. She needed to feel his quiet strength and hear the soft whisper of his breath.

"I cannot do this anymore." Catrina dropped the rag into the bowl of water and stood up. "I give up. I may as well not even be here. He does not know any better." She shook her head. "It does not do any good to sit here."

Greta darted to the bench. "Then I will take a turn."

Catrina shrugged and wandered to the hearth. She dropped onto the three-legged stool and stared into the fire. "He will not notice if you are here or not."

Greta smiled. "I know that it does good to be here. Whether he remembers or not, I know that he can feel my presence beside him."

Catrina frowned and looked back at Greta. "Oh." She studied Greta's placid expression. "But how do you know that?"

"I just *know*." Greta settled beside Jacob, dipped the cold compress in the bowl of water, and wrung it out. She returned the freshened cloth to his forehead and began to hum as she studied the rise and fall of his chest. She pressed her hand against his cheek and the coolness of his skin shocked her. "His fever has broken." She let out a long, hard sigh. "He is going to be all right."

Catrina bolted up from the three-legged stool.

Jacob's eyelids fluttered open. "Greta?"

"Yes." She placed her hand on his. "I am here." He struggled to sit up. "Shhh. Do not try and get up. You need to rest."

"I have been sick, haven't I?"

"*Ja.* Very sick. For three days now."

"And you have been here, by my side the whole time." He smiled weakly. "I remember hearing you sing. That is all that I can remember. Feeling so cold and confused and then hearing you sing. I thought that you were an angel."

Greta looked down and shook her head. "It was only me, Jacob." He reached up and touched her face, as if he did not believe that she was real. Their eyes met and locked on one another. Greta felt time stand still. Nothing existed but the intensity of his dark brown eyes.

Until Catrina flounced across the room. "Jacob! I was here too. Don't you remember?" She giggled and batted her eyelashes. "Of course you do!"

Jacob furrowed his brow. He looked over to Catrina and nodded politely. "*Ja.* Of course." His eyes moved back to Greta.

"We were so worried about you!" Catrina leaned forward to check his fever in a showy gesture. Greta sighed and stood up. "I will get you some stew. I am sure that you are hungry." Jacob watched Greta walk to the cauldron and felt startled by her beauty. *Was she always this graceful and self-assured?* He pulled his eyes away from Greta as Catrina adjusted his pillows. Jacob stared at the woman's perfect features, but his heart did not jump. His pulse did not quicken. He did not feel the joyful appreciation that filled him when he sensed the warmth that glowed from beneath Greta's Plain attire.

"I'm sorry. I don't remember you being here."

Catrina looked hurt. "I was. I made the stew. And I sat right here. For a long time."

"You were here alongside Greta?"

Catrina shrugged. "*Ja.* I was here more than she was, truth be told. She left a lot. She spent an entire day looking for weeds. And digging around outside."

"Weeds?"

Catrina shrugged again. "Yarrow."

Jacob cut his eyes back to Greta. He watched her ladle a bowlful of stew and pour fresh water into his pewter cup. "Yarrow is not easy to find this time of year. That took some work."

Catrina nodded. "*Ja.* Greta came back muddy as a

piglet." She giggled into her hand, but Jacob's stern look cut her laughter short. She cleared her throat and looked away. "I sat here with you. Do you not remember?"

"No. All I remember is hearing songs from the *Ausbund*. And the smell of vinegar. I do remember that."

Catrina wrinkled her nose. "Oh, that was Greta. She wrapped your feet in vinegar. She said something about drawing the fever down." She shook her head. "I hate the smell of vinegar, don't you?"

"Vinegar is good medicine. So is yarrow." He turned his head toward Greta. "You are very handy, Greta."

Greta blushed and carried the bowl of stew to his bedside. "It was nothing."

"You are wrong about that. I have you to thank for my recovery."

Greta shook her head. "No. I just did what anyone would do."

Jacob smiled. "It sounds as if you have worked very hard these three days."

Greta blushed again. "Catrina's grandmother stayed here as well. She just left to take care of some chores at her own cabin. She will be back soon."

Catrina's brow crinkled. "I was here too, you know."

"*Ja.*" But Jacob kept his eyes on Greta as he answered Catrina.

"I . . . I . . ." Catrina stumbled over her words while she tried to think of what she had done for Jacob during his illness. "I helped make the stew. And I sat here. Jacob, are you listening to me? I just said that I sat here, on this bench."

Jacob moved his eyes to Catrina and studied her pouty expression. *She knows how to sit. That I have noticed.* Catrina raised her chin and grabbed the bowl of stew from Greta's hands. "Thank you, dear. I will help him with this. After all, I did make it." Greta clenched her jaw. She knew that Catrina had only chopped a couple of carrots and watched her grandmother do the rest.

"I don't need any help." Jacob grimaced and shook his head. "Just hand me the bowl." Greta tried to help him up, but Catrina took over that job too. Greta stepped back and counted to ten. She knew that she would lose her temper if she stayed in the same room with Catrina Witmer for one more second.

Greta slipped out of the cabin and into the sunlight. She breathed in the brisk air and rolled up her sleeves. *I best fetch more water and carry in wood before nightfall.* She tried not to think of the beautiful young woman inside the cabin with Jacob. *She acts as if she nursed him through the sickness all by herself.* Greta sighed. *Well, I did not do it for thanks.*

Greta thought about the way Jacob's eyes locked on hers when he awoke. Her heart quickened at the memory and a soft smile formed on her lips. *He felt what I felt, I am sure of it. He does remember.* The memory stayed with her as she kneeled in the damp earth by the river and plunged the bucket into the sparkling water. As she picked her way back through the muddy field, she wondered what Catrina thought of Jacob's reaction. *I don't think she knows how to take it. I am sure that she has always been favored over other women.*

I need to be thoughtful of her feelings. If Jacob really did feel a connection with me, Catrina is bound to be hurt.

When she reached the cabin, the shutters were closed against the chill and she imagined the warm glow of firelight that flickered behind the wooden slats. *I cannot stay away any longer. I have to find a way to sit with Jacob without creating conflict with Catrina. But, I cannot just give up on Jacob! Especially now that he has given me hope.* Greta took a deep breath and opened the rough oak door.

Jacob's expression softened when he saw Greta in the threshold, her silhouette backlit by the setting sun. The golden rays bathed her in light like a Renaissance painting. He drank in her red cheeks, sparkling green eyes, and gentle smile. "Greta." His voice sounded hoarse and tired, but Greta thought she could sense the eagerness in his tone as he spoke her name.

"Jacob."

Catrina's face fell as Greta strode to Jacob's bedside. "Oh, Greta! Look at you. Really, dear. You must change into a clean apron. What on earth have you been doing?"

Greta looked down and noticed the mud stains on her skirts and the wood chips clinging to her bodice. She felt incompetent and unattractive beside Catrina's neat and careful appearance. Greta wanted to turn and run, but stood her ground and waited for Jacob's reaction as she tucked her curls back under her prayer *kappe*.

A tired half smile formed on his lips. "So tell me, what have you been up to out there?"

"I harvested your kitchen garden, carried the split

logs you left by the woodpile out back and stacked them by the door, and fetched enough water to see you through the night, should the fever return."

"Did you really?"

Greta shrugged. "It needed to be done."

Jacob's smile widened. Catrina watched with surprise as he reached up and wiped a smudge of dirt from Greta's cheek.

"You found yarrow, brought down my fever, and did my chores. And, I haven't forgotten that you saved my hen last week." He stared at her as if seeing her for the first time. The grin stayed on his face.

Catrina's expression of surprise turned to one of hurt. "I do not understand this. You only have eyes for her?" She stood up and shook her head. "This is not fair." Her lip trembled and she grabbed the rough log wall to steady herself. "I feel sick."

"Catrina." Jacob kept his voice low and even. "Catrina. That is enough."

"No. I feel sick." She stumbled away from the bedstead and collapsed onto the dirt floor. Greta gasped and rushed to her side. She felt Catrina's forehead and shook her head. "She is burning up, Jacob. She *is* sick."

Jacob pushed the quilt aside and tried to get up.

Greta put up a hand. "Don't you dare get out of that bed, Jacob Miller. You must rest." Greta bit her lip and felt Catrina's forehead again. "Is your horse still lame?"

"She is doing all right. As long as you don't push her too hard."

Greta nodded. "I am going to take Catrina home. Her grandparents can look after her."

"Can you manage?"

"Certainly."

Jacob smiled. "*Ja*. I can see that. I think that you could manage just about anything."

Greta laughed. "That is a far cry from your first impression of me, Jacob."

Jacob looked embarrassed and then returned her smile. "My first impression of you was wrong, Greta. Very, very wrong."

Greta helped Catrina through the threshold of the Witmer cabin. "You will be fine. Your grandmother will—" Greta stopped in midsentence. "Oh no." Frena Witmer crouched beside a low bedstead built into the wall of the cabin. Her husband twitched and mumbled as he lay huddled beneath a quilt. Frena felt the man's wrinkled forehead and looked up at the young woman with glassy eyes and a pale face.

Greta sighed. "I should have checked on you when you did not come back today."

The elderly woman shook her head. "You had your hands full with Jacob." She studied Catrina's ashen face. "My granddaughter has taken ill?"

"*Ja*." Greta guided Catrina to her pallet on the floor. "I am sorry."

"And Jacob?"

"Out of danger."

"Praise be."

Greta nodded, unrolled Catrina's bedding, and tucked the young woman beneath a colorful quilt. "You must rest, Frena. I will stay here to help. You go on and lie down."

Frena managed a weak smile. "*Danke*. But what about your own household? Are they still well?"

Greta nodded. "*Ja*. And Ruth will care for the twins until I return."

"You should all be fine as long as you stay out of the night air."

"Perhaps."

"Do promise me that you will not walk home after dark, when the vapors are about. You must stay here. The sun is setting." She shook her head. "Do not go back out."

"Do not worry, Frena. I will stay here and take care of you all."

The elderly woman broke into a coughing fit. She pointed a bony finger at the window and cleared her throat. "Latch the shutters. I took the oilcloth out last week during the warm spell and the night air can get in now."

Greta nodded and walked to the window. The tree line stood like a row of soldiers at the edge of the clearing. Beyond that, the sky bruised a deep purple as evening faded into night. Greta sighed as she closed the shutters against the shadows. She thought of Jacob, alone in the dark interior of his cabin, waiting for her to return. *Keep him well until I can get back to him, Lord. There are others who need me now.* Greta turned toward the sick family and took a deep breath. *Help me to help them. And please help me to do my best for Catrina—no matter how much she exasperates me!*

The hours crept by. Greta checked fevers, adjusted quilts, and offered sips of cool water. A storm rolled in and she arranged bowls across the dirt floor to catch the raindrops that leaked through the roof. Greta listened to the quiet ping of water hitting water until she dozed off by the hearth. She woke up cold, stoked the fire, and fell back asleep.

Catrina coughed and woke Greta up again. She rose from the fireside, felt the woman's forehead, and then checked on Georg and Frena.

"Greta?"

"*Ja.*" She walked back to Catrina's pallet.

"What are you doing here?"

"Making sure that you pull through this."

"You are here to take care of *me*?"

Greta shrugged. "Your grandparents, too. But they are doing all right. You are the one who causes me concern."

Catrina frowned. "I fear that I would not have done that for you."

Greta shrugged again. "I know."

Catrina's frown deepened. "That must be what Jacob sees in you."

"What?"

"Kindness." Catrina shook her head. "I have been trying to figure it out."

"Figure what out?"

"His feelings for you." Catrina broke into another coughing spell and Greta handed her a cup of water. Catrina took a few sips and handed it back. "I am getting the strangest idea that he prefers you."

Greta did not respond.

"I am beautiful. I know I am."

"*Ja.*" Greta sighed. "Everyone knows it."

"But he seemed so impressed by you when he woke up from his fever."

"Catrina, you have to see that there are more important qualities than a pretty face."

Catrina frowned.

"If you do not understand then I cannot explain it to you."

Catrina thought for a moment, then looked at Greta with a quizzical expression. "How did you know how to help Jacob when he was sick? I cannot figure out how it came so easily to you."

Greta shrugged. "I just knew. When I am around him it feels as if I have always known him. Everything just comes naturally."

"I should have known that you did not mean it when you said that you had no interest in him." She looked away. "It is true, is it not? You do hope that he will court you."

Greta looked down at her hands. She paused and wondered how to respond. "*Ja.* I do. I am sorry that I did not tell the truth earlier."

Catrina's face crumpled. She sank back into the quilt and turned her face away.

The next morning, Catrina took a turn for the worse. Greta soaked a compress in vinegar and shook her head. "I wish that I had yarrow." She searched the Witmers' cache of herbs, but found nothing that would help sweat out a fever. She had just given up when she heard a knock at the door.

"Come in."

Berta Riehl and Emma Knepp strode in. "We have heard that there is sickness in this house."

"*Ja.*"

The elderly women waved Greta aside. "Get some rest before you fall ill yourself. We will take over for a while. Abraham and Amos can manage without us for the day."

"*Danke.* But I think the best thing that I can do right now is to gather more yarrow. Catrina needs it. Jacob could use another dose too, I imagine."

Berta nodded. "Yarrow would do Catrina a world of good." She looked at the young woman and clucked her tongue. "She is not doing well."

"No. Her grandparents have begun to recover, I think. But Catrina has not been so fortunate."

"*Ja.*" Emma nodded. "Off you go then. And hurry back."

Berta put a hand on Greta's arm. "But do be careful. The rain was terrible last night. The creeks have flooded."

Greta nodded and hurried out of the cabin, leaving the warm scent of woodsmoke behind her as she stepped into the brightness of a new day.

Chapter Twenty-Four

Jacob woke up and stretched. He realized that, for the first time in days, he felt like himself again. *I wonder how long I have been asleep.* He pushed himself out of bed and threw open the shutters. A brilliant blue sky greeted him. Jacob breathed deeply. *It is so good to be up and alive.*

He turned back to the dim interior of the cabin and felt an unexpected sense of loss. Everywhere he looked he saw signs of Greta. He could vaguely remember her sitting by the fire, or hovering by his bedside. He could still feel her cool hands against his hot, fevered skin. *The cabin is so empty and still without her.*

Jacob dressed quickly and went to check on the livestock. He smiled as he rounded the corner of the cabin. There she was, humming a tune and swinging a basket as she walked across the field. Jacob raised his hand in greeting, but Greta did not see. She was too intent on her errand.

He leaned against the side of the house and watched her cut through the wild grasses. The sun shone against her white prayer *kappe* and illuminated her rosy cheeks. Jacob's heart swelled as his eyes followed her carefree movements and innocent expression. He watched as she picked her way down the hill to the edge of the creek and pause when she reached the water. Her head turned one way, then the other, as she studied the wild current rush past.

Jacob straightened up and frowned. *She is not going to try to cross the creek, is she? Not after all the rain last night.* He watched Greta take a careful step forward. The water lapped at her shoes. She hesitated and then stepped onto a stone as she waved her arms for balance.

"Greta. Don't." But Jacob knew that she could not hear him above the roaring current. He hurried down the hill. *Doesn't she know those rocks are slick with moss?* Jacob cupped his hand around his mouth. "Greta! It is not safe!"

She did not turn around. Her eyes stayed on the water as she searched for a larger, more stable rock. She switched the basket to her left hand and hitched up her skirts with her right hand. Her head nodded, *one, two, three*, and Jacob could tell that she was counting. On three, she leapt for the larger rock. Jacob's heart flew into his throat, but she stuck the landing.

Greta grinned, took another long leap, and landed safely on the far side. Jacob let out a long, shaky breath. *Thank you, Lord.* He watched her scramble up the muddy bank and into a patch of weeds. Jacob continued to make his way to the creek as he watched Greta stuff handfuls of yarrow into her basket. He grimaced as she turned back toward the water and scampered down the bank. "Wait! Let me help you!" But Greta did not hear his voice above the howl of the water. Her head stayed down as she studied the stepping-stones and she did not even realize that he was there. Jacob broke into a run. "Wait!"

The first stone sat far from the bank and Greta narrowed her eyes as she considered the distance. She clenched her jaw, whispered a prayer, and jumped for it. Her feet slid out from under her as soon as they hit the stone. Her arms spun like windmills as she tried to regain her balance, but she crashed into the water.

Jacob exploded into a sprint. "I am coming! Hold on!" He knew she could not hear him above the roaring current, but he called to her anyway. "You will be all right! I am almost there!" *Please, Lord. Do not let her drown. Please, please do not let her drown.* Every muscle burned with purpose as Jacob flew across the field and raced through the stand of trees to the edge of the bank. Greta was already gone.

Jacob stared into the churning river. *Where is she?* His stomach felt as tight as a fist as he watched for a sign of life. Seconds passed. And then Greta's head popped up downstream. She coughed and sputtered. "Help me!" But the river had carried her too far for Jacob to reach her. Greta kicked and flailed as the water sucked her under again.

Jacob took off in her direction. He stared into the empty water as his feet pounded along the bank, but he saw only the reflection of trees and sun. He tried to calculate how far downstream she must be. Long, terrible seconds passed. Jacob could only hear the roar of the current and the beat of his heart.

Greta's head appeared again, closer this time. Jacob's stomach leapt into his chest and he pushed his body to run even faster. Greta saw him and opened her mouth to shout. But water rushed between her lips and she disappeared again.

Jacob leapt over a fallen log and crashed into the creek. He could see her just beneath the surface of the water. Her hair spread out like a fan, the chestnut curls rippling in the current.

Greta's fingers clawed toward the surface, but her waterlogged skirts pulled her deeper. She could see the blue sky far above, rippling beyond the water. But she knew she could not reach it. The whitewater slapped and beat her down with cold, angry hands.

Her eyes blurred with water and her lungs burned. The creek wrapped around her like a blanket as it dragged her downward. She felt her body relax and give up. The light above the surface began to fade. As the cold dark encircled her, she knew that there was no way out. Her last thought was of Jacob. She wished with all of her strength that she had declared her love while there was still time.

As her eyes closed in defeat, Greta felt arms wrap around her waist with a ferocious intensity. Warm, living flesh burned against hers. She felt her body moving upward as strong hands pressed against the current. And then the world went black.

"It's all right. I've got you now. It's all right." Jacob felt Greta collapse against his chest. Her slim body felt as limp as a doll. He threw his weight against the current and pushed toward the shallows, one arm wrapped around her body, the other braced against the force of the water. The river slapped and knocked him back, but he fought until his lungs and legs screamed with effort. *Der Herr, give me strength.* Adrenaline surged through Jacob's body. He set his jaw, forged through the last few yards of water, and stumbled to the bank.

Jacob laid Greta's slack body on the wet green grass. She did not move. He felt a fresh rush of panic. "Greta." He ran the back of his hand across her cheek. Her pale skin felt as cold as frost. "Greta." He shook her gently. "Greta!" He could feel his world collapse and spin out of control in a horrible, unstoppable motion. "Please, Greta. Please!"

He rolled Greta onto her side and patted her back. "Come on, Greta. Breathe!" He felt her twitch. "That's it, Greta. Come on! Please!" A terrible cough erupted from her lungs. Her body shook. "That's it! Come on, Greta!" She coughed again. Jacob patted her back harder. "Greta. It is going to be all right. That's it. Get it all out."

Her eyelids fluttered open.

"Greta! Greta, darling! You are going to be all right. You are going to be all right!"

"Jacob. You came for me."

"Of course I did. Of course I came for you." He buried his face in her hair and breathed her in as he hid tears of relief. "I thought I lost you, Greta." He closed his eyes and pressed his cheek against hers. "I thought I lost you." He held her close as the warmth returned to her body, and he wished that he never had to let her go.

"I see now." He kept his arms locked around her.

"What do you see?"

"How wrong I was."

Greta smiled. "Wrong about what?"

"I was wrong to think that there could ever be anyone but you."

"Oh, Jacob!" She squeezed him more tightly and felt a deep, happy ache in her throat.

"Greta. Dear, sweet Greta. I have known it since the day I met you."

"When Rose trampled your garden?"

"Yes!" He laughed and held her even tighter. "I knew from the time I first laid eyes on you, when you landed on your backside in the dirt and tried to look dignified. I love you, Greta Scholtz. I have always loved you."

"Oh, Jacob! I have always loved you!" Greta felt so full of joy and relief that she thought she might burst. Jacob covered her face and hair in kisses, then pulled her to her feet, picked her up, and spun her around. Greta shrieked with delight as he held her aloft. He grinned and spun her around again. "You weigh no more than a feather."

Jacob set her back on her feet and pulled her to him. "Ever since the day I carried you home, I have wanted to pick you up again." Greta laughed into his chest as she stood wrapped in his arms. She could feel the warmth of his skin through his homespun shirt. "Why did we wait so long to admit how we truly feel?"

Jacob sighed and ran his fingers through her long,

wet hair, his eyes deep with longing. "I was afraid to love you." He shook his head. "After all that I had lost, I could not accept that we were meant to be together. I had to push you away." He laid his cheek across the crown of her head and closed his eyes. "Forgive me."

"And I am sorry for my pride. Ruth warned me that it would be my downfall. I almost lost you because of it. I did not want you to know that I loved you."

He let out a long, hard sigh. "*Ja.* You had me fooled. I never would have given Catrina a second thought if I had known how you really felt. I thought that you wanted nothing to do with me."

"And I thought that I was no match for Catrina."

Jacob pulled back from their embrace to look Greta in the eye. "That is why you started ignoring me?"

"I knew that I could not compete with her."

"No one can compare to you, Greta Scholtz."

"Catrina is very beautiful. And everything about her seems perfect." Greta tightened her grip on Jacob's arm. "I thought that you were in love with her."

"Never." He shook his head and pulled her close again. "I have never met a woman like you before. So full of life. So determined . . ." He grinned and shook his head again, overwhelmed that this strong, capable woman was really his.

They stood in silence for a long, wonderful moment, until Greta shivered with cold. Jacob caressed her cheek with the back of his hand. "We need to get you warmed up. No more standing outside in those wet clothes."

Greta gazed into his dark, smoldering eyes. "I do

not want this moment to end." Jacob smiled and kissed her forehead, then took her hand and led her up the embankment. "I have to take you home before you catch cold." He stayed close by her side as they walked. He could feel the heat of her body and hear the soft rhythm of her breath. "I cannot bear the thought that I almost lost you. What were you doing trying to cross the creek, anyway?"

"I was going for more yarrow. It grows on the far side of the creek."

Jacob frowned. "It was too great a risk."

Greta shrugged. "Catrina has a terrible fever. I did not feel that I had a choice. I had to do what I could to help."

Jacob raised Greta's hand to his mouth and kissed it. "You have a heart of gold."

She shook her head. "Anyone would do the same."

A troubled expression passed over Jacob's face. "I do not think that Catrina would have done the same for you. The more time that I spent with her, the more I realized that she is not Plain in her heart." He sighed. "I wonder if she will ever belong here."

Greta nodded. "I just do not know."

Jacob squeezed her hand. "*Der Herr* does. He will make a clear path for her."

"She is going to take this hard. I am sorry that our love will bring her pain."

Jacob shrugged. "I think it might be what she needs. Sometimes *der Herr* allows us to be taken down a peg to teach us how to be better people. She needs to learn that beauty is not as valuable as character. A man should choose character over beauty every time."

Greta glanced at Jacob with a twinkle in her eye. "Are you saying that I am not beautiful, Jacob Miller?"

Jacob gazed back into her eyes. His expression turned serious. "You are the most beautiful woman in the world, Greta Scholtz."

Chapter Twenty-Five

"My word!" Ruth stood up from the three-legged stool by the fire. "You look like a drowned rat!"

Greta shrugged and ran her hand over her soggy curls.

"And why are you grinning like that, when you look half drowned?"

Greta just smiled. Peter and Eliza leapt up and ran to her as they shouted and jumped up and down. "We haven't seen you in days!" They hugged her, shivered, and pulled away. "You are so wet and cold!"

"I know! I fell in the creek."

"You fell in the creek?" Ruth's face tightened. "Greta, you could have been killed. The creek is a monster today."

"*Ja.* I noticed."

"But what happened?" Peter tugged on Greta's arm.

"Well, Catrina has taken ill and her fever would not break. I thought yarrow tea would help." Greta shrugged. "But it grows across the creek."

Ruth clucked her tongue. "That was a foolhardy thing to do."

Greta shrugged again. "Catrina needs that yarrow. And I thought that I could make it."

"Oh, Greta. Always thinking of others." The old woman pressed a hand to her heart. "We could have lost you."

"But what happened?" Eliza peered up at her with big, concerned eyes. "How did you get out?"

Greta grinned and looked away.

"Greta Scholtz, that is quite an expression you have on your face." Ruth put her hands on her hips. "I would like to know what is going on!"

"Well . . ." Greta bit her lip. She felt her pulse quicken at the memory. "I could not get out. The water was so high and the current was so strong."

"What happened?" Peter bounced up and down. "How did you get out?"

"Shhh." Ruth put a finger to her lips. "She is trying to tell you."

Greta patted Peter's head and smiled. "Just when I gave up hope, I felt someone grab me and pull me out."

"Jacob!" Eliza shouted. "It was Jacob, wasn't it?!"

Greta nodded, still beaming. "*Ja*. It was Jacob. He saved me." She looked down at Eliza. "How did you guess?"

"Because he is in love with you!"

Greta's eyes opened wide. Ruth raised an eyebrow. Greta hesitated, then smiled and dropped her voice to a whisper. "*Ja*. He is. He is in love with me."

Ruth clapped her hands. "Well, it is about time the two of you figured that out!"

"What will happen now, Greta?" Eliza looked up and reached for her sleeve.

"Oh. I . . ."

Ruth put up a hand. "What happens now is that Greta will put on dry clothes and take a very long nap. She has not had a proper night's sleep for days."

"But what about Catrina? She needs medicine."

Ruth shook her head. "There is nothing to be done. No one is going back across that creek today."

"I just wish I could have saved some of the yarrow." Greta remembered the moment the basket slipped from her fingers as she struggled against the current. "You are right. There is nothing to be done. Unless . . ." She checked the pocket of her apron and grinned as her fingertips brushed against a soggy petal. *Why, look!* Greta laughed out loud. "I had almost forgotten that I tucked a few sprigs in my pocket. I cannot believe that they are still there!"

"Keep an eye on the twins for a little bit longer, Ruth." Greta spun around on her heels. "I will be back soon."

"Greta! I will not hear of it!" Ruth put her hands on her hips. "Dry off and change first. At least put on a prayer *kappe*!"

But Greta was already gone. Ruth shook her head and sighed as the door slammed shut. "She is headstrong. I will give her that."

Greta was halfway to the Witmers' when she realized how exhausted she felt. *Just a little bit farther. Catrina needs this yarrow.* Greta prayed for strength and forced herself to keep walking. She wrapped her arms around herself and shivered. *I feel so cold.* Her teeth began to chatter, but she continued to march down the path with determined steps.

Greta's body felt as heavy as stone when she arrived

at the Witmer cabin. Every muscle ached and her vision blurred. She knocked and then leaned against the threshold to steady herself. Greta heard low murmurs and shuffling inside. The door opened and Emma Knepp's shocked face appeared. "Greta? Whatever has happened?" The elderly woman took Greta by the elbow and steered her inside.

Greta's eyes took a moment to adjust to the dark, silent room. "How is Catrina?" She staggered toward the young woman's bedside. "I got the yarrow." She reached in her pocket and pulled out a handful of the weed. "I got it."

Berta Riehl stood up from the hearth. "Greta. You look like death warmed over. Sit down." Greta felt lightheaded and unsteady. She stumbled against a three-legged stool and the noise woke Catrina.

"What? Who?" Catrina's eyes opened wide. "Greta! What have you done? Just look at you! Where is your prayer *kappe*?"

"Oh. I . . ." Greta's hand flew to her head. "I lost my prayer *kappe*." She tried to smooth her tangled mass of wet curls. "I . . . I . . ." Greta felt a wave of dizziness wash over her. She reached out and tried to steady herself as darkness spread across her field of vision. Catrina gasped as Greta collapsed onto the dirt floor.

Greta sensed sunlight across her face. Muffled noises grew louder. She buried her head into the pillow and felt herself fall back into the blackness of sleep. Then she remembered. Her eyes flew open as she pushed herself onto her elbows.

"Catrina!" The word came out in a hoarse whisper. "I have to get her fever down!"

"Shhhhh." Frena Witmer appeared by the bedside and put a hand on her shoulder. "Catrina is out of danger. You can rest now."

Greta glanced around, confused. "I am in your bed?"

Frena nodded. "*Ja.* My husband and I recovered quickly, thanks to you."

Greta frowned. "I feel so groggy." She rubbed her eyes and tried to sit up.

"Rest." Frena felt Greta's forehead. "No fever, praise be. We thought that you had taken ill, but the fever never came. Instead you just slept like the dead." The elderly woman smiled. "You worked yourself to exhaustion nursing everyone back to health. You had not slept for days."

"Everyone is out of danger?"

"*Ja.* Everyone is out of danger." Frena tucked the covers back around Greta's chin. "Rest some more. I have chores to tend to, but I will be back soon." Greta watched as the elderly woman picked up a basket, opened the door, and disappeared into the sunshine. She closed her eyes and let a warm, cozy drowsiness drift over her.

"Greta?"

It was Catrina's voice. Greta opened her eyes. The young woman lay on her pallet in the opposite corner of the cabin, staring at her.

"*Ja?*"

Catrina had a strange, confused expression on her face. She slid back the quilt, pushed herself up, and padded across the room in bare feet. Her head was uncovered and her thick black hair fell to the small of her back in shining curls. Greta turned her face away from the beautiful face and beautiful hair. "I am too tired, Catrina."

Catrina frowned but did not answer. Instead she sat down on the edge of the bedstead. They waited in uncomfortable silence for a moment. Catrina sighed and pushed a lock of hair behind her ear. She looked away. "I heard what you did."

"What do you mean?"

Catrina sighed and studied her hands. "You risked your life to help me."

Greta did not know how to respond. Catrina shrugged. "I know it is true. Jacob told me."

"Jacob was here?" Greta felt her heart skip a beat as the memory of their last conversation flooded back to her. *He loves me. He has always loved me.*

"*Ja.* Word travels fast in the settlement. He came right away when he heard that you collapsed." Catrina waited for Greta to respond. When she said nothing, the young woman went on. "He told us how you insisted on getting yarrow for me, even though the creek was raging. He told us how dangerous it was and that when you fell in, you almost drowned. If he had not been there . . ."

Greta shuddered. "But he *was* there, praise be."

Catrina nodded. "*Ja.* He thought that you stayed home after that. You were so exhausted and soaked to the bone." She shook her head. "It is a miracle that you did not catch your death walking back here. You should not have done it."

Greta shrugged. "You needed the yarrow. And look at you now. It worked."

"*Ja.* It did. Grandmother says that I almost did not survive the fever. The yarrow was what made the difference." Catrina paused and swallowed. "So you see, you saved my life. And you almost sacrificed your life in the process."

Greta looked down. "I was only doing what any of us would do."

Catrina put her hand on Greta's forearm. "I don't know that I would have done it for you."

"No?"

Catrina shook her head and dropped her voice to a whisper. "No." She tightened her grip on Greta's arm. "I cannot stop thinking about it." She shook her head again. "You almost died for me. For *me*."

Greta smiled. "Don't fret. I would do it again."

"Even knowing the risk?"

"*Ja*. Even knowing the risk."

Catrina returned Greta's smile. "Now I understand why Jacob loves you."

Greta looked surprised.

Catrina laughed softly. "*Ja*. I know that he loves you. I saw it in his eyes when he came looking for you. He would not leave until he was sure that you were all right. He sat by the bedstead for hours, brooding and checking your forehead every few minutes. He did not leave until he knew that it was exhaustion and not illness." Catrina's body deflated and her shoulders sagged with defeat. "I always sensed that you had something that I did not have, something that Jacob admired." She shrugged. "The truth is, I have been jealous of you."

"Jealous? Of me?"

Catrina laughed. "*Ja*. I have everything that a man should want, but Jacob was never interested in me. Not really." She sighed. "I could sense that his heart was with you, even when he did not realize it."

"I thought he was infatuated by your beauty."

"*No.* If you had admitted your feelings earlier, I suspect that he would never have considered me." Catrina closed her eyes and sighed. "How do you do it, Greta? There is a beauty in you that I do not have, despite my looks. You have a beauty that comes from within." She opened her eyes and looked at Greta with a clear, honest expression. "How do you do it? How do you live a Plain life? It just does not come naturally to me."

"It does not come naturally to anyone, including me! We must overcome our nature to live Plain. Why, you should have seen me when you gave Jacob that cake. Do you remember that day?"

Catrina nodded.

"I felt such a need to best you." Greta chuckled at the memory. "I felt that you had stolen an idea for which I deserved credit!"

Catrina looked confused. "But why should you lay claim to the idea?"

Greta flashed a sheepish grin. "You remember when the wasps attacked me?"

"*Ja.*"

"Wasps' nests look rather like beehives, don't you think?"

"Oh, Greta, no! You were not seeking honey, were you?" Catrina clapped a hand over her mouth and broke into laughter.

"*Ja.* Honey to bake a cake so that I could impress Jacob." Greta began to laugh too. "And look how I suffered for my pride!" The two women giggled and shook until tears streamed down their faces.

Greta opened her mouth to say more but a knock at the door interrupted her. "*Ja.* Come in."

The door swung open and Jacob's large frame filled the threshold. The sun backlit his body and obscured his features, but Greta knew that he was smiling. She grinned and her heart flooded with joy. "Jacob!"

"I have come to take you home."

Chapter Twenty-Six

Jacob lifted Greta into his cart, which was small enough to navigate the narrow walking path, and draped his coat over her shoulders. Greta smiled and ran her fingers over the rough wool cloth. She loved feeling loved. Jacob shook the reins and the horse whinnied. The cart jerked and rolled forward as he walked beside it. After a while, he glanced at Greta with a nervous expression. "I forgot to ask you something."

Greta looked up at him. "You did?"

He shrugged and flashed a sheepish grin. "*Ja.* I was so happy after I pulled you from the creek that I forgot."

"Forgot what?"

Jacob tugged the reins and the cart ground to a halt.

"Why are we stopping?" Greta looked around but saw only trees. "There is nothing here."

Jacob reached into the cart and gently lifted Greta over the side and onto the ground. She stared at him without speaking. He grinned and dropped down on one knee. "This cannot wait a second longer."

Greta clasped her hands together. "Oh, Jacob!"

Jacob pulled off his beaver-felt hat and took her hand. "Greta Scholtz, will you marry me?"

"*Ja! Ja*, of course I will!"

He stood up, pulled her close, and locked his strong arms around her slender frame. "Greta." She melted into his touch as she felt the world disappear. Nothing existed but the man she loved and this moment together.

When Jacob released her she was thrilled to see that he was grinning. "Jacob, I have never seen you smile so. I hardly recognize you when you are not frowning."

"I have frowned long enough. I think I would like to start smiling now." Greta reached up and traced the contours of his face. "*Ja*. I think it is time."

He drew her hand to his lips and kissed it. "You have made me smile again, Greta Scholtz. I tried to distract myself from loss and grief by working all of the time. I tried to protect myself from more loss by pushing you away." He shook his head. "But I could not work the pain away. And I could not push you away." He tapped his chest. "You stayed here, no matter how much I fought the feelings."

He gazed into her eyes. "I was so caught up in the losses that *der Herr* allows us to suffer that I could not believe that he sends joy, too. I refused to let go for so long. But I believe that *der Herr* wants me to become a better man by knowing you, Greta. By living to support and comfort you on our journey through this world. I can never be a better man by clearing more fields or planting more corn or building a bigger barn. I can never be a better man by running away from pain. I will become a better man by softening my heart and letting you inside."

Greta placed the palm of her hand against his chest. She could feel the thump of his heart beneath his homespun shirt. "*Der Herr* has not given us a life without pain. But He has given us each other. And that will be enough."

"*Ja*. That will be enough."

Jacob kissed Greta's forehead and lifted her back into the cart. She rode in silence as she watched Jacob lead the horse down the winding path and imagined the life that they would live together.

But when the Yoder farm came into view, an unwelcome thought hit Greta. She realized that she agreed to his proposal without thinking of what would become of Ruth and the twins.

"Jacob?"

"*Ja*?"

"I should have said something earlier."

He frowned and turned to her. "About what?"

Greta bit her lip. "I want to marry you, Jacob. More than anything I want to marry you." She looked down. "But I cannot abandon Ruth and the Fisher twins. And I cannot ask you to take on so many mouths to feed. You are expecting a bride, not an entire family!"

"My dear, sweet Greta. Always thinking of others." He cupped her chin in his hand and raised her eyes to his. "Your family is my family. They will all come with you."

"Really?"

"Of course."

"You mean . . ."

Jacob nodded. "*Ja.* We will take in Eliza and Peter as our own children." He cleared his throat and turned his eyes back to the path. "If they want me for a father, that is."

"Oh, Jacob. They certainly do!"

He looked back at her. "Do you really think so?"

"*Ja.* Of course."

They rounded the curve and pulled in front of the Yoder cabin. Jacob's jaw tightened. "Well, I guess we are about to find out."

"I already told you. They will love you."

Jacob nodded, but Greta could see the doubt etched on his face. He pulled the reins and spoke to Old Bess in a low, commanding voice. Greta could not wait for the cart to roll to a complete stop. "Hurry, Jacob! I want to tell them everything!" She hopped down without his help and ran ahead. Jacob felt a pang of anxiety as he watched her bolt into the cabin. *Will the twins want to be part of my family?*

Peter and Eliza leapt up as soon as the door opened. "Greta!"

Ruth turned from the hearth and put her hands on her hips. "Well, I am glad to see that you are dry this time."

"We have news."

Jacob appeared in the doorway with a sheepish grin. "Jacob!" The children crowded closer. Greta glanced at her fiancé and he pulled her close. "Greta has agreed to marry me."

"Well, it is about time!" Ruth grinned and shook her head. "It took you long enough."

"*Ja.*" Jacob's gaze stayed on Greta as he studied her gentle eyes and freckled cheeks. "It took much too long."

Eliza smiled and stood on her tiptoes to reach Greta's ear. Then she whispered loud enough for everyone to hear, "I told you that he was in love with you!" Greta hugged the girl and laughed. "*Ja*, you did. And you were right!"

Peter watched the celebration with a finger in his mouth and a crease in his forehead. He shook his head and tightened his little fists. "No! No! No! I do not want you to marry him! You cannot marry him!" He ran out the door and slammed it behind him.

Greta's hand flew to her mouth. Jacob looked crushed, but he put a comforting hand on Greta's shoulder. "It is all right. I will go after the boy." He set his jaw and walked outside in time to see Peter disappear into the lean-to behind the cabin. Jacob sighed and followed him into the small structure. He passed through rectangles of sunlight that streamed through the cracks between logs as he looked for the boy. Jacob frowned and ran his fingers through his hair. He heard a thump from behind a sack of grain. Then another thump and a muffled sob.

Jacob eased around the sacks and found Peter wedged between the rough flax fibers and the log wall. The boy wiped his eyes with the back of his hand and looked down. Jacob sank onto the dirt floor beside him. Peter scowled and inched away. "What do you want?"

"I want to know why you are upset."

"Because you are marrying Greta. I already told you that."

"But that does not answer my question. Why don't you want me to marry Greta?"

"Because . . . because . . ." Peter's lip trembled and

a fat tear ran down his face. "Because you are going to take her away from me."

Relief washed over Jacob. "You are sad because you think that she is going away?"

Peter nodded and kicked a sack of grain.

"What if I told you that she is not going to leave you?"

Peter's eyes shot up.

"What if I told you that we want you and your sister to come live with us?"

The little boy's mouth opened in surprise. "You want me to come to your cabin to live with you?"

"*Ja.*"

A look of suspicion passed over Peter's face. "For how long? Just until you can find another home for us?"

"*No.* I want you and Eliza to stay with us forever. I want to be your father."

Peter jumped up and exploded into Jacob's arms. "Really? Do you really want to be my father?"

"*Ja.*" Jacob hugged the boy and then tousled his hair. "*Ja*, I do."

Peter looked up with serious eyes. "I am sorry about the things I said. I did not mean them." He swallowed hard. "I just felt so upset that Greta did not want me anymore."

"You know, Peter, she told me that she would not leave you to marry me."

Peter's eyes widened. "She did?"

Jacob nodded. "She did. She will never leave you." He put a hand on Peter's shoulder. "And neither will I."

Chapter Twenty-Seven

The next few days passed in a whirlwind of activity. "There is so much to do!" Greta turned to Ruth and shook her head. "And the wedding day is almost here!"

Ruth shrugged. "Everything will get done. Do not fret. The menfolk are nearly finished with the addition to Jacob's cabin. And we have already mended the linens and made more lye soap. There is just the laundry to do and the packing." She pushed a basket of dough into Greta's hands. "Here. Go do the baking. Get out and get some fresh air and relax."

"But it is not my baking day."

"No matter. We need to work ahead this week." Ruth raised an eyebrow. "Everything has been thrown off schedule, or have you not noticed?"

Greta laughed. "All right. I will try and relax. It is just that everything is about to change and I am so excited!"

Ruth patted her shoulder and smiled. "I know, dear. These are happy days."

Greta started for the door, then paused and turned

around. "There is just one thing that is still bothering me. And I do not know what to do about it."

Ruth frowned. "What is it? I thought everything had fallen into place perfectly."

"It is Catrina. I have not seen her since Jacob and I announced our engagement. I worry what will become of her. Will she stay here, feeling unloved? What if she gives up and goes back to Philadelphia?"

Ruth thought for a moment. "Catrina needs to discover why she is really here and what is truly of value. She needs to learn what it is to be Plain in her heart." She shrugged. "It is hard, but sometimes we have to suffer disappointment to find the right path."

Greta nodded, but her brow remained furrowed. "I do not want to be the cause of her pain."

Ruth shook her head. "You and Jacob were meant to be from the very beginning. The entire settlement saw it coming, did we not? And besides, I feel certain there is a man for Catrina, even though she has not met him yet. Why, with our settlement growing so fast, he could arrive any day!"

Greta swung her basket and hummed as she walked to the community bake-oven. Frost crunched beneath her feet and the sun glinted off fields of ice like a shimmering crystal wonderland. The cold air stung her cheeks, but the coming winter no longer felt barren and empty. Instead, her heart sang with expectation.

Greta's happy mood deflated as soon as she reached the oven and saw Catrina checking on a loaf of bread. Greta stopped and started to turn around, but Catrina glanced up and saw her. *Too late.* Greta adjusted her prayer *kappe* and continued walking. *Mayhap we can manage a civil conversation. Why, we even managed a good laugh, last we spoke!* She offered an awkward, but hopeful hello.

"Oh. Hello." Catrina looked uncomfortable. "I did not think that today was your baking day. I did not expect to see you here."

"*Ja*. I do not usually bake today but the wedding—" Greta stopped in midsentence and cleared her throat. She had not meant to speak of it.

"*Ja*." Catrina nodded grimly. "Of course. The wedding has thrown your schedule." She turned back to the oven, slid the long wooden paddle inside, and pulled out a golden brown loaf of bread.

"Perfect as always," Greta remarked.

Catrina's face remained hard. "A lot of good that has done me." She tucked the bread in her basket and turned away.

"Catrina, wait."

The young woman paused. She took a long, deep breath and turned around. "*Ja?*"

Greta stumbled over her thoughts. "I, uh . . . I . . ."

"*Ja?*"

Greta frowned. "I . . . I guess I just wanted to ask if you are well."

Catrina bit her lip and looked away. "I am not sure what I will do now." She shook her head. "How can I stay here? I do not fit in. I never fit in."

Greta reached out and put a hand on her arm. "That is not true, Catrina."

"Do you think that I could ever truly be one of you?"

"*Ja*." Greta nodded and looked Catrina in the eye. "I do. But it is up to you whether or not you choose to live as our people do."

Catrina hesitated. She cleared her throat and looked away. "Mayhap I should start by saying that I am sorry. I should not have competed against you for Jacob."

"Nor I. And I am sorry that I was not honest with you. How could you have known that I longed for Jacob when I told you that I did not!"

Catrina flashed a teasing grin. "'Tis true. You did create the misunderstanding." She squeezed Greta's arm. "But I did not want to believe otherwise, even when I saw the signs."

"That is all behind us now, *ja*?"

"*Ja*."

"But, will it trouble you to see me with Jacob?"

Catrina paused and shook her head. "I think not. Truth be told, I was never in love with him. I was afraid—afraid of being alone and afraid of being unloved."

Greta's expression shifted to surprise. "You were afraid of being unloved?"

"*Ja*. Of course."

"But you are so very beautiful."

"Oh, Greta, you know better than most that there is far more to a woman than her looks."

"You have caught me by my own words."

Catrina winked. "That I have."

Greta laughed.

Catrina smiled, then dropped back to a serious expression. "You know, at first I did not know that you sought Jacob's affection. And then, when I did realize, it saddened me to see how he looked at you. He never looked at me like that. I thought if I could be charming enough and beautiful enough he might look at me like that—with adoration in his eyes."

"Someone will look at you like that, Catrina! And, when he does, he will adore you for more than your beauty."

"You believe that I will find him here, in the wilderness?" Catrina laughed and shook her head.

"You never know what *der Herr* can send your way!"

Catrina's eyes danced for a moment, then she took a deep breath and let it out slowly. "I think I will stay, Greta. I want to finish the adventure that I have started."

"I am glad to hear you say that." Greta reached for Catrina's hand and squeezed it. "And I know you will be glad as well."

Snow blanketed the countryside in a clean white quilt as Jacob and Greta walked hand in hand to the Riehl cabin. When the worship service ended she would be a married woman, tied to the man she loved for the rest of her life. Greta breathed in the crisp, clear air and smiled. "The forest and fields are transformed beneath a layer of unbroken snow. And the sun could not shine any brighter. As far as the eye can see, all the world is pure and white and gleaming." Jacob grinned and looked down at her, his eyes full of love and joy. "My heart has been transformed as surely as the landscape. This is a time for renewal, Greta. *Der Herr* has restored my life to me."

Greta nodded and slid her small hand into his as they passed through the doorway of the Riehl cabin. A roomful of familiar faces waited, eager to celebrate with them. Ruth beamed as the twins fidgeted. Abraham and Amos exchanged happy I-told-you-so looks. Even Catrina was there, smiling shyly. She stepped forward and whispered quickly into Greta's ear. "I am happy for you both. I truly am." Then she slid back to her seat.

Silence fell across the room as all eyes moved onto the couple.

"Well, Greta, are you ready?" Jacob asked in a low voice.

"Oh, Jacob, I have never been more ready for anything. I want us to spend the rest of our lives together."

Jacob gazed into her eyes. "We will, my darling. We will."